WAKE

I kept beating on ~~~~~~~~~~~~~~~~~~~~~~~~~rm, but the noise wouldn~~~~~~~~~~~~~~~~~~~~~~~~ the telephone ringing, I ~~~~~~~~~~~~~~~~~~~~~ on the pillows with it.

"What?" I snapped. I do not wake up easily. Or joyfully.

"Charlie?"

The voice was masculine, but it wasn't Zack's drawl. This voice was deep. Vibrant. An actor's voice. A name rose out of the sluggish bog that is my waking brain. Bristow. Detective Sergeant Taylor Bristow.

"What time is it?" I demanded, noting that there was no daylight filtering around the miniblinds.

"Six-fifty, Charlie. Are you awake?"

"No."

"Concentrate, woman, I need your help."

I sat bolt upright, adrenaline streaking through me. "What's wrong?"

"I'm down by the old creek bed that's part of the border between Bellamy Park and Condor. I want you to come down here and see if you can identify a body."

"Somebody's dead?"

"A woman. Yes."

"Just because I've come across a couple of bodies in the past, you think I'm acquainted with every corpse that turns ~~~~~~~~~~~~~~~~~~~~~~~~kes you think I know this

~~~~~~~~~~~~~~~~~~~~~~~~~~eans pocket. Only piece of

~~~~~~~~~~~~~~~~~~~~t once.

~~~~~~~~~~~~~~~~ay. How did she die?"

~~~~~~~~~~~~~~~~."

~~~~~~~~~~~~~~~~l swung my legs over the

~~~~~~~~~~~~~~~re."

Books by Margaret Chittenden

DYING TO SING

DEAD MEN DON'T DANCE

DEAD BEAT AND DEADLY

DON'T FORGET TO DIE

Published by Kensington Publishing Corporation

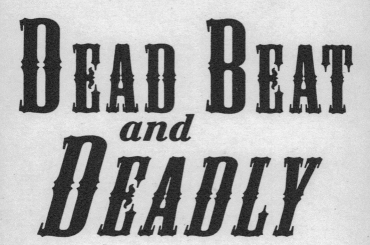

DEAD BEAT
and
DEADLY

Margaret Chittenden

KENSINGTON BOOKS
Kensington Publishing Corp.
http://www.kensingtonbooks.com

KENSINGTON BOOKS are published by

Kensington Publishing Corp.
850 Third Avenue
New York, NY 10022

First Kensington Hardcover Printing: August, 1998
First Kensington Paperback Printing: July, 1999
10 9 8 7 6 5 4 3 2 1

Printed in the United States of America

This book is dedicated to Teresa Loftin, computer wizard, web-page expert, and dear good friend.

CHAPTER 1

"Back off!" I yelled.

"Louder," the instructor said.

I filled my lungs with air, exploded it out through my mouth. "BACK OFF!"

"Yo!" he said. Leaning forward, he added in a conspiratorial whisper, "It's a euphemism, you know."

I kicked his shin, just the way he'd demonstrated in lesson one. I knew how to do that before the lesson of course; I've practiced on Zack.

"You're a quick study, Charlie," the instructor said with a weak grin. He turned his back on me and looked around at the other nineteen women standing in a circle in the middle of CHAPS' main corral—aka the dance floor. Some of them wore sloppy sweats like mine, some were tricked out in bicycle tights and tank tops, Patty Jenkins had on a spandex bodysuit.

P.J. was a regular at CHAPS—which is the country-western tavern/dance hall where all this activity was taking place. CHAPS belongs to me and my three associates, Angel Cervantes, Savanna Seabrook, and Zack Hunter.

Ever since her divorce, P.J. had been conducting a

serious man-hunting expedition, trolling the length and breadth of the San Francisco Peninsula. After showing up in sweats for the first lesson, she had discovered to her obvious joy that our instructor was an ex–military policeman with serious muscles. Hence the switch to figure-hugging spandex. It hadn't done her any good. So far, the only woman the instructor had shown extra interest in was Gina Giacomini, who managed Buttons & Bows, the Western store in CHAPS' foyer. Gina was a character in her own right, outrageously punk, bluntly outspoken. Her spiky hair had been red and green through the holidays; it was now striped blond and magenta, which dramatically set off the black lipstick and nail polish she'd taken to wearing lately, and the assortment of earrings that circled each of her ears.

Our instructor was playing with fire there, though he probably didn't know it. Gina was Angel Cervantes's girlfriend, and Angel had muscles, too. More on that later.

It had taken me a few months to find a qualified instructor who would agree to teach self-defense to women. I'd been referred to this one by Macintosh— one of Zack's poker and fishing buddies. The instructor's name, swear to God, was Duke. Duke Conway. In his parallel life he was an auto mechanic. He had dark hair, sharp features, and blue eyes that were possibly almost as vivid as mine. His kung-fu outfit looked like black pajamas. He had earned, but was not wearing, a karate black belt.

"Okay, ladies," Duke said, making most of us cringe. "Ms. Plato has shown you how it's done. Let's hear it."

"Back off!" the women said in voices varying in tone from squeak to weak bleat.

Duke sighed. "Ladies, ladies,' " he complained. "We are imagining a large male person who wishes to harm us physically, to rape us, perhaps, to steal our valuables."

I glanced at a woman named Estrella Stockton, a very pretty Filipina who was wearing a surprising amount of gold jewelry with her white, satiny long-sleeved shirt and electric blue bicycle shorts. There were gold loops in her ears, rings on several fingers, and a flat woven chain around her neck. A wide gold clip held her luxurious black hair away from her face. She needed to be prepared to protect her valuables. I didn't have to worry a whole lot about mine.

Duke started walking slowly around the circle, making eye contact, explaining all over again that it was *okay* for a woman to get mad when attacked; it was *okay* to yell, *okay* to gouge and bite and kick and stomp.

Estrella was a thirtysomething like me. We were both thin. There all resemblance ceased. She was petite. My nickname in school was Stretch. She had a perky bosom under her suspenders; my bosom is not a particularly noticeable item of my equipment.

I envied Estrella for her hair rather than her gold or bosom. Mine was just as long, but orange. As in jack-o'-lantern. And curly. Okay—frizzy.

Duke had cut Savanna Seabrook out of the pack. Savanna's a truly beautiful woman, inside and out. Zack calls her the African-American version of Dolly Parton.

Yes, I'm talking about *the* Zack Hunter—the man of every woman's dreams—used to play Sheriff

Lazarro in the long-running drama series, *Prescott's Landing.* Zack owns half of CHAPS. Savanna and Angel and I own the rest. Zack's away right now. In La-La land. We'll talk about him later, too.

"Okay, Miss," Duke said to Savanna. "This is the scenario. I'm gonna hit you and punch you." He put his hands loosely around her lovely throat. "I'm gonna strangle you, throttle you. What do you say!"

While Savanna mulled it over, I thought it would be interesting if her boyfriend were to show up. He's one of Bellamy Park's finest. Detective Sergeant Taylor Bristow. A Michael Jordan look-alike, according to Zack. (Those of you who've met Zack before will remember that almost all of his references are to television or the movies.)

"Let's hear it," Duke demanded.

Savanna attempted a snarl that turned itself into a giggle. "Back off," she spluttered.

Duke rolled his eyes. "You got any kids?" he asked.

Savanna nodded. "A daughter. Jacqueline."

Savanna's a single mother. She finally got around to divorcing her gay white husband a short time ago. Some of us can sure pick 'em.

"How old is your daughter?" Duke asked.

"Three."

"Okay. Close your eyes."

Savanna quirked a bird-wing eyebrow at me. I knew what she was thinking: *you got me into this, Charlie.* She did as she was told all the same.

"There's a guy breaking into your house right now," Duke stated.

"Apartment," Savanna corrected, looking serene.

Duke gritted his teeth. "There's a guy in a ski mask breaking into your apartment right now. He's got a gun. Your little girl's just coming out of her bedroom in her little nightie. She sees the guy, sees the gun. Scared to *death*. She screams for mommy, mommy. The guy grabs her by the arm. You run into the room swinging a baseball bat, going for the guy, what do you shout?"

Savanna's eyes had flown open and widened. Her hands curled into claws, reaching for Duke's eyeballs. "BACK OFF!" she screeched, making the wagon-wheel light fixtures vibrate.

"Works every time," Duke said smugly. "She-bear protecting her cub."

He strode to the center of the circle. "Okay, ladies," he said. "Repeat after me, loud: I can fight back."

"I can fight back," we shouted.

"Louder!"

"I can fight back," we yelled louder.

"I *will* fight back. I will *win*."

He pulled Gina out of the circle next and coaxed her until she shouted really really loud. When she finally managed it, he put his arm around her shoulders and gave them a squeeze. I glanced over at the bar, where Angel was taking inventory. Yep, he was watching.

Duke gradually worked his way around the circle. This time, the only one to fail the "back-off" test was Maisie Ridley, a pleasantly plump, middle-aged Englishwoman who just couldn't bring herself to raise her flutelike voice. She was a widow, she'd told me after the first lesson. She hadn't known the class would be all female. She was disappointed.

"There's always the instructor," I'd pointed out.

"That's true," she'd said thoughtfully. "He is quite good-looking isn't he? Certainly well built." She raised her eyebrows at me. "Somebody told me Zack Hunter owns this place. Is that true? Zack Hunter, the actor?"

"He's *one* of the owners," I corrected. "I'm afraid he's away right now." I'd disappointed her all over again.

The instructor had selected Estrella Stockton. "I can yell, no problem," she said. Actually, it didn't come out that clearly. Estrella had a bit of a speech impediment that affected certain letters. "No problem" sounded more like "No pwoblem." It was almost like baby talk, and Duke smiled at her in a paternalistic way that would have brought him serious grief if he'd done it to me.

But she was right, just the same. She could yell.

Estrella had kept herself apart from the other women during our first lesson just before the holidays, and during this one. Even in the rest room, while everyone else was tugging off jackets, swapping jeans for sweats or gym shorts, changing shoes, cracking jokes about Duke hitting on Gina, talking about what they got for Christmas, what they did New Year's Eve, Estrella put on her bicycle tights in one of the stalls, then exited without so much as a howdy.

"Estrella, isn't it?" Duke asked.

She nodded shortly.

"Okay, Estrella," Duke said. "You're really mad at me. I'm attacking you. You're much smaller than me, and you know it's no use fighting me. There's no way you can win. No way."

"Okay," she said.

"Wanna know what to do?" Duke asked.

"I know what to do," she said. "You taught us last lesson. The knee in the gwoin thing."

"Yo! You were paying attention," Duke said, smiling fondly again. He said "Yo!" quite often. I guess he was image-conscious.

He was right about Estrella paying attention. She was throwing her heart and soul into these lessons. Most of the women clowned around, not really taking it all seriously. *I* took it seriously. As I indicated earlier, I was the one who arranged for the self-defense lessons in the first place. Not too long ago I'd had a near-death experience with someone who'd wanted to interfere with my way of life. Permanently. For a period of time that was actually brief, but seemed long, I had felt absolutely helpless. And terrified. I had vowed never to be helpless again. Next time danger came looking for me, I was going to know how to cope.

I wondered if Estrella had felt helpless at some time or other. A couple of times during the first lesson, I'd thought she was following Duke's instructions a little too strenuously—as if she was venting some deeply buried anger.

Duke had his hands on Estrella's shoulders and was encouraging her to grab hold of his arms and bring her knee up. "Put your head down and push," he told her. "Push me backwards, get me off-balance, bring your right knee up, make like you're going to get me right in the family jewels. Up, down, up again, push!"

Estrella's face tightened into a mask. Pretty soon,

she had Duke stumbling. About her fifth knee raise, she connected.

Duke let out a yell and went white.

Somebody's giggle was quickly suppressed.

Estrella let go at once and said she was sowwy, weally weally sowwy. But her dark eyes held a glow of satisfaction that had no hint of apology. Maybe she had noticed that paternalistic smile after all.

"That's enough for today," Duke said hoarsely, and limped off to lean on the edge of the stage and do some power breathing.

The women crowded around the bottles of Pellegrino water Angel had set out on the bar. Angel had gone missing, I noticed. I looked around for him, saw him in the entrance, leaning against the wall, still watching Gina. She was chatting away to P.J., who had also been after Angel for a while. P.J. had given up. Gina was hanging in there. She and Angel had been going together for a year or so.

Angel Cervantes is a tough-looking hombre, relatively silent, fiercely private. Think of a man-size mahogany sculpture, cheekbones to die for. Long black hair pulled back and tied with a leather thong. Pancho Villa mustache. White western shirt, form-fitting blue jeans. Don't forget the cowboy hat made of the finest straw.

Now add spaniel-mild brown eyes. Yeah, that's the surprising thing about Angel—he's an incredibly gentle man.

"You all done?" he asked, as I passed him on my way to the rest room.

"It's more that Duke's done for," I said.

Angel's smile appeared rarely, but in this case it showed great satisfaction. "Lot of spirit in that little lady," he commented.

I have to explain something here. While I object to a woman being called a lady or a girl, I've learned to accept "little lady." I spend a lot of my time around hat hunks, aka cowboy wanna-bes, who usually adopt the mannerisms and some of the speech patterns to go along with the Stetson and boots. Being called little lady is part of my job description.

By the time I came out of the stall, the rest room was crowded. Everyone was laughing and congratulating Estrella on her performance. She looked pleased but wasn't saying much. I stood next to her as I washed my hands. She had pushed her sleeves up, ready to do the same. My gaze caught by the light glinting on her rings, I noticed ugly dark bruises on her left forearm. Four of them, finger wide.

"Those bruises look pretty recent," I said quietly, as the other women straggled out.

Her mouth tightened. She didn't look at me. "My what d'you call it—depth perception—is off," she said. She had difficulty with the "p" sounds too—a minor hesitation, but she didn't let it slow her down. "I walk into doors all the time."

"Really?" I looked in the mirror and fluffed up my hair as an excuse for sticking around. It's too frizzy to fluff, so I mainly just made it look messier. "Looks like a handprint to me," I said evenly. "Four fingers."

She had her hands under the air dryer, palms up. I could see the thumbprint now. She turned her head and saw me looking.

"You want to talk about it?" I asked.

She sighed, twitched her sleeves into place and buttoned them. "My husband," she said in a resigned voice. "He beats me all the time."

"Leave him," I said right away.

She gave me a cynical sort of glance.

"I'm serious," I said. "Nobody has to stay in that kind of relationship. There are shelters, agencies that can help you."

She shook her head. "I'm not an Amewican citizen. And I have only lived in this countwy for eighteen months. I leave him, he divorces me, I have to go back to the Philippines. I like it here. I don't wanna go back. I will never go back." She was very intense.

"I'm not sure that's so anymore," I said. "I seem to remember reading that there's a battered-wife clause in the immigration law. If you can prove you've been abused, you could get permanent-resident status. You might look into that."

She didn't look as thrilled by that as I would have expected. She simply shrugged and pulled on a down parka. "I'm okay," she said. "I'm taking this self-defense course so I can pwotect myself."

About then Gina came in. She must have been visiting with Angel. She went into a stall without saying anything. She'd probably realized Estrella and I were talking private stuff. Gina's a bit brash at times, but she can be discreet, too.

"How did you hear about the course?" I asked Estrella, being discreet myself. "You don't live around here, do you?" Most of the women had come from the

Granada apartments on the other side of Adobe Plaza, or from one of the businesses in the area.

She pulled a lipstick from her jacket pocket and applied it with confident strokes. "The instwuctor. He came by my salon, asked me to put a poster in the window."

I was immediately distracted. "Salon?"

"I'm a stylist at Hair Waising. It's a hair salon."

"Hair—" Oh, Hair *R*aising. "I know where that is. The Fairview Mall, right?" I could feel my eyes lighting up. "Could you do anything with *my* hair?"

She looked at me in the mirror, squinting professionally. She was really a very good-looking woman. She didn't smile much though. I suppose if a man was constantly beating up on me, I wouldn't smile a whole lot either.

"What you need to do is apply an antihumectant to your hair while it's still damp," she said. "Plus, you should use a diffuser to dwy it." She lifted a hank of hair away from my shoulder and studied it, frowning. "Your hair is natuwally like this?" she asked.

"I'm afraid so," I said humbly. "I tried cutting it short once, but I looked out of balance. I'm too tall for short hair."

I had looked like Orphan Annie, but I wasn't going to admit that.

Estrella pursed her lips. "We could work some Fwizz-Fwee thwough it. Twim these ends."

She sounded like a toddler, the way she talked. But her ideas sounded wonderful.

Pulling a card holder out of the front pocket of her gym bag, Estrella handed me her business card. "Call for an appointment. Tell Felicia to make it with me personally."

As we left the rest room, I asked her to wait, dashed into CHAPS' office, and brought out one of my own cards. She looked at me inquiringly. "If you decide you need to talk to someone or you need help, call me," I said.

Estrella laughed shortly, but she put my card into her jeans pocket as she headed for the exit.

"Estrella's going to have a go at my hair," I told Gina, as she walked past me.

"That's nice, Charlie."

"Is anything wrong?" I asked as Gina unlocked the door to Buttons & Bows. Gina was usually very upbeat and friendly. Always ready to stop and chat, especially if she thought there was any gossip to share.

She shrugged, entered the store, and closed the door behind her. Maybe she and Angel had a fight, I thought. I hoped Angel hadn't acted jealous because of Duke's interest in Gina. She hadn't encouraged the instructor at all. It was none of my business, of course. Which didn't mean I wouldn't be giving Angel the third degree if this state of affairs continued. My mind, like nature, abhors a vacuum.

I walked over to the main entryway and looked out through the side window. Duke's van—a squat black monster with Duke's logo painted on the sides—was already gone. Three of the women were smoking and talking at the foot of the steps. Apparently they invited Estrella to join them, but she shook her head, crossed the parking lot to a gold-colored Mercedes, and slid into the driver's seat.

A *Mercedes*. I wondered how much she was going to charge me for doing my hair, then decided that whatever it was, it would be worth it.

Estrella drove away, and I wandered back to the office, thinking about the accounts I needed to balance, wondering if there was a good movie on anywhere. Monday night was the only night CHAPS was closed. I ought to do something for excitement other than cleaning my pet rabbit's cage.

Sitting down in front of my computer, I booted it up and prepared to work, thinking that if it wasn't such a cold wet January day, I'd whisk myself off in my Jeep Wrangler, drive down to Carmel maybe.

I thought I might call the hair salon after lunch and set up an appointment with Estrella before she forgot everything she was going to do for me.

I also thought that if a man beat up on me, I'd beat him back.

CHAPTER 2

I kept beating on the clock radio to shut off the alarm, but the noise wouldn't stop. Finally realizing it was the telephone that was ringing, I grabbed the receiver and fell back on the pillows with it. For some reason I thought it might be Zack calling. I hadn't heard from him in a month or so. "What?" I snapped. I do not wake up easily. Or joyfully. And I was mad at Zack for not calling for a month. He was one of CHAPS' owners after all. Business could be going down the tube for all he cared.

"Charlie?"

The voice was masculine, but it wasn't Zack's drawl. This voice was deep. Vibrant. An actor's voice. A name rose out of the sluggish bog that is my waking brain. Bristow. Taylor Bristow. My friend, Zack's friend, Savanna's boyfriend, Detective Sergeant Taylor Bristow. Who occasionally performed in Shakespeare in the Park with that same vibrant voice. "What time is it?" I demanded, noting there was no daylight filtering around the miniblinds.

"Six-fifty, Charlie. Are you awake?"

"No."

"Concentrate woman, I need your help."

I sat bolt upright, adrenaline streaking through me. "What's wrong, something's wrong? Savanna? Are you with Savanna?"

"Nothing's wrong with Savanna. Savanna's fine."

"Something's happened to Jacqueline? Listen, I can be there in half an hour, tops. I'll just . . ."

"Charlie!"

I shut up.

"I'm down by the old creek bed that's part of the border between Bellamy Park and Condor. Still called Flood Creek even though it dried up years ago. Where the bridge crosses it. You know where that is? It's not twenty minutes from CHAPS."

"Behind the discount stores."

"You got it. I want you to come down here and see if you can identify a body."

"Somebody's dead?"

"A woman. Yes."

"Just because I've come across a couple of bodies in the past, you think I'm acquainted with every corpse that turns up in Bellamy Park? What makes you think I know this woman? What did she die of?"

His patient sigh came clearly over the line. "You sure are cranky in the morning. She had your card in her jeans pocket. Only piece of identification on her."

"Estrella Stockton," I said at once.

"How can you be sure?"

"I gave her my card yesterday. She put it in her jeans pocket. She's in my self-defense class. Filipina? Long dark hair. Slight build. Maybe 5'4"?"

"Got it in one."

"I gave her my card because she told me ..." I broke off, threw the covers aside, and swung my legs over the side of the bed. In his cage alongside, Benny, my Netherland dwarf rabbit, stood up on his hind legs and pushed his nose against the mesh. I stuck a finger through and rubbed the velvety brown fur between his ears. It's one of his erogenous zones. He started vibrating with pleasure.

"How did she die?" I repeated.

"She was murdered. Stabbed."

"I'll be right there," I said.

I made sure Benny had enough victuals to last him, and his "critter litter" was reasonably clean, threw water on my face, cleaned my teeth, and pulled on my usual working "uniform" of Western shirt, jeans, socks, and boots. Then I picked up a couple of no-fat granola bars. I don't go anywhere without breakfast. I was anorexic during one period of my life. One of the good things my ex-husband did for me was to teach me that eating right makes you feel you're in control of your life.

A few minutes later, after cramming my cowboy hat down over my night-tangled hair and grabbing my denim jacket, I locked up my loft, which is directly above CHAPS' main corral, ran down the stairs and out the main door to the parking lot.

The sun came up about the time I arrived at the creek. Not very far up. I was glad of the assistance of the nice pink-cheeked police officer who led me between the trees and down the steep bank to the dry creek bed. Good thing I had boots on, some of those weeds looked suspiciously like poison oak. The officer

also looked vaguely familiar, which wasn't surprising—
I'd spent time with Bellamy Park law-enforcement
officers before. You may have read about the murders
I've solved for them. Yes, I *know* Zack Hunter got the
credit. That doesn't mean a thing.

The January morning air was nippy around the
edges. There was litter all over the landscape. Nowadays, that seems to be the rule rather than the exception, but the area even included discarded furniture,
huge packing crates, and a couple of abandoned cars.

It dawned on me as I reached the bottom of the
bank that the packing crates and furniture and even
the cars hadn't been discarded. They comprised a resi-
dential complex.

I guess I'd read about homeless people living—
correction, *existing*—down here, as well as in a couple
of other out-of-the-way spots in Bellamy Park, but I
hadn't seen it for myself. We all drive around all day,
making a practice of not looking at anything unpleas-
ant. Might catch sight of a sunset or sunrise once in a
while, see some pretty blossom on a tree, spot a California Highway Patrol car in the distance, but homeless
people become pretty near invisible.

Bristow's red, yellow, and blue windbreaker stood
out clearly against the cluster of officers and techni-
cians busily working around the creek bed. His brown
and shapely bald head was bare. He was talking to
a man wearing a green Air Force flight jacket with
squadron patches on it and a cap with Air Force
insignia.

A few feet beyond the yellow crime-scene tape a
female officer was taking photographs. Her subject

was lying on top of an open sleeping bag, to one side of a huge packing crate that had a neat doorway cut in the front. A piece of plywood, hinged at one side, acted as a barrier against the elements.

As the photographer conferred with another officer, who was either taking notes or sketching, Bristow waved me forward and escorted me to the sleeping bag.

"That's Estrella all right," I said. She was lying on her back, looking crumpled and very dead, which is not a pretty sight. She was still wearing the down jacket, white satiny shirt, and jeans she'd had on when she got into her Mercedes the previous day. The jacket and blouse were open. She wasn't wearing a bra. The suspenders were hanging loose and her jeans were down around her knees. She had been stabbed numerous times. There was a lot of blood.

I tried several times to swallow, but my throat had closed. Silently, I told this woman I barely knew that I was sorry. As I had when Bristow told me the dead woman had my card on her, I remembered those bruises on her arm, the suppressed anger she'd vented on our hapless instructor.

"Somebody stole her jewelry," I muttered.

"There was more than the earrings?"

I saw then that her earlobes were torn. I winced. Though that was the least of her injuries. Whoever had stabbed her had wanted to make very sure she was dead. "When I last saw her, yesterday, she had on a lot of gold. A necklace. Rings—four or five possibly. A gold clip in her hair—a sort of ponytail holder."

It was gone, too.

"I take it she was raped?" I asked.

Bristow nodded, looking very solemn. "Raped, then stabbed with great violence. Someone really hated this woman." He sighed. "Whoever killed her put her in that sleeping bag, zipped it up, and threw it from the bridge up there. Not your usual robbery scenario. It landed on top of Mr. Effington's house."

He indicated the packing crate with the neat doorway cut in it.

"Mr. Effington?" I queried.

"Roderick Effington the Third." The man in the Air Force clothing had come up silently on my other side. I saw now that the jacket was fairly ancient—the knitted cuffs and collar totally unraveled—and too large for him. The man doffed his cap and bowed slightly. "Thought it was an earthquake. Five o'clock in the morning. Wham! I ran around shouting 'The sky is falling, somebody call Chicken Little.' Most undignified of me, but there it is."

I stared at him. He was of average height, thin. His pants were too long and too wide, and were stacked over his combat boots. He had a very worn and weatherbeaten face, short raggedly cut hair. Two lower teeth showed up missing when he smiled. He stank like a skunk.

He must have seen my nose twitch. "I'm sorry, Miss . . ."

"Plato," I said automatically. "Charlie Plato."

"Ah. Related to the philosopher, no doubt. Very wise man. 'The life which is unexamined is not worth living.' "

I looked to Bristow for help, but he merely smiled tightly.

"I do apologize for the odor," the odd man went on. "It's been some time since I had the opportunity to perform my ablutions." He moved around to my other side. "I'll stay downwind of you." He laughed in a gentle way. "I attended a movie last night. Came into a little unexpected money, you might say."

"Panhandling or stealing?" Bristow asked.

Mr. Effington looked shocked. "*Found* money," he said emphatically. "I decided to treat myself. Unfortunately, there was a line. But soon after I arrived, the others in the queue left, and I was able to enter. Odor is useful on occasion, Miss Plato."

"This is your *house?*" I asked.

"I have always lived in odd places," he said by way of answer. "And, like Blanche Dubois in *A Streetcar Named Desire*, I have always depended on the kindness of strangers."

"Mr. Effington was asleep when the body landed on his house," Bristow explained. "The body hit on the top of the box, then fell off onto the ground."

"The movie tired me—so much violence," the other man put in. "The sound of something hitting my roof frightened me out of a deep sleep. Once I had located the source, I tried to lift the sleeping bag, discovered it was heavy, opened it, and found that poor lady. I climbed up to the road and called 911 from a convenience store. What blessings such services as 911 are. Were I a taxpayer, I would gladly contribute."

We exited the crime scene. "I'm sure glad it was you who found my card on her body," I said to Bristow. "Sergeant Timpkin would have sent me to jail without letting me pass Go."

"After he'd clapped you in irons," he said.

Sergeant Reggie Timpkin and I had clashed a few times during his investigation of a previous Bellamy Park murder. Let's just say he was a little overzealous.

"What can you tell me about Estrella?" Bristow asked me as he fished a notebook out of the inside pocket of his colorful jacket.

"Not a whole lot. Her name is Estrella Stockton. She came from the Philippines and married an American."

"You know her husband?"

I shook my head. "She told me she couldn't divorce him because she wasn't a citizen, and she'd have to go back to the Philippines. She didn't want to do that. I extrapolated from that information that she was married to an American citizen."

"You are beginning to talk like a police officer, Charlie," Bristow commented as he made notes.

"Been hanging around you too much, I expect."

His mouth twisted in a brief smile, and I carried on, squinting into the woods as I tried to remember exactly what I did know about Estrella. "She kept to herself in self-defense class," I said. "But I got talking to her yesterday after class."

"Time?" Bristow asked.

"About eleven-thirty. The class is scheduled from ten until noon, but Estrella had accidentally kneed the instructor, and he dismissed us early. He was demonstrating how we should knee an attacker in the groin, and Estrella got carried away," I explained to his raised eyebrows. "I started talking to her in the rest room because I noticed she had bruises on her left arm that looked as if someone had gripped her real tight. Also it had seemed to me in the class that she was acting out some suppressed anger—she seemed to get a real satisfaction out of the various exercises and was very eager to learn. I thought maybe someone assaulted her in the past, or she had some kind of dangerous experience, just as I did, and that's why she was so enthusiastic about the lessons."

I paused to think some more. "Anyway, I gave her my card and told her to call me if she needed help or someone to talk to. She had a slight speech impediment, by the way. She couldn't manage the 'r' sound. It made her seem a little babyish. At first she tried to imply she was just clumsy—the old walking-into-doors excuse abused women use—but then she admitted that her husband beat her all the time."

"Did she now?" He looked over his notes and added a few more. "That's it?" he asked.

I nodded, then remembered that Estrella worked at Hair Raising and told him that. "She was going to do something about my hair," I added mournfully.

He looked at the hair in question, though the worst of the tangles were covered by my cowboy hat. "People who have hair shouldn't complain about it," he said flatly, then consulted his notes again. "You said the class was over. You were in the rest room. Did anyone else hear this conversation?"

"Gina. Gina . . ." I always had to stop and think about Gina's last name. "Gina Giacomini."

"Angel's girlfriend?"

"She didn't hear the part about the bruises. After she came in Estrella and I just talked about my hair. Then Estrella left."

"You didn't see her again?"

I shook my head, then said, "Well, I walked to the door and watched her get in her car and drive away. She drove a gold Mercedes. I guess she liked gold." Once again I felt an overwhelming sadness. "I didn't particularly like Estrella," I said, "but I did feel sorry for her."

I remembered something Bristow had told me the last time we had a conversation about a murder victim. *Look first at the victim's acquaintances and relatives, and most often you'll find the murderer.* "It's truly awful if she was killed by that husband of hers. Why on earth women put up with that kind of treatment . . ." I broke off. "I guess you'll be interviewing the husband right away," I said.

"We will certainly talk with Mr. Stockton," Bristow promised. "In the meantime, wait here while I get someone looking for that car."

As he turned away, Mr. Effington, who had been standing discreetly at a distance, joined me again. For a minute or so, we stood silently, watching the officers doing what they had to do. They were being very efficient about it. The sun was shining through the trees and into the canyon. Several people were moving around Estrella, evidently getting ready to move her body out of there. I was surprised. I hadn't seen Dr. Martin Trenckman, the county coroner/medical examiner. Perhaps he'd left before I arrived. A tall slender black woman in grey slacks and a navy blazer seemed to be in charge. Her hair was pulled up into a knot and fastened with one of those dangerous-looking clips with jaws. I ought to try a hairdo like that, I thought. Especially now that Estrella wouldn't be doing anything with my hair. Or anyone else's.

"You said you had lived in odd places?" I asked the man, looking for distraction.

"Indeed yes. A garage last winter. It became very cold, no heat at all. An abandoned bus served me for a while. My car when I had one." He sighed. "Ah well, it's healthy to live outdoors. Everyone did it when the world began. They'd get up when God turned the light on, go to bed when He turned it off."

"You mentioned found money?"

"I possess a cart I er—*borrowed* from Lenny's Market. Every day I collect things that other people discard. I sell whatever is redeemable." His smile showed the gap in his lower teeth.

I should explain here that a lot of people borrow carts from Lenny's Market. Bellamy Park may be an upscale town, but it also has quite a few elderly residents who have fallen on hard times. They might live in fancy houses and pay fancy taxes, but either they can't afford the upkeep of a car, or they can't handle the driving. So they wheel their groceries home from Lenny's. Passersby often pick up and return any carts left hanging around. Or Lenny sends out a couple of employees with a truck to round them up.

"It's very cold this week," Mr. Effington said as Detective Sergeant Bristow rejoined us. "Might I have that sleeping bag when you are done with it?"

"It wouldn't bother you that someone dead has been in it?" I asked.

He gave me a sorrowful look. "Many things bother me, Miss Plato, but beggars cannot be choosers. That

may be a cliché, but in order to become a cliché it had
to be true first. One cannot be proud when one is cold
and without funds. I liberated my last sleeping bag
during a Dumpster-diving foray, but it is wearing thin."

"Dumpster-diving?" I queried, but Bristow interrupted before I could pursue the question. "That sleeping bag is evidence," he said.

Mr. Effington sighed. "A cigar then? It has been so
long since I came across a whole cigar. I did do my
duty as a citizen, you will recall."

"I don't smoke," Bristow said. He looked at me. "I'd
like you to go on into the station and make a formal
statement."

"Now?"

"If you please."

"You would wish me to do likewise?" Mr. Effington
asked him.

I was torn. It seemed as though I ought to offer
him a ride to the police station, but much as I had
enjoyed this fascinating man's conversation, the
thought of that odor in my car was daunting.

"I'm not through with you yet," Bristow told him,
to my relief.

"It was a pleasure making your acquaintance, Miss
Plato," Mr. Effington said. "Please come back and visit
now that you know the way."

"I'll do that," I said.

"This is no place for a woman," Bristow said crossly,
then lifted his eyes to the heavens. "Now that I've said
that, I suppose you'll feel you have to come back."

He knows me.

CHAPTER 3

Angel and I teach line dances for a couple of hours every night CHAPS is open—Savanna, too, when we have a big enough crowd. Which we usually do on Wednesdays. In case you haven't seen line-dancing, I should explain that you have to have your back to the rows of learners when you are teaching, so they can do the grapevines and scoots and hitches and whatevers the same way you do. In the main corral, I demonstrate from the front and Angel from the back. There's usually quite a lot of turning involved, so the dancers need a demonstrator at each end.

The Wednesday night crowd is a good-natured crowd, friendly, mostly locals or people who work somewhere in the area and make the stopoff for dinner at Dorscheimer's and dancing at CHAPS before going home.

That Wednesday, we were teaching the Boot Scootin' Boogie, a favorite of mine, all of us laughing because instead of clapping on the fourth count, the newcomers were getting mixed up and clapping whenever it occurred to them.

Doing a quarter turn to the left, I saw Taylor Bristow coming in. I saluted. He nodded, then laughed. I turned my head to see that our earnest learners were saluting, too. "Whoa!" I yelled. "Time out. Let's start from the beginning."

I looked over at Sundancer Brown in the deejay booth and gave him a "cutting my throat" signal. We obviously weren't ready for the music yet. Sundancer nodded, removed his headset, and took off—for a cigarette probably. Angel and I positioned ourselves for a right heelstand and started talking and walking slowly through the steps of the dance, an admittedly tricky one.

Bristow took a seat and sent a smoldering glance toward Savanna, who was instructing a smaller group in the little corral on the other side of Sundancer's booth.

It was about forty-five minutes before we took a break. By then we'd boogied through two sets of music. The cowboy and cowgirl wanna-bes were getting better, though half of them were still hitching when they should have stomped and vice versa.

Savanna and I drifted over to Bristow's table. Angel headed for the bar a couple of steps ahead of our dancers. Normally, I'd have left Savanna alone with Bristow, at least for a few minutes, but I was anxious to find out how the investigation was going.

Savanna had picked up bottles of Pellegrino water for all of us. I accepted mine gratefully. Line-dancing is energetic and aerobic, you can work up quite a sweat.

"What do you hear from Zack?" Bristow asked as I sat down.

I shook my head.

He frowned. "Me neither. You suppose he's okay?"

"Zack is always okay," I said.

Time out here. As I mentioned earlier, Zack Hunter used to play Sheriff Lazarro in *Prescott's Landing*, a television drama series that went belly-up a year and a half before Zack opened CHAPS. In one of the final episodes, good old Lazarro had been run over by a bus and pronounced DOA at Prescott's Landing General Hospital.

Since his "death" Zack had done a couple of commercials and a truly dim-witted country-western musical mystery pilot that never did turn into a series. Thanks be to whoever pulled that plug.

When last seen in September, Zack was once again leaving town to go to Hollywood to join Rudy DeSilva, one of the original directors of *Prescott's Landing*, who had decided to resurrect the very popular, but, in my not so humble opinion, mindless series. According to Zack, the plan was to make out that Lazarro had only *seemed* to be dead, but had actually been in a coma for the missing years. The first episode would deal with his near-death experience and his miraculous return to life after being treated by the town doctor with experimental drugs. I don't know about you, but I can wait.

I may not have mentioned this, but I'm not mad at Zack solely on account of him being a partner in CHAPS and leaving Angel and Savanna and me to do all the work. Zack and I had come a little closer together during our joint investigation into the death of a local banker. Zack had revealed some stuff about his own background that had made me respect him more than

I had previously. But just when I'd almost convinced myself that I should stop fighting the hormonal rush his presence always activated in my body, Hollywood called him back to the fold, and he raced to answer her siren call.

"Zack's probably busy," Savanna said soothingly.

"Doing what, that is the question," Bristow said, smiling broadly.

I knew what he was thinking. The same thing I was thinking. Zack was no doubt adding more dolls to what Savanna and I had dubbed his doll brigade. Only living dolls need apply. He'd lost a couple after the last corpse incident. He was probably working on keeping the numbers up.

"So what have you found out?" I asked Bristow.

He passed a hand over his gleaming head and showed me his lovely teeth. "About what, Ms. Plato?"

I gave him a look, which made him chuckle. "She's beautiful when she's mad, isn't she, honey?" he said to Savanna.

"Charlie's always beautiful," Savanna said. Loyalty is her middle name.

I gritted my teeth, determined not to ask again. Having once glanced at Savanna's face, Bristow took a while to refocus, but eventually he caught sight of me again and put me out of my misery. It's hell having an inquiring mind.

"Nothing unusual about the murder itself," he informed me crisply. "Straightforward. Just what it looked like. Ms. Stockton was raped first, died of multiple stab wounds in the abdomen and chest. After which somebody stole her jewelry, probably to make it appear that was the motive."

How awful that such a death should be classified as nothing out of the ordinary. "She was dead when the murderer pulled her earrings off?" I asked.

"According to the medical examiner."

"Dr. Trenckman?"

"The same."

"I didn't see him at the . . . creek."

"He was busy on another case—in Condor. Deputy coroner substituted."

"Tall slim black woman?"

He nodded. "Jalena Devereau."

"Jalena?" Savanna murmured. "That's pretty. Is it African?"

Bristow shook his head. "Father's name James, mother Elena."

I narrowed my eyes at him. He'd evidently been chatting with the woman. He'd better not . . . Nah, he was gazing at Savanna again in his usual dorky way. And holding her hand under the table. It was love. No question.

"So have you caught anyone yet?" I asked.

"Expecting an arrest momentarily," he said.

"Never mind what you tell the media," I chided. "This is me, Charlie Plato, your friend, the one who identified the victim for you, thus saving you hours of investigation."

"Pretty obvious who did it, Charlie," he said.

"The husband? Because he abused her?"

Savanna made a sound of distress. I'd forgotten that I hadn't told her that part. She looked a little ashy around the mouth. Savanna has a big heart, she feels for everyone, sweetest woman I've ever known. Just a few years older than me, she was the victim of a marriage much like mine, nothing wrong with either one except my husband couldn't resist other women and her husband couldn't resist other men. She'd become my friend the day we met. She's drop-dead beautiful, especially when, like tonight, she wears one of her red-fringed shirts with her form-fitting jeans and cowboy hat.

"Estrella told me in the rest room after the self-defense class that her husband abused her," I told her. "I saw bruises on her arm and asked her about them."

"Nosy as always," Bristow said with a fond smile that took any possible sting out of his comment.

"Too many people ignore spousal abuse," I said. "I don't want to be one of them."

"To your credit," he said.

I apologized. "I didn't mean *you* ignored stuff like that," I said. "So have you arrested the husband?"

"Not yet. I've questioned him of course. Thane is the name. Thane Stockton. Weird sort. Put me in mind of the guy in *To Kill a Mockingbird*. Boo Radley."

I mentioned that Zack Hunter's references are all TV and movie connected, right? Detective Sergeant Bristow's are all literary, more usually Shakespearean. I'm not sure why that's considered the indication of a superior brain, but it seems to be, doesn't it?

Savanna squinted at me. Even squinting she was gorgeous. "Wasn't Boo Radley the one who was real quiet and gentle, but then he stabbed somebody?"

"Something like that," I said. I looked at Bristow. "Mr. Stockton doesn't have an alibi?"

"Sure he does. He was home all evening and all through the night. He had no idea where Estrella was. I asked how come he didn't report her missing, and he didn't have an answer."

"But as you didn't arrest him, I take it you don't have any actual proof that he killed his wife."

"Not yet, but I expect by the time the lab people get through with all their fuming and testing and printing, we should be able to tie him to the killing. Stands to reason. If a man was beating up on his wife, how likely would it be for someone else to come along and kill her?"

I frowned. "I don't know. It all sounds a bit too simple."

"Murder is often simple, Charlie." He raised his eyebrows. "We're mainly interested right now in where Estrella Stockton spent her final hours. Between you watching her get into her Mercedes and her body landing on Mr. Effington's head, we've drawn a complete blank. We did find her car, parked not far away from the creek. But there's no evidence of any particular value. Her husband's fingerprints and her own. No others. A few hairs on the back of the passenger seat that didn't belong to Estrella or Thane, but who knows *who* they belong to. Some friend she gave a ride to, probably. We've put out a media request for people to come forward to help us piece together her final hours. But so far nobody's telling where Estrella was that night. Apparently, Charlie, only you and I care."

He dropped into Shakespeare mode. "We two alone

will sing like birds in the cage ... and take upon us the mystery of things, as if we were God's spies."

I did mention that Bristow does Shakespeare in the Park when he's not tracking down criminals, didn't I?

I shook my head, not recognizing the source.

"*King Lear*," he said.

Before I could comment, he leaned toward me, and said, "I haven't received a thank-you card from you yet."

I was blank for all of two minutes. Then a lightbulb went on. "You mean because you kept my name out of the media reports?"

He nodded.

"I am grateful, Sergeant, I really am. We don't need any more bodies associated with CHAPS. People are going to be afraid to come here."

Actually, when news of the previous murders had been blasted all over the ether, our customer base had increased dramatically. But it seemed to me three murder connections in a row might be too much for the populace to accept.

I held out my hand to Bristow, who shook it gravely. Then I got a signal from Sundancer that it was time to get going again, and I stood up. We had a couples dance to teach now, so I suggested to Savanna she stay and talk with Bristow.

She gave me her incandescent smile and said she'd watch to make sure the waiters didn't need her help, and I had Sundancer announce we were going to have a go at The Horseshoe.

* * * *

The next morning I was again awakened from a sound sleep by a loud ringing in my ears. This time it was 9 A.M., but when you don't get to bed until going on 2 A.M., that's still fairly early. Bristow again, I thought, and growled into the telephone, "What do you want now?"

There was a silence on the other end, and I struggled to clear the cobwebs from my brain. "Excuse me, I'm not at my best in the morning," I said.

"I'm sorry. I didn't realize it was early," a male voice said hesitantly. A strange male voice, which dropped to a near mumble, "I didn't sleep, you see, not at all, not all night." He paused, then asked, "This *is* CHAPS?"

"Yes." I don't broadcast the fact that I live above CHAPS. After all, that's a lot of empty space under me. Empty *dark* space. And the buildings on either side, a bank and an office building, are unoccupied at night. My purpose in living in the loft is threefold. One: after getting so hung up on possessions that I kept putting off divorcing my husband, the infamous plastic surgeon, Rob Whittaker—yeah, the one who treats the Hollywood stars, the stars being female and "treat" being the operative word—I had vowed that I'd never own a house or fancy furnishings again. My loft was mostly furnished with stuff left behind by the Watanabes, the previous owners of the building, plus a few thrift-store purchases.

Two: I'd talked Zack into letting me occupy the loft as official watchperson, in case any vandals decided to pay CHAPS a call. I'd worked part-time as a night watchperson at a concrete factory while I was putting myself through college, so I'd argued that I had experience.

Three: I'd talked Zack into letting me live there rent-free.

I realized my caller was probably waiting for me to flesh out my answer. "CHAPS isn't open at this time of the day," I said.

"I was hoping to speak to Mr. Hunter. Zack Hunter. Is he there?"

"No, he's away."

I wasn't about to say where he was, of course. Fans sometimes get psychotically obsessed with movie and TV stars. Especially when the star looks like Zack Hunter.

"Do you expect him back soon?" the man asked.

"Not really," I said.

He made a small sound that seemed to hold an echo of disappointment.

"May I ask who's calling?" I said into the subsequent silence.

He sighed. "Some time ago, several months ago, I guess, it was on television news that Mr. Hunter helped solve a murder case for the police."

He was correct. That's how it looked on TV. That's not how it was however.

"And?" I prompted.

"I wondered if he could help me find out who murdered my wife."

I swallowed hard. There was surely only one person this caller could be. "May I ask who's calling?" I managed to get out through my suddenly dry throat.

"My name is Thane Stockton," he said.

I swallowed again. Thing was, I was supposed to go see my gynecologist this morning at eleven-fifteen. Dr. Hanssen had decided almost six months ago that I should have a cone biopsy, which for the uninitiated into women's plumbing means he wanted to cut a chunk out of my cervix and have it looked at. Yeah, I didn't like the sound of it either, but my pap smear had come back marked "questionable" a couple of times, and Doc Hanssen had done a colposcopy, which is a look-see, and had decided the results were indeterminate. So he wanted to do the biopsy to "rule out cancer."

I'd been putting off the procedure for some time, using one excuse after another. The doctor had finally gone ahead and scheduled it for January 20, which was about eleven days away. I was supposed to go in for a general checkup today.

How important could that be? I was in great shape. I could probably reschedule for Monday.

"Well, Mr. Stockton," I said carefully. "As it happens, I worked very closely with Zack on the case you're referring to. Perhaps I could be of assistance?"

I could hear him breathing, but he didn't say anything. I decided to wait him out. "Well," he said finally. "I did hope for Mr. Hunter, but ..."

He broke off, then started over. "I'm feeling rather desperate. The police seem to think I killed my wife, but I did not. So I must find out who did. You do understand that?"

"I do." I also understood that he could be trying to confuse the whole issue.

"Very well then," he said.

I guessed that meant my offer of help had been accepted. Swiftly, before he could change his mind, I told him I'd meet him at his house in a couple of hours, wrote down the directions on a scrap of yellow note-paper, and hung up the telephone.

"Looks like we're back in the sleuthing business, Ben," I told my rabbit after I'd hung up.

Ben's ears twitched. Rabbits don't have a whole range of expressions. The whiskers twitch, the nose twitches, the ears move, that's about it except when he yawns, which is really cute and shows his little buckteeth.

I lifted him out of the cage and snuggled him on my shoulder so he could nibble my hair, one of his favorite occupations. Hey, listen, most animals fixate on something. My parents had a poodle who dragged a grey fur blankie around. Made him look like he had a long beard. A friend of mine owned a Siamese cat who didn't make a move without his stuffed pink ele-phant. Ben was one of the few creatures on earth who truly liked my hair.

He pulsed gently under my hand as I petted his soft brown fur. Bristow always called him, "Ben, my man." I wondered what Bristow was going to say to me if he found out I'd visited suspected murderer Thane Stockton.

I had an idea it would not be anything pleasant.

CHAPTER 4

It was close to 11 A.M. when I emerged from CHAPS into the parking lot. Keeping my head down against the drizzle as I headed toward my Jeep Wrangler, I didn't see Zack Hunter's pickup truck until it loomed up right in front of me.

Zack was sitting in the driver's seat, rooting around in the glove compartment.

I froze in place, the way Benny does when he's hip-hopping around the loft and suddenly senses danger. Though the only danger from Zack is to my peace of mind. And body.

Those of you who know me will remember that I'm sort of mildly hung up on Zack, though I'm also dedicated to not doing anything about it. Celibacy is my watchword.

Zack had seen me standing there like a wax effigy and was getting down from the truck. A minor tremor rocked the earth under my feet. No, I'm not talking about "the earth moved" cliché—this was an ordinary earthquake-type tremor. They show up once in a while in the Bay area. If you are a true Californian, you are totally blasé about such interruptions. You might glance up to see if any buildings are about to fall on you if you're outdoors, or if the light fixtures are coming unglued if you happen to be inside a building. This one lasted no more than a few seconds.

"Whoa, Charlie—major welcome home!" Zack said.

The rain stopped. I wouldn't have been surprised to see rays of sunlight shooting down from behind the lowering clouds. "What the hell are you doing here?" I demanded.

He looked great. He always does. Unfortunately. His long legs and lean hips were packed into his jeans just right. His shirt stretched tautly across his broad shoulders. As Sheriff Lazarro, Zack had dressed in all-black clothing—jeans, cowboy hat, Western shirt, Tony Lama boots. This outfit had worked as well for Lazarro as it had for Johnny Cash, and it proved so successful in snaring the ladies, Zack had made it his signature suit, as much a part of him as his green eyes and wry smile and the straight black eyebrows that slanted whimsically upward above his nose.

As he seemed about to give me one of his full-bodied hugs, I stuck out a hand to stop him. I was still mad at him for running off the minute Rudy DeSilva, one of his former directors, crooked his pinky. Mistaking my gesture, he picked up my hand and brushed the back of it with his lips, meanwhile giving me one of the famous zinging glances from under his eyelashes.

"Charlie darlin'," he drawled. "I *surely* did miss you."

Don't let that drawl fool you. Zack grew up in L.A. and Beverly Hills. That drawl is as genuine as the zigzag scar on his left cheek, which he *says* was given him by a raging bull. Ha! More likely a cuckolded husband with pinking shears to hand.

"I asked you a question," I said.

He straightened and let my hand go, smiling his oh-so-boyish smile. "I'm home for rest and recuperation." His smile turned slightly bleak around the edges. "Seems the network pulled back some. Supposed to order thirteen episodes of *Prescott's Landin'*. Decided on a more cautious approach with six. Gonna show some in the February sweeps, then do some reruns for a spell, see how it goes."

"They aren't going to shoot any more episodes?"

"Depends on the ratin's, Charlie."

Was it my imagination, or had his voice faltered slightly? My former irritation gave way to sympathy as I noted that the bleakness had spread to his eyes. Why should I have been mad at him anyway? His career had netted him millions of dollars and the adoration of countless women. I'd been thinking of new shows and reruns from the standpoint of the viewer, not the actor. Who could blame an actor for pursuing his career to the utmost?

"Surely I'm not detecting a note of worry?" I asked. "Your ratings have always been out of sight."

Before he could answer I suddenly remembered where I was going before I saw his truck. I often have these mini fugue states when our man-in-black shows up. Hormones suck oxygen—and common sense—out of the brain. "Look, Zack, I'd love to stand and chat," I told him, "but I have an appointment."

"Charlie!" His green eyes could look so disconsolate, so *wounded*. In spite of all the pep talks I'd given myself while he was gone, I could feel a surge of activity in my nether regions that indicated vigorous interest.

"We've had another murder," I said briskly. "I'm on my way to see the man Bristow thinks may have done it. The victim's husband."

His eyebrows sloped up. "You surely weren't intendin' to go see this dude alone, darlin'?"

"Sure I was. He called and asked me to . . ." Okay, that wasn't strictly true. I sighed. "Actually, he called this morning to ask if *you* could help him solve the murder. He saw all the media hype on the last murder. Said he *didn't* kill his wife, so he wanted your help clearing his name. I explained you were gone and that I had a lot to do with solving the last couple of murders we had in Bellamy Park. So he accepted me as a substitute."

"We'll take my truck," Zack said promptly.

About to object, I realized Zack would probably be handy to have around if things took a turn for the unexpected. There were some respectable muscles under that black Western shirt. He'd also be able to get between me and Detective Sergeant Bristow if the detective felt I'd been a bit overzealous in my citizenly duty. Which he frequently did.

There was one other advantage in having Zack along. People are more likely to open up to him. All he has to do is fix those green eyes on them, slant up those puckish black eyebrows—lift that wonderfully clean-cut jaw. And there he is—Sheriff Lazarro made flesh, lawman personified. At risk of sounding sexist, I'll admit his technique works better on women than on most men, but he's still a potent inquisitor.

He was already in the truck. I hoisted myself up, handed him the slip of paper on which I'd written the directions, then filled him in on the details of the murder, the self-defense class, and how I happened to get involved with Estrella, as we headed toward Thane Stockton's address.

"So how come the network got cold feet?" I asked when I was done.

His mouth twitched at the corner nearest me. Yes, he *was* worried. "They can't decide if the reprise of *Prescott's Landin'* is certain of success. Climate's changed some. People are favorin' medical shows nowadays. Lot of young hotshots comin' up."

Was he actually admitting he wasn't a young hotshot anymore?

"I offered to play a doctor," he went on, glancing at me sideways. "How d'you think I'd look in a white coat? Should I turn in my six-shooter for a stethoscope?"

He sighed, which was an unusual sound coming out of Zack. "Rudy wants to keep me closely associated with Sheriff Lazarro until we see how it goes," he said. "So I thought I'd come home and maybe make a few commercials—a lot of big names are doing that right now. Even a couple of directors I know. Heck, I heard Brad Pitt once dressed up in a chicken suit outside a restaurant. 'Course that was *before* he became famous."

My traitorous mind wasn't paying attention. It had flashed on the last commercial Zack had shot. His body naked except for a minuscule swimsuit, he had stood under a waterfall, sensuously soaping his tanned muscles with Hawaiian Sunshine Soap, all the while gazing under his eyelashes at the camera and into the libido of every able-bodied woman in America.

About the time I emerged from this fantasy-inducing spectacle, Zack was pulling up outside wide wrought-iron gates between high stone walls. Beyond was a long avenue of palms that led to an enormous three-story-wood-and-stucco building that was a dead ringer for a French château.

"Good grief!" I exclaimed. "That house must be ten thousand square feet if it's an inch."

Zack nodded. "Pretty near. It's the old Stockton place." He reached for a switch on a post. "Real-estate lady showed it to me in passin' when I was lookin' for a place to live."

He identified himself, and the gates opened. "This dude we're goin' to see is a Stockton?"

"Thane Stockton," I said as we drove into a magnificent vista of trees, gardens, and lawns. "His wife was named Estrella."

Thane Stockton came out to meet us. He introduced himself as we parked at the foot of stone steps and exited the pickup. I'd half expected a butler, and he sort of looked the part—probably around forty-five, average height, round-shouldered, with blue eyes and a shock of sandy hair that was greying around the edges. Sort of ordinary. Not terribly attractive, but not dramatically homely either. His eyes had a melancholy cast to them. He sure didn't look like the billionaire he had to be to live in a place like this. Nor did he look like a murderer. I could easily imagine Detective Sergeant Bristow's jeering retort to *that* thought.

"And what *pre*-cisely does a murderer look like, Ms. Plato?"

There were iron bars on all the windows—wrought iron and decorative, but also substantial. To keep people out, or in? I wondered. What if there was a fire between you and the door?

Stockton followed my gaze. He must have seen me shudder. "Estrella was afraid of intruders," he explained. "She was extremely paranoid. I had the bars installed to make her feel more secure."

Maybe not so paranoid, I thought, considering she was murdered. Ironic, that. All that protection and the threat she was worried about had been fulfilled when she was outside her fortified castle.

"There's coffee," Stockton said.

"Sounds good," I said.

"I understood the young lady to say you were away," he said to Zack as we trooped through a marble-floored entry hall, and down a long corridor, past a sunken pastel living room. Though gnashing my teeth over being called a young lady, I managed to take an admiring look at the grand piano in the far corner, the light-filled paintings on the walls.

Beyond a formal dining room that could have seated thirty people, we entered a huge kitchen that featured a lot of copper pans on a rack hanging from the ceiling, an enormous stove, a side-by-side refrigerator-freezer. While Zack explained his unheralded return, I noticed a bunch of words on the refrigerator door. I'd seen an ad in a catalog recently for magnetic poetry, and that's what this was. A couple of hundred words and parts of words, backed by magnetic strips, stuck randomly on the refrigerator. The idea being you could pick out what you needed to write your poems.

I read the first two lines aloud. " 'Dead beat and deadly/ I whisper of death in purple shadows.' Who's the poet?"

"I'd hardly call myself that," Stockton said. "I just find it relaxing to put words together." With one rather large hand, he swept the words into the general mass.

Would there be any way to match up his fingerprints with those bruises on Estrella's arm, I wondered. And had he really written those lines, or were they Estrella's work?

We sat at a butcher-block table next to a window with a wonderful view of the extensive back gardens. There were snapdragons, primroses, and daffodils overflowing baskets hung on trellises above manicured green lawns through which paths wandered. Bright variegated tulips nodded in circular beds here and there. We'd had a lot of sunshine the previous week. Flowers had been exploding all over Bellamy Park.

"How long had you and Estrella been married?" I asked Thane Stockton to get things going.

He shook his head in a helpless sort of way. "Two years," he said, with the drawn-out sound of someone saying "too long." He poured coffee for all of us, reached back to the counter, and set the carafe on the coffeemaker to keep warm.

"You met here in Bellamy Park?"

He looked down at the table and traced one of the blocks with a long index finger. When I'd just about decided he wasn't going to answer what had seemed to me an innocent enough question, he glanced shyly up at me, his mouth grimacing slightly. "I found Estrella in a catalog of prospective brides on the World Wide Web," he said.

Zack's eyebrows slanted. Taking off his cowboy hat, he set it carefully on an empty chair, crown side down, then sat back as though he'd decided this was going to take a while.

I stared at Mr. Stockton for several seconds, too shocked to speak.

"He said prospective brides, Charlie," Zack said. "Didn't say nothin' about white slavery."

"But that's the same as mail order," I said. "You're kidding. Tell me you're kidding."

Mr. Stockton shook his head. "It's quite common, Miss Plato. There are many businesses marketing the addresses of foreign women to American men. The publications on the Internet are no different. They are full of photographs and descriptions. For a price you are sold the address of the woman of your choice—or women if you wish to make a further selection." He paused. "Please note that they sell only the addresses. Not the women."

"That's a very fine distinction," I said. I was having to hold back a tirade of anger about this whole idea of women being offered for sale like a bunch of cattle.

"The women place the ads themselves," Stockton pointed out in his mild voice. "Nobody forces them to advertise. Usually, they want to improve their situation in life. Or perhaps get away from the demands of their families. They are quite free to turn the man down or accept him. No coercion is involved."

"It still stinks," I said.

He flushed, and I apologized. "I'm sorry, Mr. Stockton, I don't mean anything personal. It's just the idea of ordering a wife from a catalog. I thought it was bad enough when I learned about it in history lessons at school and on television shows about frontier days. I had no idea it was still going on."

"You must understand, Miss Plato, that this is not the same thing at all. The man writes to several women. If he's lucky, they write back. He narrows his choice after a few letters. He sends photographs and information about himself. It's like a pen-pal club. When he decides which woman he prefers, the courtship proceeds in the same way it would if you were introduced by a friend, or met the woman at a party."

"Then why not meet a woman at a party?" I asked.

"I don't go to parties," he said sadly. He was silent for a minute or two, then he looked at me directly. "Let me try to explain my reasoning. At first when I stumbled across this arrangement on the web, I was merely curious. The first site I looked into featured Eastern European women, but they did not seem at all attractive to me."

Zack was looking at him as if he were some rare creature he had never seen before. Of course, to Zack the idea of paying for an introduction to a woman would be completely alien. And unnecessary.

"Then I found a Philippine site," Mr. Stockton went on. "The women seemed lovely. Small and dark-haired, dark-eyed. I began to take the idea more seriously. There was a lot of talk in the web site about their ladies having traditional values. From what I read, I thought I would be getting someone who would be a proper wife, a real wife, loving and, well—docile. Demure."

Zack shot me a glance. I caught it out of the corner of my eye. He was obviously expecting me to explode. But I wanted to hear what Thane Stockton had to say. This was no time to be ranting about the so-called liberation of women.

"I take it Estrella didn't measure up," I said.

Stockton flushed again. There was a kind of innocence in his blue eyes I hadn't noticed before. Something unworldly there. "I want you to understand, Miss Plato," he said. "I don't go out much. I don't have much of a social life. And American women, most American women, terrify me. They seem so confident always, so absolutely sure of what they want and where they are going."

"And you don't like that."

"It's not a case of liking, or not liking, it's a case of timidity." He moved his head from side to side in that helpless way again. "I am a very shy man, Miss Plato. I was lonely. Forty years old. I wanted someone to share my home. I wanted children. Estrella said she wanted the same. We wrote to each other for three months, then I went to the Philippines. She was . . ." He hesitated. "Enchanting. She seemed everything I was looking for. So sweet, so charming."

That didn't sound like the Estrella I had met.

"And so beautiful," he concluded.

Okay. I could concede that.

He excused himself for a minute, returned carrying a large photo album bound in white fabric. The first photograph in it was of Estrella, breathtaking in white lace, with a veil over her long dark hair.

"We were married in the Philippines," he said.

"Her family approved?" I asked.

He shook his head. "She had no family. They were all dead. That was why she wanted to leave the country, she said. She had only bad memories."

"So you married and brought your bride here?"

"Surprisingly quickly. I learned later it often takes a new bride a year to get the necessary papers to come to the United States, but I spoke to an old family friend, and he managed to get Estrella here in six months."

Old boys' clubs can do wonders.

"At first it was wonderful," he went on. "We were very happy. At least, *I* was very happy. Estrella felt somewhat overwhelmed by this house, she said. She wanted me to sell it and buy a smaller one. She thought it would be more comfortable. But of course, I could not, would not, do that. And then I found out about Estrella's shopping. I'd had no idea a woman could spend so much money so quickly. I had to speak to her, to explain that we couldn't afford to spend so much. I discovered to my horror that she had formed the impression I was an extremely rich man."

I glanced around the kitchen, out of the window at the grounds. He interpreted my thoughts. "This house, I know. It looks as if I'm extraordinarily wealthy. My family was one of the old California families. And it is true, I am not a poor man. But unfortunately, my father made several foolish investments and lost a great deal of the family fortune. When my parents died, the house came to me along with a trust fund my grandfather had set up. It's enough to maintain the house and pay taxes and buy food and quite a few luxuries besides. But it's by no means inexhaustible."

"Your wife didn't like findin' out you weren't as rich as she thought?" Zack suggested. He was sitting forward now, looking more like tough-minded Sheriff Lazarro than his own mild-mannered though macho self. Sometimes old Lazarro just takes over. Sometimes I think Zack himself isn't sure if he's being Zack or playing his old role.

"She was furious," Stockton said with a rueful twist to his mouth. "She immediately went out and got a job, so she could continue her shopping expeditions. To shame me, she said. She'd worked as a hairdresser in Manila, so she had no trouble finding a job at a salon." He shook his head. "I didn't want her to work. I wanted an old-fashioned wife. Someone who would take care of me, love me, love my house."

If he hadn't looked so pathetically wistful, I might have kicked him on the shins for such sexist remarks.

His story continued. Estrella had gone to work at Hair Raising. She had met other American women. She had started acting like American women. Wouldn't do this, wouldn't do that. She took driving lessons, demanded a car of her own. Went shopping more than ever. Spent all her money on jewelry, clothes, cosmetics.

"When I protested that I wanted her to stay home, to be with me, she was not at all pleased. We had words and . . ." Stockton paused and shook his head again, then swallowed painfully, his Adam's apple bobbing.

Zack and I exchanged a glance. His eyebrows canted

up inquiringly over his nose. I shook my head. I didn't want to say a word. I thought I knew what was coming. A confession that Thane Stockton had begun abusing his wife.

But what he said was, "That was when Estrella started beating up on me."

CHAPTER 5

"Oh, come on now," I protested. "I saw Estrella's bruises. On her arm. You were the one doing the beating. She told me so."

"She told . . ." He looked totally shocked. "You *know* my wife?"

I'd forgotten that I'd failed to mention that particular fact. "Not exactly," I admitted. "I met her when she took the self-defense classes I started at CHAPS. The last class was the day before she . . . died. We were in the rest room. I saw bruises on her arm when she pushed up her blouse sleeves to wash her hands."

He closed his eyes briefly. When he opened them again they seemed even bluer, like those of a child. "I had to hold her arm to stop her from attacking me with a broken bottle," he said. "It had a very jagged edge. She was threatening to cut my face. I know I'm no beauty but still . . . I had to hold her off until she calmed down. As for that self-defense class . . . after the first one, she made a game of practicing the techniques on me. Kneed me very hard in . . . well, it was very painful, I had to go to the doctor."

"Did you tell the cops about this?" Zack asked. He

was maintaining his wise Sheriff Lazarro investigator attitude, but I was pretty sure he wasn't buying Thane Stockton's story.

Mr. Stockton shook his head slowly. "How would it look, me letting myself be abused? I couldn't bear the humiliation of police officers knowing. If the media got hold of it . . . I could imagine the headlines. The Stockton name . . ."

His clear blue eyes met mine directly. "In any case, do you think for one minute they would have believed me? Estrella was small. Much smaller than I." He sighed deeply. "She was a wicked, wicked woman. I was afraid she was going to be the death of me."

"So you killed her in self-defense, is that what you're sayin'?" Zack asked.

Mr. Stockton looked at him hopelessly. "I didn't kill my wife, Mr. Hunter. I came to hate her, but I did not kill her."

You can't always go by innocent blue eyes. It seems easier for blue eyes to look innocent than any other color. I know just how to put an innocent expression in my own.

I suddenly remembered the satisfied expression in Estrella's dark eyes when she kneed our hapless instructor in the groin. It had seemed to me she was venting anger. Maybe substituting her husband's woebegone face for the instructor's confident features. Was that why she'd gone after Duke so enthusiastically?

"I'm a fairly useless sort of person," Mr. Stockton went on, seemingly engrossed in gazing at his hands on the table. "I never expected to have to work at anything; I was raised to be wealthy. My father taught me it was my duty to take care of this house and the gardens, to preside at charity board meetings—though I never liked that part and gave it up after his death. I love this estate, Miss Plato, Mr. Hunter," he added, looking up at us again. "I was so afraid Estrella was going to get us deeply in debt. She regarded a credit card as something that should be used to the full extent of the allowed amount. I was afraid she would go so far as to lose this house for me. I couldn't live, wouldn't *want* to live without my house."

I was tempted to tell him it was stupid to get attached to a house—I'd stayed in my former marriage longer than I should have because of my fondness for the Tudor house on Puget Sound that Rob and I had owned. I knew better now. I wasn't about to get too attached to anything.

I took a sip of coffee. Kona blend. My favorite kind. "Did you tell the police you were afraid Estrella would lose your house out from under you?" I asked.

He shook his head. Well, at least he'd had the sense not to make his possible motives too clear.

"I do paint," he added, with some pride. "Watercolors, not oils. Oils are harsh, don't you think? Watercolors are nice. Soft shadings. Delicate tones."

"You did the paintings back there?" I asked, gesturing toward the hall we'd come along.

He nodded. I realized that the paintings I'd seen in passing had been mostly of this house and its surrounding gardens. Bristow was an astute detective. He might very well have extrapolated Mr. Stockton's motive from the paintings.

"I've known women beat up on men," Zack said

slowly, gazing down into his coffee mug as if he could see his future in it. No, not his future—his past. I remembered suddenly the terrible things he'd suffered as a child. He'd evidently been thinking over Thane Stockton's claim that Estrella had abused him. "There was an episode on *Prescott's Landin'* too," he went on.

That was the Zack I knew—relating real life to TV. His credo was "Life imitates art," though he'd never have phrased it that way. He seemed to believe that everyone in the whole world was taking part in a TV show. Actually, I sometimes believe that myself.

The episode he was referring to was not one I'd ever watched. I avoid television whenever possible, preferring to get my entertainment from books, especially mystery novels. Evidently in this particular show, Sheriff Lazarro had investigated the killing of an elderly man in a nursing home and had discovered that one of the nurses was the guilty party. She had been abusing patients for years, but they'd been too intimidated to complain.

This was hardly the same sort of situation, but it was obviously influencing Zack to give Thane Stockton the benefit of some doubt.

"The nurse was the mother of the administrator of the home," Zack continued. "That's why everyone was afraid to tell. They were afraid the dude would turn on them."

Mr. Stockton nodded, looking at Zack now as if he had suddenly sprouted wings and a halo. "Estrella had men friends," he said. "She used to say she'd get them to finish me off, so she could inherit this white elephant and sell it."

He glanced at me, looking forlorn again. "She was talking about my house."

"Do you have any proof that she was having affairs?" I asked, thinking at the same time that he was making it look worse for his side, rather than improving his situation.

He shook his head. "The most recent ones she mentioned were a bank guard and the instructor you had for those self-defense classes. I forget his name."

"Duke? Duke Conway?" He was losing me rapidly. "No way," I said. "The only woman Duke showed any interest in was . . ." I broke off, not wanting to say anything about Gina in front of Zack in case he might bring it up in front of Angel. "Another woman altogether," I finished lamely, then tried a trick question. "Did Estrella tell you about Duke after that last lesson? Did she mention that she got carried away in the demonstration of the knee-in-the-groin technique?"

Zack winced, almost audibly.

Mr. Stockton frowned. "I didn't see Estrella after that lesson," he said. So much for my trickiness. "She didn't come home. I told the police I didn't report it because I thought she might have left me. She'd threatened to often enough. Like the day before when she came at me with that bottle." His mouth moved dejectedly. "I was hoping she *had* left me."

He'd avoided falling into the hole I'd tried to dig for him, but he was digging one of his own.

He sighed. "I guess she was lying about the instructor, then? It was so difficult to know when to believe her. That baby way she had of talking. I found it enchanting at first, irritating later. I think she often exaggerated it. 'The instwuctor man,' she called him. Sometimes she told the truth, sometimes she lied. She told me after the first lesson, the one before Christmas, that the instructor was tall, dark, and handsome, not like me. And he had a black belt in karate."

I nodded. "The black belt part is true. And you could call him handsome, I guess."

"She said she'd get him to beat me up if I kept nagging her about money. He could do a really good job, she said. She told me she was sleeping with other men, too. Some man she met on a trip to Las Vegas. Another one the hair salon ordered supplies from. A man who worked in her favorite jewelry store. Maybe she lied about them all. I don't know. I don't think she was trying to make me jealous; I think she was trying to scare me, make me afraid of these men who would beat me up if she asked them to. The one from Las Vegas was a member of a Filipino gang, she said."

He looked abjectly miserable. I still wasn't sure I believed everything he was saying, but if any of it was true I felt very sorry for him.

"The thing is, you see," he went on heavily. "It wasn't just threats. She'd fly off the handle over the littlest thing. If I asked her where she was going, when she got all dressed up to go out. If I said one word about her shopping. Mostly I just tried to keep away from her, to defuse the situation. She would *do* things. Awful things."

"What kinda things?" Zack asked.

"She poisoned my dog with antifreeze. Took her to the vet and had him get rid of her. She was a lovely dog—a golden cocker spaniel. We used to play tug-of-war with an old doggy blanket, and she'd come out with me when I worked in the gardens. She never quite accepted Estrella, barked at her every time she came home. Estrella said her death was an accident, and maybe *I'd* have an accident one day. Maybe I'd die, she said, and it would be good riddance."

"But she was the one who died," I pointed out.

He stared at me, his face draining of color. "Yes," he whispered. "She was the one who died."

"You must have staff here," Zack said briskly. "Friends maybe. Did any of your friends witness your altercations with your wife?"

"They weren't exactly altercations, Mr. Hunter. Altercations implies participation by two or more people." He looked sad. "Estrella was careful never to do anything in front of the people who work for me. I employ only day people—some garden helpers, a few women who come in to clean and do laundry. We keep a great deal of this house closed up, dustcovers, that sort of thing. So there's not as much work as you'd think. None of my people are here today. I like to have the place to myself sometimes."

He hesitated. "Estrella was always very nice to the people who work here. She might not have liked the house, but she loved having servants. They liked her very much, too." He sighed. "As for friends, yes, I have a friend. He didn't ever see Estrella doing anything to me, but he did see the results. He's my doctor. Adler Hutchins. We see each other often. He likes to play outdoor chess."

"Outdoor chess?" Zack and I queried at the same time.

Mr. Stockton stood up, scraping his chair back in sudden eagerness. "I designed it myself and made all the pieces, would you like to see it?"

The chessboard was in the side yard. Concrete had been colored alternately black and white, set up in squares that covered a fairly large area. Lined up in their proper places were foot-high kings, queens, bishops, knights, rooks, and pawns, all carved of weathered wood, set on flat bases.

My dad would have loved it. He'd played chess with the head waiter when things had been slow at the Greek restaurant he and my mom had owned in Sacramento. When my parents' Cessna crashed on the way to Tahoe one stormy Thanksgiving, the head waiter had asked if he could keep the board and pieces. He wanted to glue them in place in the positions they'd left them in when Dad went off to the airport.

Mr. Stockton demonstrated a couple of moves for us, maneuvering the pieces with a pusher on the end of a broomstick handle. The pieces were beautifully balanced. They glided effortlessly.

"Dang!" Zack exclaimed admiringly.

"Did Estrella play?" I asked.

"She wasn't a patient person," her husband said.

Yes. Well, I'd never had the patience to sit down and learn the game either. Now I wished I had. *Later*, I'd kept telling my father.

As we trooped back toward the house, we heard a loud buzzing sound. "The gate," Mr. Stockton said, and went off to let whoever in.

A couple of minutes later, Detective Sergeant Bristow drove in. We were waiting at the foot of the steps—

Mr. Stockton, Zack, and I. "Will you help me?" Mr. Stockton asked as we watched Bristow get out of his car.

"I'll call you," I said, not wanting to commit myself.

He nodded as if satisfied.

Bristow and Zack did the complicated hand-slapping thing that men do when they like each other but are too macho to show it. "Zack, my man," Bristow said. "I'd no idea you were due back."

"It's a long story," Zack said.

Bristow fixed his sights on me, his eyes narrowing. "May I ask, Ms. Plato, ma'am, what you might be doing here?"

"You didn't ask Zack that question," I pointed out.

"I assumed you persuaded him to accompany you, or else he gallantly offered you his protection."

I swallowed my outrage. It does no good to get outraged at Bristow. He just puts it down to feminine wiles and ignores it. "He invited himself along," I said mildly. "I simply came to offer Mr. Stockton my condolences on the death of his wife."

Mr. Stockton flashed me a grateful glance that was not lost on Bristow.

"Uh-huh," Bristow said, drawing out the first syllable to show he wasn't buying.

"I have a couple questions, Mr. Stockton," he said evenly to our host.

The man swallowed.

"It has come to my attention that your late wife drew out a considerable amount of money from her checking account on the day before she died. At about 4 P.M."

Mr. Stockton looked mournful, then nodded. "It was probably the money I acquired a week ago by selling an oil painting my father once accepted in lieu of a debt. I never liked it, but it was well thought of and extremely valuable."

He held his palms upward in a helpless gesture. "I'd intended doing some necessary repairs on the roof with that money. But Estrella insisted she must have it, that she needed it to pay a debt. She—"

He broke off, swallowed, and started again. "She forced me to endorse the check and give it to her. I suppose she must have deposited it in her own account."

Bristow polished the top of his head with one lean brown hand. "She forced you." His voice was flat.

"Perhaps I haven't quite told you the whole story of my marriage," Mr. Stockton said slowly.

"It seems possible," Bristow said.

I was very interested to see if Thane Stockton would tell Bristow the same story he'd told Zack and me, but Bristow turned to me, and said, "You *were* just leaving?" with an emphasis that left me in no doubt it would be prudent to agree.

Zack and I drove up the long driveway in silence. After we exited through the gates and turned onto the road, I said, "Well, what do you think?"

Zack shook his head. "Seems hard to believe, but I sorta believe him."

"Mr. Stockton, you mean?"

"Yep. Doesn't seem like a murderer to me."

"Murderers don't always go around dripping blood from their incisors."

"I know that, darlin'. But he seemed such a shy sorta guy."

I nodded. He'd seemed very gentle, certainly. But people could be very deceiving. Take Zack for example. He could make a woman feel she was the most important person in his life. And then another woman would drift past and beckon and he'd point like a bird dog on the first day of hunting season.

"Bristow thinks he's like Boo Radley in *To Kill a Mockingbird*," I told him.

"I remember that movie," he said.

"I think Bristow was talking about the book."

"It was a book?"

"It won a Pulitzer."

He looked blank, then rallied. "Gregory Peck won an Oscar for the movie."

Oscars and Emmys he knew. Pulitzers were outside his range of vision.

Zack shrugged. "Seems like there were things in Stockton's story that could be checked, so I figure it's not too likely he'd tell them if they weren't true."

"You mean about him going to the doctor when his wife supposedly kneed him?"

"And her poisonin' the dog with antifreeze. And havin' affairs. People notice that kind of thing."

He'd know all about that last part, of course.

"All of those things give Thane Stockton *more* reason to have murdered Estrella," I pointed out.

He was silent for a moment, no doubt struck anew

by my intelligence. Then he said, "All the same, I think I'll do what he asked."

I stared at his lean profile. He had on a seriously focused, hard-jawed Sheriff Lazarro expression. "I didn't hear him ask you to do anything."

"*You* told me, Charlie. You said he wanted me to look into his wife's murder, find out who really did it." One of his sexy under-lowered-eyelid glances zinged at me sideways. "We're a good team, darlin'. We could take it on. Together, Charlie. We do very well together."

Yeah right. Until Hollywood or some other woman, *any* other woman, distracted him.

"Don't call me darlin'," I said automatically, but my heart wasn't in it. I wanted to do just what Thane Stockton had asked us to do—look for the murderer. I'd discovered in the past that I enjoyed matching wits with people who had something to hide. And I was good at it.

I also wanted to know if Thane Stockton was guilty or innocent. And whether or not he'd told the truth about his wife abusing him. That look of satisfaction in Estrella Stockton's dark brown eyes was still etched on my memory. It seemed possible Stockton was telling the truth. On the other hand, he also seemed to be the most likely suspect. Sometimes worms *do* turn.

CHAPTER 6

"Cigars were invented in Spain, using Cuban tobacco seed, some time in the eighteenth century," Roderick Effington III said, sniffing blissfully at the box I'd brought him. "Soldiers returning from the Napoleonic wars brought them back to England and France, thus creating a demand. Here in the United States, they didn't really become popular until the Civil War."

Opening the box, he gazed at the neat row of golden brown cylinders nestled within. "Lovely quality," he said, with a smile for me that showed the double gap in his bottom set of teeth.

Roderick Effington III had moved into the attic of a fairly decrepit house since Estrella's murder. A handsome African-American man known only as Gateway had given us this address when we inquired at Mr. Effington's old packing-case homestead, which Gateway had appropriated. The peeling front door had been opened by a somewhat disheveled elderly woman who was extremely drunk. "Call me Bonnie," she'd suggested without explaining if it was a first name, last name, or wishful thinking.

The attic decor was minimalist in design. I was

sitting on a vinyl-covered bean bag whose plastic beans were leaking through the seams; Zack sat—gingerly— on an apple crate, Rory on the rolled up sleeping bag I'd brought him, his back propped against the wall. If you could call it a wall. There was no wallboard, but the sunlight streaming through the single high window glinted cheerily on the foil-backed insulation that had been stapled to the two-by-fours.

Mr. Effington, still dressed in his padded flight jacket—it was chilly in the attic—was smiling mischievously at Zack now. His aroma was marginally less offensive. I thought he'd probably taken a bath, but his clothing hadn't. Apparently the house had a working bathroom. I was resisting a visit.

"Whilst staying with friends fortunate enough to own a television set, I saw several of your performances as Sheriff Lazarro," Mr. Effington told Zack. "I must reluctantly inform you that when you lit that cigar Deputy Krenshaw gave you to celebrate his son's birth, you did not follow proper procedure. Would you care for a demonstration?"

Zack produced his wry smile. "Always willin' to learn," he drawled graciously. "Long as you don't expect me to inhale. Made me toss my cookies when I did it on the show."

"In that case, I shall ask you only to watch. I abhor waste." Selecting a cigar, he rolled it gently between his fingers, holding it to his ear, then passed it to Zack, who did likewise and passed it back.

"You need to make the cut clean and level, not too high on the shoulder," Mr. Effington instructed. Taking a guillotine-style cutter from one of his jacket's pockets, he demonstrated. "I believe you used your teeth?"

"Got the job done," Zack pointed out.

Not deigning to answer, Mr. Effington produced a Zippo lighter, held the cigar steady over the flame, rotating the end, until it was charred all the way around, then drew on it to ignite it.

For a minute or two, he smoked in hedonistic silence, his head wreathed in a pale blue cloud.

Luckily there was enough of a draft coming through the open door that I could risk breathing in once in a while.

"How come you moved, Mr. Effington?" I asked when it seemed the lesson was over.

He took the cigar from his mouth and blew lightly on its glowing end. "You must call me Rory, Miss Plato," he said graciously. "I shall call you Charlie, shall I? I'm quite sure we are going to become great friends."

I was beginning to remember why I'd liked him at our previous meeting. I realized, however, that he'd avoided answering my question. "Why did you move?" I asked again.

Sorrow shadowed his eyes. "I decided discretion was the better part of valor." He paused. "I was mugged."

Abruptly, I sat forward on my bean bag, which made a very rude sound and spewed forth some more of its stuffing. "Somebody attacked you?"

"While I was sleeping. In my packing-crate villa under the bridge." He showed the gap in his teeth again. "I thought I was experiencing a repeat of my dream about the sky falling. But the damage to my cranium was undoubtedly real." Turning his head, he took off his cap, pushed up his raggedly cut hair, and showed a sizable lump that had spread a purple bruise onto the back of his neck.

"What did the mugger hit you with?" Zack asked.

"As I passed from sleep to semiconsciousness and did not call for a forensic unit, I've no idea. It felt like a hammer. Could have been a bottle, I suppose. There were many such around that sylvan glade. The attacker left immediately, at a fast trot, so I was unable to ascertain the precise nature of the weapon."

"You don't seem too worried," I said.

"Mugging is one of the occupational hazards of homelessness," he said cheerfully.

I frowned at him. "The media interviewed you after Estrella's body landed on you," I reminded him.

"They did indeed. My fifteen minutes of fame as foretold by Andy Warhol."

"So maybe whoever murdered Estrella saw the interview, thought you might have seen him killing her, and tried to finish you off."

He tilted his head to one side and drew thoughtfully on the cigar. "A possibility," he conceded. "Though I have no knowledge of anything that might constitute a threat to anyone." He shrugged. "It seemed politic to remove myself for a while. Perhaps I should have a word with Gateway. I'm delighted he sent you both to me, but I wouldn't want him to make a habit of handing out my address."

His eyes twinkled. "I'm very grateful for the cigars and sleeping bag," he said, patting the bag he was sitting on. "As I believe I mentioned at our last meeting, I obtained my last one while Dumpster-diving."

"Sounds like an interestin' sport," Zack said. "What do you dive for? Food?"

Rory smiled. "I have eaten from Dumpsters, I must admit, though I prefer a handout from the back door of a restaurant. Once food hits the Dumpster, it tends to become mixed together and hard to recognize. Unappetizing, to say the least."

"And you don't know if the handler washed his hands," I said solemnly.

"Exactly." His eyes twinkled back at me. I do love a man who has a sense of humor. "Mostly, I dive for clothing or furnishings. Pans. Books." He indicated a couple of planks balanced on bricks that had at least twenty books piled on them. "I'm very selective about my Dumpsters," he continued. "The ones near apartments are best. People move out of apartments more often than out of houses and they often discard excellent goods. Sneakers, a portable radio, tape recorder, sunglasses. You'd be amazed how wasteful people can be."

"I'll bear that in mind next time I'm near a Dumpster," I said, and received another twinkle.

"You truly get *inside* a Dumpster?" Zack asked, having acquired a faint green tinge like that on a cauliflower.

"It's the only way," Rory said. "One has to sift through the dross to find the gold. And the heavier, more useful stuff tends to settle to the bottom."

I looked around the almost empty attic.

Rory intercepted my glance. "You are wondering

where my treasures went?" he asked, then continued without waiting for an answer. "I discarded all my belongings when I moved from the creek. It does the heart—and the character—much good to begin again from scratch."

I had done much the same when I left Rob Whittaker and our wonderful Tudor house on Puget Sound. I had left behind my favorite walnut library table, my antique linens, my beautiful little rocking chair, and my entire collection of 243 blue willow dishes, which I had amassed piece by piece at antique shows and flea markets. As I mentioned earlier, I had sworn I would never allow myself to get attached to things again.

It occurred to me that there wasn't much of a dividing line between Rory's approach and mine. Which was a disconcerting, but not unacceptable thought.

"You come by your Air Force togs in a Dumpster?" Zack asked. Rory shook his head. "They are legitimately mine own," he said.

There was a short silence, during which he finished his cigar and extinguished it in a large ceramic ashtray that was the shape of Texas. It had a crack through its middle, but had evidently been repaired, no doubt by Rory.

"Now that you understand about Dumpster-diving, I have a story to tell you," Rory said.

There was a note in his voice that caused me to lean forward again, wincing when the bean bag belted out another raspberry. Zack gave me his wry smile, the one that usually made my innards go *Whomp!* Oddly enough, this time it didn't. Maybe my hormones were finally getting the message that I was not, repeat not, ever going to have anything sexual to do with Zack Hunter.

The resident little voice in my head, which no doubt came direct to me from my subconscious, said, "Ha!"

I fixed my attention on Rory, who was looking very solemn. "Two–three months ago," he said slowly, "I was inside a Dumpster, conducting an inventory by flashlight—in the employee parking lot behind the Fairview mall."

Hair Raising, the salon where Estrella worked, was in that mall. Rory had all my attention now.

He'd heard the woman before he saw her, he told us, the click of her high heels on the concrete had drawn his attention. Then a car door slammed shut, and a man's voice said, "Hi Estrella," in rather an arch way.

There was a gasp, then a silence. Then the woman exclaimed, "Mother of God! What are you doing here?"

"Looking for you, sweetheart," the man said.

"About then I peeked out," Rory said. "It was late in the evening, and, unlike the front lot where the customers park, the back lot was unlit. Just a little light was diffused through the back windows of a couple of stores. However, the man flicked a lighter, and I saw that the woman had a cigarette between her lips. I saw her face, but the man was taller than she and his lighter did not illuminate his features. He had short hair. He wore dark clothing. Judging by his silhouette I would say he was wearing jeans, a jacket, and a baseball cap."

Rory paused for a minute, thinking. "Baggy jeans."

He could be describing himself, I thought.

The man could have been someone Estrella hadn't

seen in a while, I reasoned. Or just someone she hadn't expected to see in the parking lot. Or even her husband. Exclaiming "Mother of God," could be due to a severe shock, or Estrella might merely have been startled when the man spoke to her out of the shadows.

"Is that all they said?" Zack asked.

Rory nodded. "They got in a car and drove away. His car, I guess." He shook his head at me as I leaned forward again. "No, Charlie, I was not able to see the license number. The car was facing in my direction, and as soon as the man switched on the headlights I ducked down. I had no way of knowing the incident would turn out to be significant, remember. I didn't even notice what kind of car the man was driving, except that it appeared to be very old. The engine sounded as if it were running on gravel."

"Did Estrella seem reluctant to get in the car?" I asked.

"The man did not drag her in by her hair, if that's what you mean. He did take her arm. He might possibly have carried a weapon. I didn't see one, but that doesn't mean he didn't have one."

I stood up. Cautiously, Zack did likewise. Rory stayed where he was, evidently unwilling to give up his comfortable perch.

"You must have recognized Estrella's face the minute you opened that sleeping bag," I muttered.

Rory nodded.

"Did you tell Detective Sergeant Bristow you'd seen her before?"

He smiled sweetly. "I have made it a lifelong practice to tell law-enforcement officers no more than they ask for," he said.

He glanced up at me, his hazel eyes bright as a bird's. "Do not mistake me. I have only respect for police officers—I was almost one myself. I believe we *need* a police force. I would not wish to live in anarchy."

He coughed slightly. "Police officers tend to have rather suspicious minds, however," he continued, sounding professorial. "This is especially noticeable when they are dealing with people who are not property owners. When they have nothing else of importance to occupy them, they tend to move us along in order to appear to be taking action against the homeless problem. This approach does not inspire people such as myself to confide in them."

"Where to next?" Zack asked, when we were back in his pickup.

I thought about it. The following day would be a Saturday. Hair salons were usually open on Saturdays. "Sufficient unto the day," I said. "Let's give it up for now."

Everyone, male or female, was delighted to welcome Zack back into CHAPS' fold. Savanna showed her affection with a warm hug to her ample bosom, Angel's brown-velvet eyes gleamed as he shook hands, Sundancer spun like a Spanish dancer in the deejay booth, stomping his feet, waving his arms like a mad symphony conductor, the cord attached to his headset whipping the air. Sundancer is not only a dedicated Zack Hunter fan, he's terminally weird.

The Friday night crowd assumed a perkiness that I hadn't even realized had been missing. There is something about a celebrity presence that injects electricity into the air, making people stand up a little straighter, dance a little more gracefully, smile wider, laugh more often.

"Stick around and dance some," Sundancer announced as usual, after Angel and I were through giving line-dancing instruction. Everybody seemed inclined to do just that; one of our most popular live country groups, Lonnie Tremayne and The California Rangers, was coming on stage.

Zack invited me to do a two-step with him. I accepted warily. Lonnie sang an Alan Jackson number that said he was in love with his baby even though he didn't know her name. Typical male sentiment. Savanna, aka Earth Mother, beamed upon Zack and me from the sidelines. I supposed Bristow must be working tonight.

"Feels real good," Zack said, his right hand pressing warmly against my back.

What felt good? My back? Dancing with me? Holding me?

"Yes," I said noncommittally. We needed to open the plaza door, I thought—all of a sudden there didn't seem to be enough air in the main corral.

"Bein' back at CHAPS, I mean," Zack said.

"Oh."

Angel was just coming onto the floor with Gina. She looked quite cute in a denim romper and cowboy boots if you ignored her weird makeup and the half dozen necklaces she was wearing. Angel's brown eyes glowed again as he looked down at her spiky punk hair. With Angel that's as close to a smile as he gets without actually turning one loose. Gina kept her head down. Her mouth seemed a little on the pouty side. That could have been a side effect of her black lipstick, or else the difficulty between them hadn't been settled yet.

"Hard to know where I want to be sometimes," Zack added after he'd twirled me a couple of times and brought me in close again. "Miss you and Savanna and Angel when I'm away, miss actin' when I'm here."

"Quite a dilemma," I said coolly. Whenever my bones start melting around Zack he says or does something that firms my spine right back up. Being missed in a lump with other people is not the stuff romantic dreams are made of.

At the same time, Zack's arm was pressing more and more intimately, forcing me ever closer.

Whenever I'm around Zack, there's an ongoing battle between my brain, which contains a formidable supply of common sense and self-esteem, and my body, which experiences a debilitating increase in hormonal activity in his presence.

So far, my brain has won out, but occasionally surrender seems imminent.

Did I mention that sometimes people who live alone get lonely?

CHAPTER 7

There was a Dumpster in the parking lot behind Hair Raising all right. And an elderly beat-up Ford parked nearby. I made a mental note of the license number.

"Looks like the set of *Steel Magnolias*," Zack murmured as we hesitated inside the entrance to the salon.

"Nobody here looks like Olympia Dukakis or Shirley MacLaine or Sally Field, not to mention Julia Roberts," I said.

ZZ Top rock was blasting out of the sound system. The women inside the salon were so busy yelling at one another over it, it took a minute or so for someone to notice us. It took another moment for me to realize that the plump blond woman who switched off the music and came forward was Maisie Ridley, the Englishwoman who had shown up in my self-defense class. I hadn't known she worked with Estrella—which would make her a source.

"Hello, Charlie!" She sounded as surprised as I felt.

Before I could respond, she added, "Oh, my goodness gracious," in her flutey voice, and turned every head in the place.

"Zack Hunter!" one of the clients exclaimed, placing

her hand over her plastic shampoo cape in the region of her heart.

Seven pairs of eyes stared in wonder—three customers, two stylists, one very pretty young Filipina manicurist with the most improbably long and thick eyelashes I'd ever seen, one gaunt redhead standing immobile with a pair of shears in her hand.

Zack lifted his cowboy hat and repositioned it at its sexiest angle. "Afternoon, ladies," he drawled.

A collective sigh stirred the air.

"Did you wish to make an appointment?" Maisie asked our man-in-black with a hopeful smile.

His answering smile cut through her like a laser—you could almost see her inner parts reverberate just the way mine do under like circumstances. "Had a haircut couple days past," he said, sounding truly regretful.

"I could give you a manicure," the petite young woman with the eyelashes offered, leaping to her feet.

"Well, now, that would be mighty nice," Zack agreed.

Next thing, the manicurist's customer had declared her polish to be dry, gladly surrendered her seat, and the young woman was holding Zack's hand and examining it minutely, while Maisie, the former customer, and the rest of the women smiled fondly at them both. I appeared to have disappeared. This often happened when I was accompanied by Zack.

"Are you the manager?" I asked the redhead with the shears, who was the only one not wearing a peach-colored smock. She started, but rallied quickly. "The owner," she corrected me. "Felicia Godfrey."

Felicia appeared to be fortyish. She had spent a lot of time on the suntan bed that was advertised in huge multicolored print in the front window. Her red hair was cut Sassoon style, fitting her head like a gleaming cap. She wore big glasses, a pale denim jacket trimmed with studs, beads, and gold appliqué, skintight jeans, and sandals with very high heels. How could she work all day on those heels, I wondered. She was very thin, even skinnier than me, the kind of thin you get when you starve yourself—the way I used to.

Setting down the shears on a nearby table, she came toward me. "Are you with Mr. Hunter?" she asked.

It seemed petty to argue that Mr. Hunter was with me, so I nodded. "We want to talk to you about Estrella Stockton."

Maisie's eyes shone with tears. "We feel just awful about Estrella," she said.

The other stylist and the customers nodded in unison.

"Anybody have any idea who might have killed her?" Zack asked. Subtlety isn't exactly Zack's thing.

They all shook their heads, except for Felicia, who looked worried. Zack's new admirer began filing his nails. I raised my eyebrows at Felicia.

She tilted her head to the wall beyond Zack and the manicurist, indicating a pair of chairs whose hood dryers had been pushed up out of the way. I followed her over there and accepted a mug of coffee. Zack declined politely.

Felicia didn't seem too eager to start talking. "Nice jacket," I lied, to get things going.

She shrugged absently. "I buy all my clothes in Las Vegas."

"Great city," Zack said.

The women beamed at him as if he'd said something infinitely witty.

"Did Estrella ever go with you?" I asked, remembering that Thane Stockton had mentioned Las Vegas in connection with his wife. I tried to stir my grey cells into coming up with the reference.

Felicia nodded. "Couple of times, but her husband didn't like her shopping there. Real spoilsport, that man."

The memory that had surfaced had something to do with Estrella telling, or lying to, her husband about affairs she'd had with various men. The one in Las Vegas had supposedly been involved with some Filipino gang that was based there. "Did she get involved with any men while she was there with you?" I asked.

Felicia made a puffing sound through her lips that I interpreted as negative. "We went for the gambling and the shopping," she said. But her eyes didn't quite meet mine.

"Thane Stockton says he found Estrella through the Internet," Zack said.

"That's true," Candy the manicurist said. "I came by the same route." She giggled. "Right out of cyberspace, that's me and Estrella."

Felicia shook her head. "Those two. I can't imagine doing such a thing. Though of course, I was born and bred down the road in East Dennison, so I didn't have to figure out a way to get to the U.S. That's not to say I believe in all this love malarkey though. I made up my mind early on that I was going to marry an older man. Somebody stable."

She and Maisie exchanged a glance and giggled. "Mr. Godfrey's stable all right, so stable he's almost mummified, but he's a good old guy, can't do enough for his baby. Not rich, but he set me up in this business, which is all I ever wanted."

Felicia's marriage wasn't the one I wanted to discuss. "Estrella's husband was a spoilsport, you said?"

She nodded. "He wanted her to stay home all the time. Nice house, lots of money, but always crying poor mouth. Estrella was *not* happy. Not with her husband at least." There seemed to be a significant note in her voice.

"There was another man then?"

"Not in Las Vegas," she said firmly. Too firmly? "But right here in Bellamy Park? Maybe." She leaned toward me conspiratorially. Her perfume was very strong. "I've been thinking I should maybe tell the police what I know," she said. "Nobody's been here yet, but I figure it's only a matter of time, right?" She leaned back and narrowed her eyes. "You're not with the police, are you?"

"Zack and I are just sort of helping out," I said, hoping the vague answer would satisfy her.

She glanced at Zack. He'd taken off his cowboy hat, rolled up his shirtsleeves. The little manicurist was massaging cream into his cuticles now. Slowly. One might almost say sensuously, her cheeks as flushed as if she were running a fever. Zack looked gratified. He liked women a lot, was always happy in their company—especially when they seemed about to swoon.

Felicia leaned toward me again, then frowned. "You ought to try bleaching those freckles," she said, gazing at my nose.

"Maybe someday," I hedged. I have no quarrel with my freckles. They've always been there, a part of me. I think they look kind of cheery. With my orange hair I'd look awful with a tan, and a dermatologist once told me that tan skin is unhealthy skin, so I don't go out of my way to acquire the bronze look that's so prevalent in California. Freckles are my substitute.

Felicia took a sip of her coffee. After arranging her thoughts for a couple of minutes, she said, "It was like this. I was in Paulie's Place. You know it? Local bar."

"I know where it is."

"This was maybe three months ago," she went on.

I felt a thrill of anticipation go through me. Rory had said the incident he'd witnessed from the Dumpster in the parking lot was two or three months ago.

"You saw Estrella with a man?" I asked.

She nodded. "They seemed to be having a good time," she said. "I couldn't tell much about the guy— they were sitting at a corner table, and he had his back to me. And the lighting's peculiar in there, and well, to be honest, I didn't have my glasses on. Sometimes when I go out I leave them home. I look prettier without them, people tell me."

To demonstrate, she took them off and blinked at me myopically. In my opinion, people who need glasses should keep them on. Without them their eyes look strained. "Your husband was with you?" I asked, wondering if his eyesight was keener than hers.

She laughed as if I'd said something uproariously

funny. Maisie turned our way. "She wants to know if I was in Paulie's Place with Mr. Godfrey," Felicia said as she replaced her glasses.

Maisie chuckled.

"Like I told you, I married an old man," Felicia said. "I mean *old*. My husband doesn't go out much. So I go out with my friends."

"I see."

Maybe she thought I sounded disapproving. When she spoke again she had a defensive note in her voice. "I'm very good to that old man," she said.

"I'm sorry," I said. "I didn't mean anything. It's just the idea of arranged marriages and loveless marriages ..."

"I make that old man very happy," she went on. "I take care of him. He's the one tells me to go out and have a good time. He feels guilty because he got sick right after we were married."

She laughed. "I guess you could say I was too much for him. He couldn't take the excitement. Heart went bad on him about the third time we did it."

I couldn't think of anything to say to that.

"Candy there, *she's* very happy," Felicia said, indicating the manicurist. "Like she said, she came here the same way as Estrella, all arranged on the Internet, miracles of technology. But her husband is young, a real looker, great bod, a good worker, too. Brings home real money. Pretty soon they're going to start a family. You never saw people look such goo-goo eyes at each other."

Candy flashed her a shy smile. Zack slanted his eyebrows at me.

We were getting way off the subject.

"Did you know Estrella's husband?" I asked Felicia.

"Never met him." She pondered a while. "Estrella and I weren't what you'd call best friends. I mean, we worked together, and we got along fine, except Estrella had a quick temper and would get mad at a customer if she looked at her sideways, but we didn't pal around a whole lot. Except that couple of times we went up to Vegas, and then we didn't stick together the whole time."

"So she *could* have met someone there?" I asked.

She shrugged, then set down her coffee mug on the nearby counter and called out to Maisie. "Didn't you meet Estrella's old man once?"

Maisie dusted off her customer's shoulders with a whisk brush and came over. The customer turned her chair and scooted it forward so she could watch Zack getting his manicure. Evidently she wasn't in any hurry to leave.

"Were you a cyberspace bride, too?" I asked Maisie.

Her laugh trilled out. "Goodness gracious, what an idea," she said. "No, no, my dear, I met my late husband on an American Air Force base in England. A dear friend of mine took me to a dance, and there he was." She looked at me very directly. "I was *not* a war bride," she said firmly. "I'm not *that* old. Tom and I met in 1968."

Zack had apparently lost interest in the conversation. He was concentrating all his attention on the little manicurist. Surprise, surprise. She was glancing up at him from beneath her eyelash extensions as she buffed his fingernails, blushing less hectically, more prettily.

Candy. I hoped her marriage was as strong as Felicia thought it was. Dandy little Candy, complete with clippers, cuticle cream, and buffer, would fit right into Zack's doll brigade along with Flyin' Missy, his own personal flight attendant, Good Golly Miss Molly, aka Molly Carstairs, his costar on *Prescott's Landing*, and half a dozen others whom Savanna and I had nicknamed at one time or another.

"Estrella's husband is not what I'd call dishy," Maisie said, when I'd almost forgotten what we'd been talking about originally. "Older than Estrella. A bit dull—tow-colored hair, pale eyes."

Felicia shook her head. "The man I saw Estrella with did not have fair hair. He had dark hair. Straight hair. Not very well cut." She wrinkled her forehead and pursed her lips. "Estrella seemed very excited that night. She had a big bruise on her arm. I asked about it the next day, and she said it was a present from her husband when she told him she was going out."

"She often had bruises," Maisie said.

The other stylist chimed in as Felicia nodded. "One time she had to wear latex gloves because of the bruises on the backs of her hands."

"I'd forgotten that, Jody," Felicia said.

Jody nodded. "She didn't want her clients seeing her with bruises. Said it wouldn't be good for business."

"Well if the backs of her hands were bruised, you'd think Estrella was the one doing the hitting," I pointed out.

Jody and Felicia looked at me as if I was crazy. "It's not good to speak ill of the dead," Jody said accusingly.

I apologized. "Anybody have any idea who that old

beat-up Ford in the parking lot belongs to?" I asked, to change the subject. Dredging the license number from my memory I rattled it off.

"That's my car," Felicia said, laughing when I grimaced and apologized again. "I recognized the description, didn't I? Had that old beater six years now. I always mean to look for a newer model, but it does keep going."

She frowned. "How come you want to know?" she asked.

When cornered I tend to wriggle. "I used to have one just like it," I lied. " 'Wondered if it might even be the same one. I traded it in on my Jeep Wrangler a few years back and . . ."

My voice trailed off. Why on earth was I making stuff up when there was no need? "I heard from someone that Estrella got in a car like that two, three months ago, with a man, right there in that parking lot."

Felicia looked startled, then glanced at Maisie with a puzzled frown. Maisie shrugged and went off to collect some money from her customer, who had finally stood up and approached the cash register.

Felicia's face cleared. "Hey, wait a minute. That's right. Estrella borrowed my car for a couple of days when her Mercedes was in the shop for its annual overhaul. Three months back." She laughed, took off her oversize glasses, and polished them with a tissue she took from her jacket pocket. "Estrella hated driving my old clunker, but she needed transportation, and her old man was having one of his mean streaks. He'd cut off her funds every once in a while, and sometimes she'd run low on her own money. I borrowed my step-daughter's pickup until Estrella gave my car back. I love that truck, vroom, vroom, so no problem."

The story seemed a little complicated. I wondered if she was telling me the truth.

"She ever say anythin' about killin' her husband's dog?" Zack asked.

There was a shocked silence, then Maisie laughed nervously. "He had a dog she didn't like. A spaniel of some kind, I believe. Evidently it barked a lot. Sometimes it would snarl at her and curl its upper lip. Once or twice she said she was going to drown the nasty little thing, but I'm sure she wouldn't really . . ."

Her voice trailed off, and she paled as if she suddenly wasn't all that sure.

I looked at Felicia. She shook her head and shrugged. I threw out a few questions to the other stylist, but didn't get much in the way of answers. Estrella, according to her coworkers, had been a very private person, not given to talking a lot about her own life except in explosive little bits when she was mad about something.

Driving me back to CHAPS in his pickup, Zack said he'd questioned Candy, using a technique he'd learned on *Prescott's Landing*, acting like she must know something but was maybe afraid to tell and she shouldn't be afraid, because he wasn't going to quote her anywhere that mattered and she'd feel a whole heap better if she got it off her chest.

"So then she said she hadn't liked Estrella, said she was hard and quick-tempered, said she hadn't had much to do with her. But she remembered Estrella sayin' the man Felicia saw her with in Paulie's Place was her old boyfriend from the Philippines. It was good to talk about old times and good old days, Estrella told her."

"Did Candy say when this was?" I asked.

"Said it was around the same time Estrella had to take her Mercedes into the shop." He did his squinting into a dust-storm impression, then added, "Estrella said her old boyfriend had made jokes about her drivin' that old car, but when she picked him up in her Mercedes later he was blown away."

Zack *hadn't* spent all his time flirting. I felt apologetic and impressed. He'd managed to get more helpful information out of Candy than I'd pried out of Felicia and Maisie. He'd make a great prosecuting attorney, if he could be sure of all female witnesses. They'd pour their little hearts out to him.

"Sweet little thing," he said, and I was pretty sure he wasn't talking about Estrella.

"Dandy little Candy is happily married," I told him sharply.

He grinned sideways at me. "What are you implyin', darlin'?" he asked.

As if he didn't know.

CHAPTER 8

At nine-forty-five on Monday morning, I was cleaning out Ben's cage, wishing I didn't have to go see my gynecologist. But Matilda, Doc Hanssen's elderly receptionist, had threatened to bill me anyway if I canceled out again.

Ben was happily hip-hopping around my loft, pausing to gnaw on the baseboard from time to time. If I ever moved out of there I was going to have to replace that baseboard. No big deal, I'd helped my dad stain and install the baseboards in the Greek restaurant he'd owned in Sacramento.

Usually Ben senses when anyone's about to hit CHAPS' front doorbell even before the extension Sundancer rigged up sounds off in my loft, but I had a Tracy Byrd CD blasting on the portable player I'd picked up at the Salvation Army thrift store, and all I heard was a faint dong. Ben's ears barely twitched.

Luckily, I'd gotten up early in order to get some stuff done before my gynecology appointment, so I was showered and dressed in sweats and sneakers, though my hair was still wet. I hadn't yet followed Estrella's advice about using a diffuser to dry it with—I kept forgetting to buy one.

First scooting Ben back into his cage, I trotted down the stairs and opened the heavy door to Gina Giacomini, she of the blond-and-magenta hairdo. "Hey," I said.

She smiled. "Mislaid my key."

"What brings you out so early?" I asked. Usually she kept Buttons & Bows open the same hours as CHAPS.

Her already round eyes grew rounder. "We aren't having the self-defense class this week?"

"Good grief!" I closed the door behind her. "I forgot all about it. I guess my subconscious figured that after Estrella was killed, we'd do without it for a while."

"Did your subconscious tell Duke that?" she asked. "He seemed to think it was still on."

I gazed at her blankly.

"The instructor," she said.

Well, I knew who Duke was—I was wondering when he'd talked to Gina about the class. Her comment implied a certain intimacy that worried me. Gina was Angel's girlfriend. I didn't want to see Angel get hurt.

Before I could get nosy, the doorbell rang again. Duke was on the other side of the door this time, all done up in his kung-fu pajamas, bristling with macho charisma, ready for action. Behind him in the parking lot a red Jeep Cherokee was disgorging four women. A Chevy station wagon was just pulling in.

I groaned.

"Charlie forgot about the class," Gina told Duke.

"You wanna call it off?" he asked me. He grinned at Gina, running a hand over his hair. Primping?

"Maybe we could grab some breakfast. I didn't get around to eating since dinner last night."

"Me neither," Gina said, smiling prettily up at him. Ho!

"The class is on," I said firmly. "I just had a moment of mental aberration."

We went on in to the main corral, leaving the outer door open. More women were arriving at the plaza door, having walked over from the Granada apartment complex. Pretty soon, most of them were in the rest room changing into the gym clothes of their choice. I took a couple of minutes to duck into my office and call Dr. Hanssen's office. Matilda was not happy with me. She did reschedule though, for that afternoon at 1 P.M. She said it was my very last chance. Her choice of words sounded ominous.

"Today we are going to talk about weapons," Duke announced when he'd got us drawn up in our circle. "First we'll decide what kind of weapons women have on them all the time. Anyone care to begin?"

"Fingernails," Savanna said. She had some; I didn't. Not that I chewed them, I kept them cut back for typing on the computer. Long nails get in the way.

Several women made threatening claws of their long nails and laughed.

"High-heeled shoes," Gina said.

I didn't have any of those either. I figured at 5'10" I was high enough.

Duke's smile for Gina was approving and a little on the cocky side. Uh-huh. Something was definitely going on.

"High heels are a terrific weapon," Duke said. "Pull

the shoe off, jab that heel in the attacker's throat or his eye. You can use a pencil the same way. Or a tightly rolled-up piece of paper."

I meditated briefly on whether I could ever, under any circumstances, gouge someone's eyes. You may remember there have been a couple of occasions in my recent life when I needed to defend myself, so I could actually put myself back in those situations, imagine the people who had threatened me, and project the scenario.

No. There were probably women in the world who could gouge people's eyes out. I wasn't one of them. Ergo, I needed some other method of defense.

Duke walked around the circle like a drill sergeant, hands clasped behind his back, looking at each of us in turn. "No matter how big or strong the attacker is, there are weak points all over his body." He made jabbing motions with his right hand. "Get him in the eyes, the temples, the knees, anywhere on the neck, under the nose, under the chin, in the throat, the diaphragm." To demonstrate this last, he pressed his fingers into his own flat midriff, just below where his ribs separated.

"And of course, in the groin," he added. I was willing to bet we were all, including Duke, thinking of Estrella. Everyone had seen the story of Estrella's murder in the news, of course. I'd heard the women discussing it as they waited for the class to get started.

"My handbag would make a good weapon," Maisie Ridley said into the sudden silence. "It's too bad Estrella never carried a handbag." Her eyes filled with tears. I felt a lump form in my own throat.

"Hey, listen," Duke said earnestly. "What we want to do is make sure any of you get in that same position as Estrella, you'll *know* what to do."

That made sense, and we rallied and paid attention. We learned we should carry a whistle at all times. A loud whistle. Duke just happened to have some for sale. I bought a small one for my key ring, a longer one on a black cord to go around my neck when I was working out alone in the gym.

We sat on the floor, and Duke passed around a selection of guns for us to examine. I'd never held a gun before. I was surprised at the familiar way one of them seemed to fit in my hand. It was matte and black and efficient-looking, a Walther PPK 9mm pistol, Duke told me.

I thought that if I ever owned a gun, which I had no desire to do, that would be the gun I'd want. It puzzled me that I'd even think about it. I guessed that Estrella's death had affected me even more than I thought it had. And, of course, Estrella's was the third murder I'd run into.

Fourth.

No—fifth.

I began to wonder morbidly if the old Grim Reaper might be edging closer to me.

"Yo, Charlie," Duke yelled, and I realized I was still holding on to the gun and staring down at it. I passed it on to Savanna and took the next one coming around— some little silver metal jobby with a rose on the grip, came in a gold fabric case. Meant for a woman, I supposed. Not this woman. I couldn't imagine carrying a gun decorated with a flower.

Looking up, I saw that Angel had arrived and was busying himself around the bar. I hadn't expected him to come in this morning. But then again, I hadn't expected the class to be held. Complete with handsome instructor.

I watched Angel for a few minutes as the guns went on around the circle of women, saw him glance several times from Gina to Duke. Under his drooping mustache, his lips were set tight.

Gina's mouth had a compressed look about it, too.

When we were on our feet again, Duke showed us a canister of pepper spray. It was a small silver-and-black cylinder that looked a lot like a travel-size container of hair spray. It came in a black-vinyl sheath and would fit easily in a purse or pocket.

"The effects range from severe blepharospasm— a twitching or spasmodic contraction of the eyes, to involuntary closing of the eyes," Duke told us, sounding like a manual. He went on to talk about other effects, none of which sounded remotely pleasant, then told us we could buy canisters from him, but he wanted us to experience the effects first.

"Follow me," he said, and we did, like a bunch of lambs voluntarily going to the slaughter.

Duke led us to the ladies' rest room, went inside and squirted some spray around, then told us to walk through and breathe in.

The flock of lambs dutifully did that, too, and came out doubled over, weeping and coughing and choking and cussing Duke.

Duke handed a folded whiter-than-white handkerchief to Gina, whose eyes were streaming, and let the rest of us cough until we recovered. The inside of my nose was burning. Likewise my throat.

"Very funny," I said to Duke, whose blue eyes were bright with amusement.

"Best you get some idea now," he said. "You're less likely to spray indiscriminately and get in the way of it yourself."

Which, I had to admit, made sense.

"Is this stuff legal?" Savanna asked between choking coughs.

Duke nodded. "As of January 1996, you don't even need a permit in the state of California. Don't try to take the spray on an airplane, though."

We all trooped back to the main corral, Angel watching covertly from under the brim of his cowboy hat. I wondered if he was keeping an eye on Gina's and Duke's auras. Months ago, he'd talked to me about people's auras, surprising me. I hadn't known Angel was into that kind of mystical stuff. I wondered what color people's auras would be if they were boffing each other. Passionate purple, maybe? Ravishing red?

"Visual acuity will return within five minutes for most people after they've been sprayed," Duke said. "Quicker if they flush their faces with cool water. You get accidentally sprayed, wash it off fast. Respiratory functions will return to normal in a couple of minutes. You don't need to worry that you're maiming somebody for life. It wears off, okay? The person doesn't even need medical treatment. So if the day comes you have to use this stuff, do it directly in the attacker's face in short, fast bursts, then take off running. It will disable him, he will be incapable of aggression, but not forever.

You have maybe thirty minutes to make your getaway. Forty-five minutes outside." He held up a hand, palm out as if to stop traffic. "And remember, ladies, always remember, the bad guys can buy pepper spray, too."

We spent the next few minutes lined up to buy our canisters. Savanna murmured that she thought Duke was doing pretty well out of this class, what with the fees we'd paid him and the probable markup on the whistles and sprays. She bought one all the same. I bought two. I could see myself using *this* weapon. Disable—yes, maim—no.

I followed the women into the rest room when the class was over. Duke had thoughtfully gone back in and opened a window, and it was okay to breathe. Standing in line behind P.J., who you'll remember was one of our Granada neighbors and the CHAPS regular who had the most notches on her male-catching belt, I brought Estrella's name into the general conversation.

Everyone, including P.J., seemed to have decided, on the strength of media accounts, that Thane Stockton was to blame for his wife's death. None of them had known her personally, so had nothing to offer as far as other men she might have known.

When I came out of the stall, Maisie was washing her hands, and the rest of the women had left. We talked generally about Estrella as Maisie lathered up and rinsed and dried. "The police don't seem to be ready to arrest Thane Stockton," she said as she combed her Dutch-bobbed, assisted blond hair.

"You think he's guilty, too?" I asked.

"I'm not sure." She put her comb away in her large shoulder bag, then leaned a hip against the sink, apparently in no hurry to leave.

I dried my own hands. "Everyone else seems to be quite sure he did it."

"Well, it's possible, I suppose," she said slowly. "Estrella told us often enough that Thane beat her up, but the one time I met him, he seemed sort of frightened around her. I don't think wife beaters usually get frightened around their wives. Besides which . . ."

I hate when people hesitate right when they're about to say something interesting.

Maisie glanced at the stalls as if to be sure they were all empty, then walked over and opened, then closed the door. "I don't really know a whole lot more than Felicia told you," she said, "but I do know this— that Estrella was having an affair with an old boyfriend from the Philippines. She told me about it. When I thought about it after you came to the salon, it occurred to me her Filipino friend might have been the man she was with at Paulie's Place."

Which confirmed what Candy had told Zack.

"Did Estrella mention his name?" I asked.

Maisie shook her head. "It seemed to me she was careful not to. She told me . . ." Again a hesitation.

Patience is not one of my virtues, but I've learned if you let a silence lengthen, people will fill it eventually. So I checked my hair in the mirror, discovered it was its usual kinky mess, checked my teeth to be sure I hadn't left any cereal between them this morning, checked the color of my tongue, which my dentist had said was an indicator of health. It was a nice-looking pink, which surely meant I didn't have cancer.

Maisie cleared her throat. Whenever I read that sentence in a book, I imagine someone hawking and spitting, and it turns me off the character, but Maisie did it very delicately—like a kitten coughing. I could almost hear the word "Ahem."

"Estrella never said to me that she was afraid of her husband, but she said she was a little afraid of this old boyfriend, even though he was crazy about her. She said her fear gave an edge to the sex." Maisie's cheeks flushed pink as she pronounced the last word. "Estrella said having . . . sex with him was like starring in a snuff film. Evidently she'd done that to make money when she was in her teens."

She hesitated. "You know what a snuff film is, Charlie? People make films of people having . . . sex and the man would supposedly strangle Estrella at the same time and it would look as if she died right as the man . . . had orgasm. Have you ever heard about such a dreadful thing, Charlie?"

"I guess so," I said. "It's not something I've ever wanted to know much about."

"Nor I," she said with feeling. "I think Estrella enjoyed shocking me, so I was never sure how much to believe of what she told me. I caught her out in a couple of little lies—nothing important, but it indicated to me that I should take whatever she said with the proverbial grain of salt."

She frowned. "She *said* her old boyfriend wanted her to divorce Thane and marry him. But she thought he was just after a share of whatever money she could get out of Thane in a settlement, so she told him no."

"And she never once mentioned his name?"

"Never." She paused to think. "I do recall her once calling him by a nickname of sorts. The empty man."

"Weird," I said.

CHAPTER 9

Angel doesn't often smile. When he does it's a real treat for the eyes, though you have to be sure you don't blink. The smile is wide and white against his bronze skin, but it switches off before you can catch your breath.

He'd looked fairly grim the minute before I presented him with the extra canister of pepper spray I'd bought from Duke. But I never paid attention to his "mean" look. It made him effective as a bouncer, but didn't go more than skin deep.

"What am I supposed to do with this?" he asked.

I had to admit the little silver-and-black cylinder looked pretty useless in his big fist, but I'd experienced firsthand what one tiny inhalation could do. "I thought it might come in handy if one of our wanna-be cowboys got out of hand."

Angel shook his head and tried to give the pepper spray back to me. "I'm touched that you're concerned about my safety, but I have two good hands that can do the job just fine. This'll do more good in *your* pocket, Charlie."

"I have one for myself. I want you to keep that one under the bar."

He sighed one of those male "I guess we have to humor the ladies" sighs, but gave in graciously. "If it'll make you happy, Charlie."

"It will."

I hitched a hip onto a barstool and accepted the bottle of Pellegrino water he offered me.

"How goes the detective business?" he asked.

I raised innocent eyebrows and took a swig of mineral water.

"I saw you follow the ladies into the rest room, Charlie."

"And you jumped to the conclusion that I was going to question them? You don't think I have the same needs as other women?"

"I *know* you, Charlie," he said solemnly.

I set my bottle down on the bar. "Okay, you've got me. Zack and I have been asked to try to find out who killed Estrella."

"By Taylor Bristow?"

"Give me a break, Angel. Bristow's tolerant of what he refers to as our interference, but he's not going to egg us on. It was Estrella's husband who asked for our help."

"Isn't he supposed to be the killer?"

"That's the general impression. But I'm not sure he did it. Neither is Zack. He's not the type."

"What type is that, Charlie?"

Well, I had to admit I didn't know. "I guess it's a gut instinct," I said.

"Women's intuition," he said slyly, expecting to get a rise out of me.

I disappointed him. "Maybe so," I said.

He opened a bottle of Pellegrino water for himself. "So how are you and Zack going about this investigation?" he asked.

Angel was always interested in how such things were managed, and he was a good listener, so I explained how Zack and I had talked first to Thane Stockton, then to Rory and the women at the hair salon, ending with a reprise of my conversation with Maisie.

"Probably the police are moving much faster than we are," I told him. "They can throw a bunch of information in a computer and come up with a likely suspect. All we can do is ask questions of anyone who knew Estrella and hope something will pop out of the woodwork. If we knew the name of this mysterious Filipino boyfriend of Estrella's, we might be able to track him down, but all I have is a very vague description that could fit a lot of people, and now the nickname."

"The empty man," Angel said softly, with a faraway look in his eye. He definitely has a mystical bent. It shows up every once in a while. I thought maybe I ought to take him to meet Thane Stockton, see if he could sense any violence in his aura.

Angel stroked his Pancho Villa mustache while he thought deep thoughts. Then he asked, "How would you do that?"

I blanked out.

"You said you could track the guy down if you knew his name."

"Oh that." I gestured for another bottle of Pellegrino, then hoisted myself fully onto the barstool. "There are search organizations that can find people. I read a newspaper article about them. Usually they look for people who are not so much missing as lost track of. Not necessarily criminals."

Angel narrowed his eyes at me and pondered for a while. The skin was tight over his high cheekbones. He can get very intense sometimes. "Like for instance," he said, "I have this ... friend ... an old schoolfriend. I really liked him but I moved and he moved and then I got to thinking I'd like to see him again. So I could go to one of these search places and get help?"

"That's the idea," I agreed, then looked at him curiously. "Is this old friend someone you knew back in Texas?" I asked in my most innocent voice.

In a rare moment of candor, when he and I were first acquainted—in the early days of CHAPS—Angel had told me that when he was in his early twenties he'd worked on a ranch in Texas and competed in rodeos. That's almost all he'd ever told me about his past.

Angel's face is all planes and angles, naturally bronze in color. His hair is black, pulled back and tied in a ponytail with a leather thong. He always wears a cowboy hat made of fine straw. Between the shadow cast by the hat and the fact that sometimes his eyes are so dark it's hard to see the pupils, added to the disguising element of his drooping mustache, it's not easy at any time to tell what Angel is thinking.

I was quite sure he was going to brush me off and refuse to answer my question, but instead, after a fairly long silence, he said, "Not Texas, no. Someone I knew in Mexico."

He'd never actually told me he'd lived in Mexico, so I was surprised, but worked to hide it. I nodded as if I'd known it all along. "It might be difficult to trace your friend in Mexico," I said. "The article dealt only with organizations in the States."

His mouth tightened fractionally, but then he said, "I heard he came to the United States. My friend."

"Oh. Then it should be possible. The only thing I remember offhand is that Social Security will send letters on to lost friends or relatives, free of charge, if there's a really important reason. But the article had addresses and phone numbers of the different organizations, I think. I'll try to find it."

His smile peeked out again, but in a more restrained manner this time. He looked relieved, but whether that was because of the information I'd given him, or that he'd managed not to give away any really important secrets, I didn't know.

"So how are things going with you and Gina?" I asked breezily when it seemed the search topic was done with.

The upper edges of his cheekbones acquired a streak of red. "Fine," he said.

I kept my gaze fixed on his face.

"Not so good, Charlie," he said, and got very busy washing a bar towel in some sudsy water in the left-hand section of the bar's three-holer sink.

"You worried about her and Duke Conway?"

He didn't answer right away. Actually, he didn't answer—but the question he asked told me I was on the right track. "What d'you know about this Duke character?"

"Not a whole lot. He was recommended by Macintosh. Zack's friend? The one who has the children's program on TV—*Spreading Circles?* He helped out with the election campaign last year."

Angel was nodding as if he had Macintosh placed now. "Anyway," I went on, "Macintosh teaches a computer-skills class at the high school." Macintosh had also taught me all I knew about computers. He was really aptly named, though he'd confessed he preferred a PC to a Mac.

"He told me the PE teacher had brought Duke out to the school after they had that scare with the sexual predator who was released from prison and was hanging around. He said Duke was real good with basic defense maneuvers, which was what I was after. He did a stint in the Army. Duke, not Macintosh."

I didn't mention that Macintosh had taken part in the course himself because he lived with the fear of "gay-bashing." Macintosh hadn't come out yet. It was impossible for him to do so, involved as he was with kids—people do get uptight. They seem to expect gays to attempt to seduce everyone in sight.

Angel carefully rinsed his towel in the middle sink, then dipped it through the disinfectant in the third, wrung it out, and hung it behind the bar to air dry. "What d'you think of him?" he asked in a voice that was apparently supposed to sound casual.

"Macintosh?" I asked, with assumed innocence.

He looked at me.

It was a tough question. I wasn't really sure how

I felt about Duke. "He's okay, I guess," I said finally. "Knows what he's doing as far as the class goes. Seems a mite too full of his own testosterone."

"You notice him trying to make time with Gina?"

Another toughie. It was like this: although Angel was always the gentlest of men underneath that tough-looking exterior of his, I often got the impression that maybe the tough-looking exterior was the real Angel and the gentleness was assumed. I had nothing on which to base this except that old gut instinct I was always talking about.

Angel was a man of contrasts. When we found the skeleton in CHAPS' flower bed August before last, Angel fainted on top of it. Gave us all a turn. He said it reminded him of a body he'd discovered when he was a kid.

On the other hand, several times over the going on two years we'd worked together, I'd watched Angel evict a kid who'd shown up with a false ID, or a guy who'd had a few too many beers, or a prostitute who had tried to ply her ancient trade. None of them had ever argued with him, or tried to give him a hard time. He had that kind of presence.

Not being quite sure of how he'd react, I wasn't sure I wanted to say anything about Duke and Gina. But then again, Angel and I were friends. And when a friend asks me something I tell the truth.

Usually.

Most of the time.

"He seemed interested," I admitted.

He nodded, looking glum. "She's interested, too," he said.

"Oh."

I'd have sworn Gina was madly in love with Angel, but then I've been known to be wrong about people. And there had been a time I was madly in love with Rob Whittaker, who was now relegated to ex-husband status without any regrets on my part. People change. Emotions change. You wake up one day, and say, "What was I thinking?"

"I'm sorry, Angel," I said lamely.

He shrugged. "No big deal," he said. He disposed of our water bottles in the trash can behind the bar, wiped the bar counter down with a spotless cloth. I couldn't read any expression at all on his face, but the atmosphere felt cold suddenly, as though a storm front was coming in from the ocean. Sometimes I sense auras myself. I was almost relieved when the telephone rang.

Angel picked up the handset, and said "CHAPS" very sternly. "It's for you, Charlie," he said.

"I'll take it upstairs," I said. "I want to check on Ben." What I really wanted was to escape before Angel could ask me any more questions relating to his love life.

It was Thane Stockton, wanting a progress report. I'd been talking to him most days—telling him some stuff, holding back on other stuff, not naming names.

Of *course* I didn't trust him. What did you think? No matter how unlikely a suspect he seemed to me, it *was* possible he had murdered his wife. Bristow believed he had, and Bristow was an experienced cop. Mr. Stockton *could* be using me to find somebody who knew too much and needed murdering.

Carrying my mobile phone into the bathroom, I

turned Benny loose. He thundered off into the sitting area and disappeared under the sofa. I'd suspected for some time that he was pulling stuffing out from underneath, but hadn't got around to checking behind the skirt. Probably the couch would collapse before I'd remember to look.

"We don't really have much to go on yet," I told Mr. Stockton when he got through apologizing profusely for taking me away from my work. I certainly wasn't going to tell him his wife had apparently been having an affair with an old boyfriend from her homeland. Not without being there to watch his face and his body language. He had admitted that he wasn't sure if she was lying about having affairs or not—if he had known for sure that she was, his motive for murder was fairly strong.

I found I was shaking my head as I told Mr. Stockton who Zack and I had talked to so far. I just couldn't cast this tentative man in the role of a killer who would stab his wife as violently as Estrella had been stabbed, wrap her up in a sleeping bag, and toss her over a bridge.

"I'm glad you called," I told him when he started in apologizing again. "I have a question for you. Zack and I met Candy at Hair Raising. Did Estrella have any other Filipino friends, either male or female?"

He was silent for a while. I pulled out green onions and no-fat mayonnaise from the refrigerator, took a can of tuna in springwater and a can of ripe olives out of a cabinet, and fished in a drawer until I found a can opener.

"She didn't belong to any Filipino clubs," Mr. Stockton said at last. "She always said she'd left the Philippines because she wanted to get away, and she didn't want any reminders of the place."

That hardly squared with Estrella telling Candy that she and her Filipino "friend" had been talking about the good old days.

"One time I listened in on the telephone when she was talking to some guy," Thane Stockton went on. "They spoke in English, but he was Filipino. I could tell by the way he talked—and they mentioned several places in the Philippines. When I questioned her, Estrella told me he was one of her lovers, one of the men who was going to come by and beat me up one day."

They'd had a really happy marriage, Estrella and Thane Stockton. All the same, this was interesting stuff. This male caller could very well be the "old boyfriend from the Philippines." This most certainly qualified as a clue.

"I said I was going to tell the police that this man was threatening me, and then Estrella laughed and said she was joking, he was just a security guard at the bank. He'd called to tell her she'd left her wallet on the counter. I told her I'd heard them discussing the Philippines, and she said they'd talked at the bank a couple of times."

I could almost see him shaking his head in that helpless way he had.

I remembered suddenly that he'd talked about a bank guard early on. I'd been distracted because he'd mentioned Duke Conway at the same time, and I hadn't ever followed up on the guard.

I craned my neck backward to see what Ben was up to. He was lying flat out on his side on the floor in front of the sofa, all stretched out. Quite suddenly, he flipped himself over to the other side, then back. First time he ever did that I thought he was having a fit. Almost had a fit myself. Turned out to be a rabbit habit—maybe some kind of aerobic exercise bunnies indulge in. He saw me watching him and came hopping over, then thundered off again, wanting me to play. "In a minute," I called to him, holding my hand over the telephone mouthpiece.

"Did you get the guy's name?" I asked Mr. Stockton when it seemed nothing more was forthcoming. I fully expected him to say no, or to tell me he'd only heard a nickname. That was the way things were going in this case.

"Domingo," he said. "Estrella called him Domingo. I don't know if that was his given name or last name."

"And the bank? Estrella's bank?"

"The Bellamy Park Bank. Downtown."

As soon as I hung up I was hot to trot. But first I needed lunch, and so did Ben, and then ...

And then I had to go see Dr. Hanssen. My appointment was less than an hour away. No way could I weasel out of it again. I'd probably do well to wait until tomorrow for any possible confrontation with this Domingo character anyway. Maybe I could plan overnight some clever way to get the security guard to admit he was a killer.

It occurred to me about then that if Domingo turned out to be Estrella's murderer, it might be a good idea to have someone with me as a witness, and a bodyguard to make sure Domingo didn't cap his career by becoming *my* murderer. I hadn't quite graduated from the self-defense course yet, and it might not look so good to enter a bank flourishing a canister of pepper spray. Someone might jump to the wrong conclusions.

Sighing, I picked up the phone again and punched in Zack's number.

CHAPTER 10

Bellamy Park's main drag is San Pablo Avenue. It's a wide street, attractive and upscale, lined with trees and wooden planters, overflowing at this time with daffodils and sweet williams, primroses, and violas. Yeah, I know it was only January, but that's one of the advantages of living in California.

There are clothing boutiques, artsy-crafty shops, sidewalk cafés, bookstores, upscale children's emporiums, and a lot of antique stores on San Pablo Avenue. The latter sell only fine antiques, of course. I used to haunt such stores when I was married and living on Puget Sound. Rob and I furnished our wonderful Tudor-style house with the most amazing finds. That house was so hard to leave, I've taught myself never to look at another antique, so on San Pablo I keep my gaze on the brick sidewalks.

As Zack and I approached the Bellamy Park Bank, I thought about the death of its former president six months earlier. How could I not? Zack and I were very much involved in the case—Zack more personally than I.

And now we had another dead body.

I don't use that bank, so I hadn't been in it before. We keep CHAPS' money, and I stash my own, in the bank next door to CHAPS on Adobe Plaza. This one was sort of historic—it was built on the site of a former Wells Fargo office. It was a little pretentious, like many of the buildings in Bellamy Park, all white, with tall windows and Grecian columns and wide steps leading up to it.

The guard's full name was Domingo Romero. He was very smart in a dark blue uniform. Possibly mid to late thirties, I thought, average height but sturdy, dark-eyed and dark-haired, round-faced, swarthy complexion. His black hair was cut in a circle on top, very short on the sides with zigzag inscriptions. I was fascinated. I hadn't seen them close up before. You know what I mean—where designs have been cut in? I immediately wanted to ask him how often he had to have them done over. Whether it cost a lot. How difficult it was to do.

When we first stopped in front of him, I thought he was going to go into cardiac arrest. He literally hyperventilated. No, it wasn't a seizure of guilt. It was the effect Zack's arrival often has on Zack-worshipers. No doubt about it—Domingo was a fan.

Zack was unfazed. He's used to that kind of reaction. Which explains why he's not too lacking in self-confidence. "Any possibility you and I could have a *discussion*," he said to Domingo when it seemed the younger man might be able to breathe again.

"You mean here?" Domingo squeaked.

Zack looked around. It was eleven o'clock. The bank wasn't busy, but every teller in the place and a couple of female customers were gazing our way. I was pretty sure it wasn't my orange hair they were fascinated by.

Zack zapped them with one of his under-the-eye-lashes looks and turned back while they were still reeling. "You aimin' to take a break soon?" he asked, sticking his thumbs under his belt. Evidently Sheriff Lazarro had taken possession of Zack's body on the way in. "You wanna meet us outside in the alley?"

Domingo swallowed, his eyes widening.

"This isn't *High Noon*," I assured him. "Zack just means we want to talk to you in private."

"Five minutes?" Domingo croaked.

"Try to get hold of yourself," I advised him kindly as Zack exited the building. "Zack Hunter didn't really come down from Mount Olympus, only from Adobe Plaza."

Domingo looked at me blankly.

Zack was waiting for me on the sidewalk, making passersby do double takes. Most of them appeared to think they were mistaken about his identity. According to local media reports, Zack was in Hollywood, happily laying up new and exciting episodes of *Prescott's Landing* against the future. Some people tried to appear unimpressed. Zack Hunter was just another Hollywood star to them. They kept looking back over their shoulders all the same. One young woman was so startled she stepped out into the crosswalk while the hand was lit up and almost got run over by a Lincoln Continental with tinted windows.

"Hey," Domingo said behind us.

We walked through the alley to the parking lot. "This is my friend Charlie," Zack told Domingo. That's

the only time I get worshipful looks, when Zack intro-
duces me as a friend. It's not a bad experience. "She
wants to ask you a few questions," Zack continued.

Apparently Sheriff Lazarro had gone off duty
already.

"It's about Estrella Stockton," I said.

"Oh man," Domingo exclaimed. "I just knew the
minute I saw that story on TV somebody was going to
open their big mouth and tell the cops I knew Estrella. I
just knew it." Surprisingly, he suddenly broke into a
singsong rhythm, "Estrella, Estrella, where you at.
Wish I'd never met you, that's that."

"We're not the . . ." Zack began, but broke off when
I quelled him with a glance.

"How *well* did you know Estrella?" I asked Domingo.

He opened his mouth and closed it again. I thought
he was going to sing some more, but instead he patted
the breast pocket of his uniform shirt and pulled out
a pack of generic cigarettes. His hands shook as he lit
one, but I didn't think it was Zack who was causing
the tremors now. Which could mean Domingo Romero
was just a little nervous about being associated with
a dead person, or else he had something to hide. Interesting.

"I didn't know her all that well, you know?" he said
in a whining voice that sounded completely untruthful.
"I mean I didn't know her outside the bank, not really.
She was a customer, you know? One time she said
something to me in Tagalog, and I answered, so after
that we'd go have a cup of coffee on my break, lunch
maybe twice, a cigarette out here sometimes. Once I

took her for a ride on my Harley." He gestured vaguely at the vehicles in the parking lot. "Sometimes we'd talk, you know?"

Zack preempted me. "About what?"

Domingo raked his fingers through his circular top-knot and blew smoke out of his nostrils like a dragon. "Home. Manila. The Philippines. Like that."

"You knew her from home?" I asked.

"Nah. Like I said, I didn't know her until she spoke to me that time. We were both glad to be in the States, you know? But sometimes, well it's only natural, sometimes you get homesick. It's nice to talk to someone knows what you're talking about, you know?"

Estrella hadn't said anything to her husband about having nostalgia fests with the bank guard. The bank guard wasn't saying anything about having an affair. But Estrella had told Maisie she was having an affair with her old boyfriend from home. Actually, I was beginning to have my doubts about *that* story, because Domingo didn't quite fit the role. And he'd denied knowing her in the Philippines.

"When did you arrive in the U.S.?" I asked. "Two—three months ago?"

He dropped his cigarette butt on the ground and stepped on it. A cocky grin appeared on his face. Evidently he was going to try a different tack. "I look like I just got off the boat?" he asked. "I've been here thirteen years. Since I was sixteen."

"You ever take Estrella to Paulie's Place?" Zack asked.

I gazed at him with genuine admiration. I'd forgotten for the moment that Felicia had told us that's where she'd seen Estrella with her "old boyfriend from the Philippines."

Domingo curled his upper lip and shook his head. "Nah. I don't drink. Ever. Hate the taste of the stuff. Makes me sick. Not barf sick—ill. If I want to socialize, I hang out at The Grange, you know?"

Okay, that confirmed the impression I'd been receiving ever since we'd met this guy. The Grange was an espresso bar in Dennison that was very popular with gay men. Right on cue, as I stared at him, Domingo gave Zack a bright-eyed sideways and upward glance with a flutter of eyelashes that could only be construed as flirtatious. "Hey," he said languorously. "I heard you owned a place out near Condor. Some country-style place."

"CHAPS," Zack said.

"Yeah, that's what I heard. Maybe I'll come out there sometime. Bring my friend. We like to dance. Never did try line-dancing. Looks fun on TV, you know? You have karaoke?"

I shuddered.

"So when *did* you first meet Estrella?" I asked.

"Six months ago?" Much of what he said ended on a questioning note. I was beginning to find it irritating.

"The bank was closed July Fourth," he went on. "Estrella spoke to me the next day—asked me if I enjoyed the holiday? Said something about the fireworks not being as noisy and smoky as New Year's Eve in Manila."

"You're only twenty-nine?" I asked abruptly, my subconscious having done some mathematics while I was busy elsewhere.

He gave me a knowing look. "You thought I was older? Everybody thinks so. I had a rough life. My mom was a Filipina, my dad a GI. After we came to Condor, Daddy didn't stick around too long. Mom took off a year or so later. I ran the streets. Old story, you know?"

I saw some fellow feeling on Zack's face. Zack's official bio implies he's always been an overprivileged resident of Beverly Hills, and had attended the best schools, but during the last investigation we'd become embroiled in, he'd admitted to me that he'd grown up on some of the meaner streets of L.A.

"I was lucky," Domingo said. "I ran into a cop took me under his wing. Like Mother Goose, you know? Got me to stay in school, helped me get a job as a waiter. Later on, got me into this job."

"A Condor police officer?" Zack asked.

I was amazed at the good questions Zack was asking today. There must have been an episode of *Prescott's Landing* with a scenario like this one.

"They call him Big John," Domingo said. "His name is John Avila."

Zack glanced at me, and I could almost read his mind. We could tell Detective Sergeant Bristow about Domingo's cop friend and he might feed us whatever *he* found out about Domingo from the guy.

"Did you ever call Estrella at home?" I asked Domingo to get us back on track.

He started playing air guitar, his mouth pursed as if he'd zipped his lips. I was beginning to discern a pattern here.

"Estrella's husband told us a Filipino man called one day from the bank," I told him.

"That's what got you on my trail?" he asked, reverting to a singsong rhythm again.

I nodded.

His eyes narrowed suddenly. "What's all this got to do with you, anyway?"

That always happens. Just when you settle in to asking the right kind of questions, the questionee gets suspicious and wants to see your license. Which of course I didn't have.

"I was a friend of Estrella's," I said. "A client."

"Yeah?" He cast a doubtful glance at my hair. I wasn't wearing my cowboy hat. Everybody's a critic.

Zack sent his wry grin my way, and Domingo forgot all about being suspicious of my motives. He looked ready to swoon instead. "You gonna give me an autograph after all this?" he asked our man-in-black.

"Do it right now," Zack said. "Gratitude for whatever information you can give us."

To show what a good guy I was, I rummaged in my jacket pocket and pulled out a pen. Domingo offered the back of his hand, but Zack shook his head and the guard hauled out a wallet and dug a receipt out of it.

"Zack and I have been hired to investigate Estrella's murder," I said as Zack signed his name with a flourish on the back of the receipt. Hired wasn't quite the right word, I supposed. No one had mentioned any kind of pay scale.

"You're PIs?" Domingo asked, obviously awed.

"In a way," I said vaguely, hoping my expression was secretive enough to discourage any more exploration of *that* subject. I wasn't really lying, I assured myself. We *were* investigating, and we were certainly private.

"That was me telephoned the house, you know?" Domingo admitted. "I called to tell Estrella she left her billfold on the counter at the bank. She said afterward her husband had listened in. He killed her, huh?"

"We don't . . ." Zack started, but I cut in.

"What makes you say that?" I asked.

"Stands to reason. He was the one beat her up. Always jealous, she told me. Put her through the third degree if she was two minutes late getting home from work. Didn't want her to have friends, you know? Made her have sex with him all the time when she didn't want to."

I tried but could not imagine Thane Stockton demanding sex at *any* time, never mind *all* the time. "You ever meet him?" Zack asked Domingo. Similar thoughts must be going through *his* mind.

Domingo shook his head, then looked at his watch. "Look, man, I gotta go. I told my boss you wanted to talk to me about a bit part in a movie, he said I could have twenty minutes, you know?"

"That was inventive," I murmured. "You're sure you never went with Estrella to Paulie's?" I persisted.

"Never set foot in Paulie's. Swear to God." He started edging away.

"One more question. Did she ever mention having *another* Filipino friend?"

"Well, there was Candy, at Hair Raising."

"I mean a male friend. A very close male friend. Someone who *might* have taken her to Paulie's."

"A Filipino?" About to say something more, he
zipped his mouth again as something flickered in his
eyes. Almost immediately his face closed down into a
bland mask. "I don't know what you're talking about,
lady," he said, and for once there was no questioning
note.

"I just want to know if Estrella ever mentioned a
male Filipino friend," I said.

"Some dude who took her to Paulie's Place," Zack
added so there couldn't be any mistake.

Domingo hesitated, no doubt about that. But he
could just have been thinking. The closed look in his
eyes could have been due to concentration.

"Nah, I never heard anything about that," he said
at last. His voice had changed. His eyelids were
twitching. I wouldn't have been surprised to see his
nose grow six inches.

"Well then, did you ever see any *evidence* that
Thane Stockton was abusing Estrella?"

"Hey, you said one more question," he complained.

"That's the last one, I promise."

He heaved a dramatic sigh. "One time I picked
Estrella up on my Harley outside her gates. I gave
her a lift to where she worked. Her Mercedes was
in the shop. She was all, like, what's the word—dish
something—mussed up. She said Thane had been at
her again. There was blood on her blouse, you know?"
He turned away. "That's it, lady," he said.

Blood on her blouse. Estrella's blood or her husband's? I wondered.

CHAPTER 11

"What do you think?" I asked Zack as we headed for his pickup.

"No question," he said with a brisk nod. "The dude's gay."

"I didn't mean that. Do you think Domingo was telling the truth about never going to Paulie's, and not knowing Estrella in the Philippines and never hearing about some other Filipino friend of hers?"

"Hard to tell."

Why had I thought Zack might have picked up some subtlety I'd missed? Subtlety and Zack were complete strangers to one another.

I'd found it hard to tell, too, but my instincts were screaming that Domingo had not played straight with us. No pun intended.

"I think maybe he either knew something about Estrella's Filipino boyfriend," I said as I climbed into the pickup, "or else he knew that he was the guy she was talking about. His eyes sort of twitched. Did you notice?"

Zack grunted noncommittally. Which probably meant he hadn't.

Apparently he took for granted that he was invited to lunch. He got out of the pickup with me when we arrived at CHAPS, accompanied me up to my loft, took his hat off, let Benny out of his cage, and sat down with him in my flea-market rocking chair.

The apartment immediately became smaller and lost all its air. Zack has that effect on places.

On my places anyway.

Benny always looked very small in Zack's long-fingered, beautiful hands. The rabbit was fairly small to start with, of course. If a child were to draw Benny, she'd first make a small circle for his head, then a much larger circle for his body and a tiny cotton-ball circle for his tail, then add a few whiskers to his cheeks and put two ears on top of his head, close together and sticking straight up, though not as far up as those of bigger rabbits.

Benny always looked relaxed when Zack held him. His nose didn't even twitch, and I'm here to tell you a rabbit's nose twitches a *lot.* Let's face it, our man-in-black is loaded with far more than his share of charisma; everybody falls under his spell. I could feel my own chemistry perking like a coffee commercial as I put some turkey sandwiches together and tossed a salad, and Zack wasn't even looking at me.

While we ate, and Benny hopped around my loft, we discussed everything we'd found out about Estrella so far and decided the only avenue left to explore was Thane Stockton's friend, Dr. Adler Hutchins. We'd check on him the following day.

I debated telling Zack I was going into Doc Hanssen's clinic the following Monday for the biopsy I'd been putting off, but I decided Sunday would be soon enough to let him know. Mostly I was trying not to think too graphically about having a bit of my innards chopped out and scrutinized for cancer cells. After all, there wasn't much I could do about it at this point, except go through with it, but I kept having this cold wave of fright wash over me at unexpected moments.

Zack helped me clear the dishes from my rickety table to the sink. When we both reached for a plate at the same time, our hands met. And paused.

Whomp! went my stomach. It always responded like that. Evidently even Zack's four-month absence hadn't reconditioned any of my reflexes.

Zack's eyebrows did their trademark slant, indicating a question. There was only one question he was likely to be asking in a private situation like this. Normally I would quell a question like that with one frosty glance, but I guess I was feeling vulnerable about the forthcoming medical procedure and all I could manage was a doubtful kind of head movement somewhere between a nod and a shrug.

Which was all the invitation our man-in-black ever needed. Next thing I knew my upper parts were nicely surrounded by a strong manly arm.

Zack's free hand cupped my chin, his thumb gently brushing my mouth. "Did you miss me, darlin'?" he asked softly.

"Sure," I croaked. "We all did."

His hand moved to the back of my head and pressed it to his chest so I could hear his heart beating. His other arm tightened. I could feel him breathing into my hair.

It had been a long time for me. Some months ago it had seemed likely that my long dry spell was going to end with the help of one of Zack's poker partners, but that moment had passed, and the poker partner had left town shortly afterward.

So here I was again, letting myself get all steamed up over Zack Hunter, when I knew damn well if Rudy DeSilva or one of Zack's other directors called right this minute to say they were going on with *Prescott's Landing,* or thinking of starting some new series, Zack would round up the wagons and head on out of town without a backward glance.

Which wouldn't be as bad as if I succumbed and then had to watch him react to the next gorgeous female to walk through CHAPS' door and crook a finger.

It wasn't that Zack *chased* after women. He just couldn't *resist* a woman who let him know she wanted him. He never had resisted. I *knew* that.

I'd like to think I was about to draw myself regretfully but firmly out of his sphere of influence, but to tell the truth, I don't know if I was going to or not. The question became moot because Ben suddenly went into his "Something wicked this way comes" act, which so surprised Zack that he loosened his hold on me, and I managed to step back from the edge of the abyss.

Benny does this thing where he pushes up on his front legs, very stiff. His ears stand rigidly at attention. His eyes widen and become glassy. Lastly, he thumps the floor with his rear right foot, very fast, very hard, very loud, two maybe three times.

"Whoa!" Zack exclaimed.

And then the doorbell extension sounded off on the wall and Benny scuttled into his cage in the bathroom.

"I think he's equipped with radar," I told Zack. I am always astonished at the sixth sense animals seem to possess, though I did wonder as I trotted down the steps to CHAPS' main outer door whether Ben's attention-getting fit had been brought on by jealousy and the doorbell was merely a coincidence. Whatever the cause, I was grateful to have my sanity restored.

Moderately grateful.

Detective Sergeant Taylor Bristow was at the door, dressed in a yellow polo shirt, jeans, and yet another dazzlingly colorful windbreaker. He gave me his Michael Jordan smile, so at least I knew he wasn't angry with me. I've never actually seen Bristow angry, but he's big enough and built well enough that I never want to. He's also a Shakespearean actor, remember, so he probably knows a few fairly forceful imprecations.

I took him upstairs, which surprised him until he saw Zack up there. Usually we all get together in the main corral when Bristow drops by.

He did look questioningly from me to Zack with a sort of interested glint in his amber eyes, but I squelched his speculation with a glance. "Thought I'd find out how your end of the investigation is going," he said with a flash of his eyes in my direction as he seated himself on my rocker.

Zack was on the sofa with Benny cradled in his hands. Evidently he'd coaxed him out of his cage so he could reassure him all was well. I could see Benny vibrating gently with pleasure.

I sat down on the sofa next to Zack. I don't have a

whole lot of furniture, and I felt pretty safe with Bristow there. "What makes you think we're investigating anything?" I asked.

Bristow smiled.

As I said before—he knows me.

"I heard you'd visited Hair Raising," he said.

"You went there yourself?"

He nodded. "Maisie and Candy told me about a Filipino friend of Estrella's. Hot and heavy friend according to Maisie. Felicia said she'd seen Estrella with a man not her husband at Paulie's Place. Wasn't sure if he was Filipino on account of the funny lighting and him wearing a cap. Couldn't quite picture his face anymore, she said. All three said they'd told you all of this."

He shook his head as if in puzzlement, then narrowed his eyes at me. "Odd thing, Ms. Plato. I cannot recall that you reported this information to me."

I swallowed.

Zack rescued me, at the same time digging our hole deeper. "We checked the guy at the bank out," he said. "Domingo something. He says he never took Estrella to Paulie's Place. Says he was never in Paulie's Place."

"Domingo Romero," I supplied with a sigh.

"What's the look for?" Zack asked.

"What guy at what bank?" Bristow demanded, sitting forward so suddenly that Benny's ears twitched, and his eyes rolled.

I took Benny from Zack, put him into his cage in the bathroom with a Romaine lettuce leaf to chew on, came back and sat down and clued Bristow in on Domingo Romero.

He kept his gaze fixed on my face for a minute or two after I was through talking. I braced myself for the lecture, but it was not forthcoming. "None of the women at Hair Raising mentioned anyone named Domingo," Bristow said. "They didn't know the name of the Filipino friend Estrella was fooling around with. Where did you hear about Domingo?"

This was not a question I wanted to answer.

"Client privilege?" I asked without much hope.

Bristow snorted. "Last I heard neither of you had a PI license, which I might remind you is a requirement in the state of California." He glanced at Zack. "Acting credits accumulated by Sheriff Lazarro don't count."

That last comment sounded fairly jocular, so I thought he possibly wasn't too irritated with us after all.

"Thane Stockton hired us," Zack offered before I could stop him. He often takes the wind out of my sails like that. Times I've kicked him on the shins for it, and he was close enough, but I didn't want to do it in front of Bristow. He might have had me up for intimidating a witness.

"My number one suspect," Bristow said in a voice layered with sarcasm. "I'm working at closing in on him, and you're working to get him off. What do you mean, hired?" he added, his eyes glinting with something that was not affection. "I'd better not hear that any money changed hands."

"We're just trying to do the dude a favor," Zack protested.

"He *asked* us to help prove him innocent," I butted

in. "That's not supposed to be necessary in our system, but it seems to be becoming more common."

"Not too likely to prove him innocent if he's guilty," Bristow said, sounding smug.

"You've found more evidence that looks bad for him? You've discovered he really was abusing Estrella? You got the DNA results?"

He rubbed a hand over the back of his bare head, looking rueful. "That was not Thane Stockton's seminal fluid inside Estrella's body," he said.

"Well then—"

"That does not rule out the possibility that he killed her," Bristow pointed out. "He confessed to me that Estrella was beating him up, and it appears that the bruises on her body and his would bear out that claim."

"He has bruises?" I exclaimed.

Bristow nodded. "The fact that she was possibly abusing him does not make him automatically innocent of her murder, Charlie. Quite the reverse. Also, the fact that it was someone else's seminal fluid makes it *more* likely her husband killed her rather than less."

He was calling me Charlie again. A good sign.

"But you haven't arrested him?"

He shook his head. "One thing that causes me to pause is the fact that when I first spoke to him about his wife's murder, he said to me, 'I did not kill my wife.' "

I nodded. "He said the same thing to me when he asked me to help find her killer." I looked at him curiously. "You mean you took his word for it, just like that?"

"Not completely, but you see, Charlie, most guilty

people won't come right out and say they didn't do a crime. They'll say, 'I'm innocent of all charges,' or 'you can't prove I did anything wrong,' or 'I have no knowledge of it.' "

"Politicians do the same thing. They waffle."

"Right. So when a man says 'I did not kill my wife,' straight out like that, I am forced to consider that perhaps he didn't."

"Husbands don't take kindly to dudes boinkin' their wives," Zack said solemnly, having pondered through our exchange. "They usually get more agitated with the dude than the wife though."

Bristow laughed. "Know that for a fact, do you?" he asked.

"You might say that," Zack drawled with a wry grin.

I was tempted to kick both of them.

"It's possible Thane came across Estrella boinking someone else, hung around and killed her after the guy was gone," Bristow said. "Or she could have *told* him she'd just boinked someone else, and *then* he killed her. He *says* he has no idea who the murderer could have been. Says Estrella went where she wanted to when she wanted to. She was always making up stories about getting laid, but he never really believed her. He says."

"He overheard a phone call Estrella had from Domingo," I said. "Afterward, Estrella told him Domingo was one of her lovers, then she laughed and said that wasn't true, he was just a guard at the bank and he'd called to tell her she'd left her billfold on the counter. According to Domingo the billfold part was true, but the rest wasn't. Domingo also said Estrella complained all the time about Thane's jealousy. Which she may have done, but who knows if she was lying? I'm not at all sure Domingo told us the truth about the other stuff. Either he did know Estrella in the Philippines, and he was the old boyfriend, or he knew something about some other Filipino man in her life."

"You have knowledge of *another* man?" Bristow asked.

I shrugged. I didn't want to tell him what Rory had seen from his Dumpster. He might think it suspicious that Rory had withheld that information from the police. Maybe it was, but I wanted to think about it before telling.

"What makes you think this Domingo Romero lied to you?" Bristow asked.

"His eyelids twitched," Zack told him.

That earned him a look. He smiled his wry smile and raised his hands palms up. "Don't blame me, Charlie told me that's how she knew Domingo was funnin' her."

Bristow rolled his eyes.

"Okay," I said. "How about some quid pro quo here?"

"There's no law on the books that says a law-enforcement officer has to provide information to an informant," Bristow said with one of his clever smiles.

"It's part of the friendship law," I said. "I give you a present, you give me a present. That's how it works. You pay for dinner out this week, I pay next week."

He laughed. I can usually make him laugh. That's part of the friendship syndrome, too. "You have to admit," I went on, pressing my advantage, "Zack and I have come up with a lot of good stuff."

He tilted his head and shrugged slightly, which I took for agreement. "I'm quite sure you haven't been idle while we've been digging around," I added.

A couple of gentle nods this time.

"So what have you come up with?"

He frowned, then did a sort of "what the heck" grimace. "I've discovered that Estrella was married before, to a Filipino."

"The old boyfriend," I exclaimed. "That must be who she was with in Paulie's Place the night Felicia was there." A thought struck me. "Did she get a divorce?"

"Divorce isn't legal in the Philippines."

"You mean she committed bigamy? Wait a minute— her husband found out she married Thane Stockton and followed them to the U.S. You said she drew out some money from the bank the day before she died. The first husband was blackmailing her because she was still married to him. She paid him, and he killed her."

Bristow had a fond expression on his face, but it did not look as if he was impressed by my brilliance.

"What?" I demanded.

"You read too many mystery novels," he said.

Zack laughed.

"It wasn't that way?" I guessed.

"Far from it, Charlie." Bristow leaned forward, his face going serious. This was going to be the straight skinny, I could tell. "Estrella's first husband—one Carlos Rosales—fell from a tenth-story window of a hotel where he and Estrella were spending a vacation. He died on impact."

I stared at him. "You think Estrella killed him?"

"Estrella was shopping at the time."

"Thane Stockton said she was a compulsive shopper," Zack reminded us.

"No one saw Carlos fall," Bristow continued. "The detective I spoke to suspected Estrella's grief wasn't as deep as it should have been in the circumstances. But he couldn't come up with enough evidence to indict her. Nor did there seem to be any reason for or evidence of suicide. Carlos's death was ruled accidental. Estrella collected a very large amount of insurance. Less than a year later she came to California as Thane Stockton's loving wife. The detective thought she probably wanted to get away before she gave herself away."

"Do you suppose Mr. Stockton knew how her first husband died?" I asked.

"According to himself, he knew she had been married before, and widowed, but he had no idea there were any suspicious circumstances surrounding the man's death. When I acquainted him with the facts, he seemed to feel he'd had a lucky escape."

"Wow!" was all I could find to say.

Bristow stood up. "I guess I'll go have a talk with Mr. Romero at the bank," he said. He leveled a glance at me. "You've told me everything?"

"Domingo intimated he was a bit wild when he was a kid," I said. Part of my mind was already probing the information Bristow had given us, checking it for significant details. "He told us he was taken in hand by a Condor cop called Big John Avila. You know him?"

"Maybe."

"Domingo's gay," I added. "I'm inclined to think that would rule him out as Estrella's Filipino lover. Unless he's bisexual."

"I'll rule him out when I'm good and ready," Bristow said. He hesitated. "Is that it?"

"That's everything we've learned about Domingo so far," Zack said.

Evidently Bristow thought about that as he headed across the room. He paused in the doorway and turned around. "I have an idea that was too selective a statement. What do the Hardy brother and Nancy Drew have in mind for the near future?"

Zack and I exchanged guilty looks. "We thought we might try to find some of Thane Stockton's friends," I said, which was skirting the truth in a way, but only because I didn't want Bristow going after Dr. Adler Hutchins before I'd had a chance to talk to him.

He frowned, and I was afraid he was going to forbid us to go on with our investigation. If he did that, we'd have to quit; I wasn't going to get afoul of the law if I could help it. But all he said was, "Keep in touch," which was as good as saying, "Go for it," as far as I was concerned.

I remembered him saying during a previous investigation that I could possibly ask questions and get into places where police officers governed by regulations were not allowed to tread. I had an idea that as long as I didn't trample anyone's toes, he'd pretty well leave me alone.

Just as Bristow was closing the door, and I was letting my tummy relax, he turned back one more time.

I tightened up again, but then I saw that a much softer expression had come into his eyes. "Savanna told me about you having to go in for some kind of medical procedure Monday," he said. "Sure sorry to hear that, Charlie. I'll be rooting for you."

I thanked him and he finally left. There was a silence next to me. Then I felt an arm go around my shoulders. "What was that about a medical procedure?" Zack asked.

I explained about the Class III pap smear, the indeterminate colposcopy, and the biopsy that was on for Monday.

"But you'll be okay?" Zack asked when I was done.

"Sure," I said with a lot more confidence than I felt. "I had a pre-op checkup yesterday. Everything else was in good shape, the doctor said, so probably it's just a false alarm."

Evidently he detected the note of doubt. Pulling me into his side, he tucked my head down on his shoulder. "I'll drive you," he said.

"I have to leave here at 9 A.M."

Zack was no more a morning person than I was.

"I'll be here at eight-forty-five," he insisted. "You shouldn't be alone for somethin' like that."

He began rubbing my back gently. I love having my back rubbed. It makes me want to purr like a contented kitten. And for once there was no sexual suggestiveness in Zack's attitude. This was a friend offering support to a friend. I relaxed and accepted the comfort.

CHAPTER 12

According to the snippety woman at his voice-mail service, Dr. Adler Hutchins was out of his office and another doctor was taking his emergencies. No, she could *not* give out his home phone number, but she would leave a message for him, asking him to call me, if I wanted to inform her of the nature of my problem.

Thinking rapidly, I said I wished to talk to the doctor about Zack Hunter.

"Zack Hunter," she gasped.

"The one and only," I said, and hung up.

I checked the local directory and discovered the doctor's home number was listed. My jubilation was short-lived; the same snippy voice answered. I hung up again.

While I was pondering what to do, I went downstairs to see if the mail had arrived. It had. I put it on my desk in the office and thumbed through the usual collection of catalogs and bills and charity requests. The only personal mail was a flyer from my ex-husband in Seattle. An invitation to his new plastic-surgery clinic's open house. Rob liked to keep in touch. "Any chance you can come?" he'd written across the top left corner. I still felt an emotional lift when I saw his signature. Even when love gets shattered, it's a difficult habit to get over.

There was also a very cutesy card for Benny from his vet, Dr. Lansing, reminding him he was due his semiannual checkup. It was written in rascally rabbit talk. I took it upstairs to the loft and showed it to Ben. "What do you think?" I asked. "Does that make you want to barf?"

He wiggled his nose—affirmatively, I decided.

"It would take our minds off my medical problems," I suggested. I had the phone in my hand and was about to punch in the vet's numbers when a thought struck me, and I called Thane Stockton instead. "I got to thinking about your dog," I said. "You told me she was poisoned, and you thought Estrella did it."

He sighed. "I don't have any proof, Miss Plato, if that's what you are looking for. There was antifreeze in the garage and the can had supposedly developed a leak, which seemed unlikely. I thought at the time Estrella must have punctured the can and forced the fluid into Champers. Champers was a finicky eater, I couldn't imagine her voluntarily ingesting something like that. The first I knew about it, Champers was throwing up."

"Champers?"

"Champagne. The dog's name was Champagne, but I called her Champers for short."

Champers. It was my day for cutesy. "So you took her to the vet? What did he or she say?"

"He." Silence vibrated along the line. "I don't drive, Miss Plato. Estrella took her in."

So she said. Maybe she dropped her off in the bay. "Did you talk to the vet about her?" I asked.

"No. Estrella told me Champers had died on the way there and the vet sent her right over to the Humane Society for disposal. I was upset for a long time."

This man wasn't to be believed. He'd given over complete control of his life to that woman. "Do you at least know which vet Estrella took her to?"

"Oh yes, of course. The Andersen Clinic. Dr. Brian Andersen. Just a minute, I'll look it up." He hesitated. "Are you going there?"

"I thought I'd take my rabbit to him, maybe ask him about your dog at the same time," I said. "Don't bother looking," I added. "I've found the phone number. I'll talk to you later."

"Okay," he said, sounding helpless again. That man needed someone to take him in hand, give him some assertiveness training.

I was able to get Ben an appointment for one-fifteen. The clinic was a thirty-minute drive away. If Dr. Hutchins called, he could leave a message on *my* answering machine.

"Nothing wrong with this rabbit," Dr. Andersen said after a very thorough examination. "Whatever it is you're doing, keep doing it."

He grinned at me as he put Ben back in his cage. "You think that's worth thirty bucks?"

We'd been mildly flirting all through the examination. Dr. Brian Andersen was around my own age, my height, Scandinavian appearance, nice open face, clear blue eyes—no wedding ring. Not to-die-for, but you wouldn't slam the door in his face if he came calling.

"A friend of mine gave me your name," I told him, suddenly afraid he'd wash his hands and leave before I got to the real point of my visit. My former vet with the cutesy cards always dashed off as soon as he was done.

But this guy appeared to have all the time in the world. Sitting down on his rolling stool, he raised his eyebrows.

"Thane Stockton," I said.

He got a real funny look on his face. "Isn't he in jail?"

"He hasn't been charged with anything, in spite of what the media say."

He seemed real thoughtful.

"I heard about his dog," I said.

His head came up. "You mean he actually *told* you he wanted her euthanized for no reason?"

"Whoa!" There was a chair in the corner of the examining room. I decided I needed to sit down, too. Benny was happily nibbling on a veggie-flavored bunny bite that looked like a carrot.

"Something's wrong with this picture," I said.

The vet frowned. He was really quite cute, I decided. "I'm not sure I know what you mean, Ms. Plato."

"Charlie."

He had a nice smile, too. Dimples. "Charlie."

"It's like this," I said. "The dog story *I* heard was that Estrella fed the dog, Champers, some antifreeze. The dog threw up. Estrella brought her to you, but she died before she got here, and you shipped her off to the Humane Society to be disposed of."

His eyes had widened. "Who told you that?"

"Thane Stockton."

For a moment he just sat back and stared at me. Then he stood up, and said, "Come with me."

Ben was probably safe in his cage, but who knew what animal might shoulder its way in here. I picked up the cage and followed the vet to the other end of the clinic and into his office, where he was greeted lovingly, but in well-behaved fashion, by three dogs— a couple of sleek black Labradors and a small-size, but beautiful, cocker spaniel. "Say hello to Champers," the vet said.

"I think I need to sit down again," I said.

"Me too." He grinned and sat in his office chair, gesturing at its twin on the other side of the desk. The dogs settled around his feet.

I put Ben's cage on the desk and sank down on the chair. "You first."

"I've never met Thane Stockton," he said. "One of his employees always brought in the dog for shots or whatever. I guess he's too important to do such things himself. I've heard the Stocktons were one of the early families in these parts. Wealthy, I understand."

I nodded. "Mr. Stockton is pretty well off, but he doesn't think he's anything special. Far from it. He doesn't drive. I don't know why. Maybe he has poor eyesight. I imagine that's why he didn't bring the dog himself. Way he talked, he really loved that dog."

He leaned forward. "It sure didn't seem that way to me. Mrs. Stockton, Estrella Stockton, brought

Champers in one day—six—seven months ago. The poor little dog was upchucking—seemed she'd eaten something that didn't quite agree with her. But it certainly wasn't antifreeze. She recovered within twenty-four hours."

"But you didn't give her back?"

"Mrs. Stockton told me she and her husband had decided the dog was too much trouble and expense and should be euthanized. I told her I wasn't about to euthanize a healthy dog. She told me to send it to the Humane Society—and she did say 'it'—and to let them do away with it. Again, her words. Then she flounced out. When the dog recovered, I called Mr. Stockton but was told by one of his employees that he was indisposed and could not be disturbed. I meant to call the following day, but by then I'd decided if they wanted to kill that sweet little animal that badly, they'd probably find a way to do it. So I kept her and waited for one of them to call. They never did. The next thing I heard about the Stocktons was that Estrella was dead, and her husband had apparently killed her."

"He said he was very upset about the dog, so that was probably why nobody wanted to disturb him. As far as the murder's concerned, there's no actual evidence against Mr. Stockton yet. The question is, which one of them was lying about the dog?"

I looked at him directly. "I'd like you to treat this as confidential, but there's some possibility that Mrs. Stockton abused Mr. Stockton. However, it could have been the other way around." I shook my head. "I can't possibly tell him the dog's alive—he'd want her back.

Sure did seem to care about her—he told me he used
to play tug-of-war with her, with a piece of blanket or
something."

His eyes lit. "She taught me that game, brought
me an old towel and shook it at me until I grabbed it.
I'll be darned."

"I'll have to tell Detective Sergeant Bristow," I
went on. "He's the officer in ..."

"Taylor Bristow? I met him when that disgusting
animal-mutilation business was going on. I'll be happy
to tell him what little I know. There didn't seem much
point if Stockton was already under arrest, and I didn't
want to risk ..." It was his turn to look straight at
me. "I'm not giving her back if there's any possibility
Estrella Stockton was telling the truth."

"I wouldn't want you to."

We chewed it over a little longer, then his receptionist came in and told the vet he had a couple of patients
waiting. We both stood up and shook hands, and I
picked up Benny's cage. The cocker spaniel stretched
herself as if she was bowing and looked up at me as if
she'd understood everything we'd talked about. "She
looks sad," I said.

"Spaniels do." He reached down to pet her, and her
entire rear end wiggled with joy.

"Don't hesitate to call if you're ever concerned about
Benny's health," he added.

"I won't." I hesitated. "You don't send out cute
reminder cards in bunny talk, do you?"

"God no," he said without hesitation, then laughed.
"You were going to Dr. Lansing?"

I nodded.

As he held open the door, we made eye contact again. Hmm, I thought. "You gave your home address and phone number to my receptionist?" he asked.

"Yes. Oh—I guess I'll stop on the way out and pay her."

"I wasn't asking for the payment, though I'm always happy to have money. I was asking for myself."

"Oh." I gave him an appraising look of my own.

"Divorced," he said. "By mutual agreement. No rancor, no kids."

Oh, I do love a straightforward man. "Me too," I allowed, then added. "I do have some stuff going on right now though. Could you hold off for a month or so?"

"I'll try."

He probably thought I was in a relationship that was coming apart at the seams. Well, that was okay.

"What's your connection to Thane Stockton?" he asked as we walked down the hall.

"He asked for my help. He swears he's innocent."

"You're a private investigator?"

"Not exactly. Mostly just a nosy female."

He laughed, then held out his hand again. We'd reached the door to the waiting room. "I enjoyed meeting you, Charlie."

"Likewise, Doctor."

"Brian."

"Okay."

We exchanged another grin. Then he said, "If Mr. Stockton is cleared and can clear himself with me, I'll be happy to return Champers to her rightful owner.

In the meantime, I'll take good care of her and wait for your call."

"That was very interesting," I told Ben as I settled him in my Jeep Wrangler.

He hunkered down. Apparently, he hadn't thought so.

CHAPTER 13

The snippety woman had followed through. Dr. Adler Hutchins, Thane Stockton's friend, called me back early Friday afternoon and explained that he and his wife were staying in San Francisco because his daughter had delivered a baby a couple of days earlier. A strong healthy boy. "Fool insurance company wanted to kick Jeannie out last night," he said testily. "Had to threaten 'em within an inch of her deductible to make them agree she could stay until today. We've just brought her home."

I explained what Zack and I wanted to talk to him about.

"Why should I talk to *you?*" he asked.

I could be crotchety, too. "Because Thane Stockton asked us to clear him and you're Thane Stockton's friend and he needs all the help he can get."

There was a pause. I could hear a baby wailing in the background. "Too distracting here for a decent conversation," the doctor grouched. "Good set of lungs on that kid," he added, sounding a little mellower. "I do want to help Thane any way I can, poor guy's suffered enough. Let me think now, where would be a good place ..."

I was pleased with the way this was going—I would much rather talk to the doctor one-on-one, where I could watch his reactions to my questions.

We finally agreed to meet the following morning at Dr. Hutchins's daughter's house and play it by ear. "That way my wife and daughter will get to meet Zack Hunter," he added. "They went ballistic when they heard his name—wouldn't forgive me I let an opportunity like that pass. Wear something comfortable," he advised just as I was about to hang up. "I need some fresh air. Been cooped up for too long. We can maybe fly a kite or take a hike."

Saturday dawned bright and breezy, with a cheerful edge of warmth to the air. I always feel my spirits lift when I go to San Francisco—not just because of its heart-stopping hills and fascinating architecture, but because it's a *manageable* city. From many locations you can see all of it and grasp its identity—and beauty—in a way that isn't possible with cities built on flat land.

The doctor's daughter lived in the Marina district, not far from the wonderfully ornate Palace of Fine Arts, overlooking the Bay. The area had suffered extensive damage during the 1989 earthquake, but it appeared to be in great shape now.

I felt as if I'd been granted an unexpected holiday as I stepped down from Zack's pickup in the short driveway and took a deep breath of salt-scrubbed air. Kites were bobbing and weaving high above Marina

Green, the breeze was whipping creamy foam into the crests of the waves in the Bay, sailboats were scudding exuberantly along, sails billowing.

The house was Hollywood Mediterranean in style, pastel-colored, with a tile roof and overwrought iron-railed balcony, the living quarters built above the garage and daylight basement.

Dr. Hutchins opened the door to us. He was very short, balding, wiry-looking, fiftyish. He was dressed in sweats, as Zack and I were, and all ready to go, but Zack wanted to see the baby first.

Baby's mom, Jeannie, was a picture-perfect bru-nette in a floating and astonishingly sheer negligée I would have thought existed only in movies. It was so revealing, I couldn't think why she'd bother to wear it. Okay, maybe I was a little envious—her long straight hair was the kind I've always yearned for. She was happy to show off her new baby and gigglingly thrilled to meet Zack Hunter. There didn't seem to be a daddy around at the moment. Which was probably just as well.

Zack is great with babies and rabbits. He knows just how to hold them so they feel most secure. This baby still had his birth wrinkles. He looked like a gnome in a little knitted suit and a knitted blue hat fastened on one side with a pom-pom. One big hand supporting the babe's wobbly head, Zack held him right up to his face and spoke to him man to man, while the simpering mom and beaming grandmom looked on, and grandpa clicked his camera. I imagined this kid years from now looking at the photos, and saying, "Zack who?" The thought made me feel sad. Though there was really no reason to think Zack Hunter wouldn't still be a household name twenty years from now. Look at Paul Newman.

"A woman I dated had a baby," Zack said when the doctor commented on his easy way with the infant. My face must have shown shock—he sent me a look. "Not *my* baby, Charlie, she already had him when I met her. Sweetest baby you could imagine. Time he was two years old, hoo-ee could that kid throw a temper tantrum! Mom too." He laughed, and the baby gurgled as though appreciating the joke. "Decided to move on," Zack said, as he handed the baby back to his mother. I was surprised she didn't ask him to autograph the kid's diaper. He'd have done it, too.

Dr. Hutchins had decided we should hike rather than fly a kite. I was relieved. I've never seen the point of kite-flying. My opinion—it's right up there with golf. No meaning to either one. Shoot me down in flames if you will.

To my delight, the walk he'd chosen led us to the Golden Gate Bridge, which I'd hiked over long ago with my parents—an event I remembered with pleasure. I also remembered being disappointed by the rust orange color of the bridge, but my dad had explained solemnly, the way he always explained things, that the "Golden Gate" pertained to the gap in the coast ranges that formed the mile-wide entrance to the Bay, and not to the bridge.

Dr. Hutchins's legs were short, but he set a lively pace, and talked the whole time about how the bridge was constructed. I'd heard it all before, but it was still invigorating to walk on that span high above the water, the wind blowing my hair into tangles that would take forever to unsnarl, glorious views all around, automobiles and trucks and recreational vehicles thundering by within inches of the pedestrian pathway, joggers passing in both directions.

"So what made you pick on me?" Dr. Hutchins asked when we stopped at what he said was the exact center of the span.

We all leaned on the rail and looked down at the water far below. A couple of guys were riding wave runners down there, a few more dashed about on Jet Skis.

"Seemed a good idea to talk to Thane Stockton's friends," Zack said.

The doctor laughed. His face had enough wrinkles to show he'd spent too much time in the sun. He was as gnomelike as his new grandson, but he had a charming humor to his expression. "You won't have far to go," he said. "I'm it."

Zack looked blank.

"You're Mr. Stockton's only friend?" I asked.

"I'm afraid so, Charlie." He'd put us on a first-name basis right away, but I didn't seem able to call him Adler. My parents taught me to call all authority figures—doctors, teachers, lawyers, ministers, and whoever, by their proper titles—Mr. or Mrs. or Miss, Doctor, Reverend—whatever. I couldn't seem to shuck the habit. Except where Detective Sergeant Taylor Bristow was concerned. It had always seemed more natural to call him Bristow than anything else.

"You've known Mr. Stockton a long time?" I asked.

The doctor shrugged. "Year or so. Way I met him was he called and asked me to come see him because he wasn't feeling well. This was maybe six months after Estrella arrived in this country."

"You make house calls?" Zack marveled.

When Dr. Hutchins laughed, all the lines on his face gathered together. "Not as a matter of course. Too many patients to do that. I'm one of that rare breed, Zack—a general practitioner. If I were to make house calls all the time, I'd be on the road, stuck in traffic, two-thirds of the day."

He shook his head. "Those days are gone, I'm afraid. But Thane is an exception. I grew up on the peninsula. The Stockton name is a well-known one, the Stockton place one of the buildings we take out-of-town visitors to see. From a distance, mind you. 'No trespassing' signs all over the place when old man Stockton was alive. Thatcher Stockton that was. Thane is no more welcoming."

"Odd names, Thane and Thatcher," I commented.

"Old English," the doctor said. "Family came from England a few eons ago."

"Stockton said his father lost a lot of the family fortune," Zack said.

"Dumb investments," Dr. Hutchins said.

"He said his father expected him to take care of the house and grounds. Did he mean that literally?"

"All the way. Thatcher Stockton made a servant of the boy, I understand. Hardly ever let him off the property, except to go to some charity board meeting or another, which Thane hated." He sighed. "I blame Thatcher for the way Thane turned out."

He was standing between us at the rail. Both Zack and I had to stoop a little to talk to him and to hear what he was saying before the wind whipped his words away. We exchanged a glance above his head.

"The way he turned out?" Zack queried.

"Thane Stockton is an agoraphobic," Dr. Hutchins said.

I half expected Zack to say, "Say what?" but he surprised me. He often does. "We had an agoraphobic in an episode of *Prescott's Landin'*," he said, his eyes glinting with pleasure that he was able to show off some knowledge. "It means 'fear of the marketplace,'" he told me kindly. "People who have it are scared to go into public places or open spaces and such. Our episode was about a young single mom," he told Dr. Hutchins. "Started with her havin' panic attacks in the grocery store, then she got scared of drivin' her car, pretty soon she wouldn't leave the house for anythin'— leastways not until old Lazarro talked her into comin' out on a date."

There was a reminiscent gleam in his green eyes. "Beverly Arnott played the part," he continued. "Story lasted just a couple episodes, but she relished the opportunity to visit *Prescott's Landin'*, she said."

Beverly Arnott was an ingenue with a reputation for sexual hijinks that didn't quite equal Zack's, but then she was probably fifteen years younger. Care to speculate on what extracurricular activity these two stars of the television screen engaged in when the cameras were unplugged?

The doctor was nodding. "You've got it, Zack. Thane

can't bear to leave the grounds unless there are exceptional circumstances."

I remembered Mr. Stockton saying with great feeling that he couldn't live if he didn't have his house. All the same . . . "He went to Manila to marry Estrella," I pointed out.

"And suffered agonies for it," Dr. Hutchins said flatly, then backed down a little. "According to what he told me, anyway. You understand this is all hearsay. I only know what Thane has chosen to tell me."

"We're not in a court of law," Sheriff Lazarro aka Zack Hunter said.

"Estrella told me she was a battered wife," I volunteered.

A freighter was coming toward us down the center of the channel.

"I saw the Blue Angels strut their stuff here once," Dr. Hutchins said, watching the ship. "Exciting performance, though they didn't fly under the bridge, which was a mite disappointing." He sighed. "The best part of the show, in my opinion, was done by four biplanes. They did all kinds of stalling, twisting dives, smoke streaming. Now that's the kind of flying I could go for."

"Estrella said her husband beat her up all the time," I said.

"Ha!" he said, then looked at me curiously. "You knew Estrella?"

"Not well." I explained about the self-defense class. "She told the people she worked with at the hair salon that her husband abused her. Gave the same story to a guy she knew at a bank. And I saw her bruises."

He was nodding. "Thane told me that was the story she was giving out to her friends. I only met the woman a few times, and then for only a few minutes, but from all Thane told me she seems to have been a dreadful woman. Cruel, bad-tempered, spiteful. Obviously she married him to take advantage of his wealth and position. There was certainly no love in her, for all the tender letters she wrote him before he went to meet her. She even killed his dog."

I glanced at Zack. I'd told him the previous evening about my visit to the Stocktons' vet, leaving out the part about Brian Andersen's dimples. I'd also called Bristow and passed the story on to him. We'd agreed between us there was no need for anyone else to know the dog was still alive until the truth could be established.

The lines on the doctor's face had gathered in a different formation this time—a mask of disgust. He hadn't liked Estrella one bit.

As if he'd realized I was interpreting his expression, he changed it to one of forbearance. "Fortunately, I have several Filipino friends," he said lightly. "Estrella was an exception. Please don't judge other Filipino people by her behavior."

I wondered if he knew Estrella had been married before and that her husband had died in suspicious circumstances. I couldn't see where his knowing or not knowing would make a difference, and I didn't want to muddy those waters either. I still wasn't sure what I thought about this bombshell that Bristow had dropped on us, though it hadn't been far from my mind since he told us about it. It seemed to me the most

likely ingredient that prior death had added to our
mixture of suspicions was the possibility of a revenge
motive. If someone thought—or knew—that Estrella
had killed Carlos Rosales, and that person had been
related to, or a friend of Carlos, then he, or she, might
have followed Estrella to California in order to kill her.

Which brought us back to that Filipino friend of
Estrella's with whom she'd talked about "the good old
days." Some good old days *they* had been.

Dr. Hutchins was watching my face, I realized.
"Sorry," I said. "I drifted off. Was there something
more you wanted to say?"

He nodded. "What I *can* tell you with assurance—
and believe me, this is *not* hearsay—is that *someone*
was beating up on Thane Stockton. He told me it was
Estrella, and I had no reason to doubt him. In the past
year I've treated him for black eyes, a broken leg,
fractured ribs, and a profound blow to his genitals."

Zack winced.

"Aren't you supposed to report stuff like that to
the police?" I said.

He gave me an upward scoffing look. "You really
think Thane would admit to the police that Estrella was
punching his lights out? Not Thane Stockton. Stockton
pride would not allow him to tell anyone. At first, he
even tried to convince *me* that he was accident-prone.
Joked about it. Quoted Don Marquis—the archy and
mehitabel writer—said he was 'so unlucky he runs into
accidents that started out to happen to someone else.' "

He glanced at Zack, saw that he'd gone blank again,
and explained, "archy was a cockroach who typed stories when no one was around. He couldn't use the shift

key so there were no capitals or punctuation in the stories."

If anything, Zack looked blanker.

"But you *knew* Mr. Stockton was being abused," I said, making it a statement rather than a question.

He nodded. "Finally got him to admit it, after we'd been friends for a few months."

"D'you think he killed her?" Zack asked.

"He says he's innocent," the doctor said.

"What do *you* think?" I asked.

The freighter was close enough in now that I could make out people moving around on her deck. The wave runners and Jet Skis were flanking the huge ship now, providing her with an unofficial but exuberant escort. She was still heading straight down the middle, aimed right at us.

The doctor watched the freighter with great attention. He seemed to be selecting and rejecting words, his mouth twitching slightly but continuously, as though he were trying them out for size.

My brain was on red alert. Anytime an answer needed this much thinking about, it was going to be suspect.

"I cannot think but that it would have required more courage than Thane Stockton possesses to kill Estrella and put her in a sleeping bag and then drive outside the gates of his estate to dispose of the body," Dr. Hutchins said. "Nor can I imagine him lying in wait for her somewhere and following the same sequence of events."

Which was a fancy-schmancy way of saying he wasn't going to commit himself to a direct yes or no.

"What if you ignored the method the killer used?" I asked.

He pondered again for several minutes, then shrugged.

I persisted. "What if Estrella had been found buried somewhere in the grounds? Would you be more inclined to believe her husband could have killed her?"

His eyes squinched tight as he looked at me, then he looked away very abruptly. "Answers to hypothetical questions aren't always dependable," he said.

"You think he's *capable* of murder?" Zack asked. Evidently Sheriff Lazarro and I were entertaining the same impression—Adler Hutchins was going evasive on us.

There was another long silence, broken only by the sound of the traffic behind us and the approaching vessel's engines. "We're all capable of it, Zack," Dr. Hutchins said at last. "Given the right provocation."

An image popped up in my mind of Savanna curving her fingers into claws when Duke talked about her daughter being threatened, followed by the memory of Estrella kneeing our poor self-defense instructor in the groin. I thought about how I felt when I walked into my ex-husband's examining room with an urgent message and found him consulting with his extraordinarily beautiful patient—an international model—from on top of her prone form, the pants to his grey Armani suit draped around his ankles.

Most of us have murderous impulses when unduly provoked. Was it too much to wonder, recalling Thane Stockton's humiliating experiences at the hands of his wife, if he was indeed guilty of murdering her?

"I still can't understand why you didn't report Estrella's behavior to the police," I said.

"Thane told me if I did such a thing, I could no longer be his friend," Dr. Hutchins said.

Zack shook his head. "I feel sorry for the dude, but there's no doubt in my mind he's seriously weird," he said. "I guess you can't refuse to be his doctor, but he said you visit and play chess on that outdoors setup he made."

The doctor nodded.

"Why would you *want* to be his friend?" Zack asked.

"I wonder where they're going?" Dr. Hutchins said.

I was puzzled for a second, then realized he was referring to the freighter, which was now almost directly below us. There were a number of crewmen performing various tasks on deck, some of them looking up. On impulse I waved and they waved back, one so boisterously he knocked his cap off. It was picked up by the wind and blown overboard before he could catch up with it. I wondered if he had a spare with him. Would the poor guy have to do without his cap for however long it would take him to get to where he was going? Or would there be some kind of store on board? I'm forever pondering dumb questions.

The ship disappeared under the bridge, the wave runners and Jet Skis peeling off in formation.

As if the whole purpose of our excursion had been to wave good-bye to the freighter, Dr. Hutchins decided it was time to leave. We started hiking back, looking west once in a while to see how far the freighter had gone. When we reached the end of the bridge, the doctor said, "I have a definite hankering for a Polish dog. And I know a hot-dog stand on Ocean Beach that serves the very best. Would you care to join me?"

Zack agreed so eagerly I figured he probably hadn't bothered with breakfast. I didn't have the heart to start lecturing about fat content and the possibilities of bacteria inherent in eating from a hot-dog stand. Nobody ever listens to me anyway.

We hiked back to Zack's pickup and took off. We were almost at the beach before Dr. Hutchins finally answered Zack's question as to why he was Thane Stockton's friend. "Being a friend doesn't always have to be easy," he said.

That was a nice sentiment. Would it include refusing to face up to the possibility that said friend had brutally murdered his wife?

Loneliness had encouraged Thane Stockton to rise above his agoraphobia long enough to travel to the Philippines and go through whatever was necessary to get married there. Despair would hardly be a weaker motive. Would it have been strong enough to take him, in the early hours of that morning, beyond the grounds of his mansion to the bridge above Flood Creek?

Remembering that sudden expression of disgust on Adler Hutchins's face when he talked about Estrella, I even entertained the possibility that the doctor had bumped her off. Some people were big on doing favors for a friend.

CHAPTER 14

Sunday nights, CHAPS was less crowded than usual, probably because Zack wasn't there to be swooned over or stared at—Sunday being his poker night.

This particular Sunday had been an even prettier, much warmer day than Saturday, so I wasn't surprised when CHAPS was even slower than expected. Probably a lot of our patrons had headed for the great outdoors. I'd spent an hour or so jogging around the streets of Bellamy Park myself, until I started sneezing my head off. Some kind of pollen, I supposed, or else an unusual number of cats had been rubbing up against the trees. I'm superallergic to cat dander. That was one of the reasons I'd acquired a pet rabbit.

When Savanna and I had finished leading our boys and girls through the Cherokee Kick and the Tush Push, we picked up a bottle of mineral water apiece and headed over to one of the booths at the side of the main corral. About the time we were beginning to cool off, a cowboy wanna-be swaggered over.

"Yo, Charlie, Savanna," he said.

I hadn't recognized Duke Conway out of his kung-fu jammies. Savanna gave him her killer smile, which made him blink. Showed how strong *he* was—most men hyperventilated. "We on for tomorrow, Charlie?" he asked, without taking his gaze off Savanna's face— a face that is certainly worth gazing at.

I'd forgotten the self-defense class again. "I'm not going to be here," I said. "Maybe we should call it off for a week."

"I can come over early and take care of everything," Savanna offered. "Jacqueline's preschool class has a date with the zoo. Baby-sitter's going with her. I'd be coming to the class anyway."

"Jacqueline?" Duke asked. Evidently he'd forgotten the scenario he'd constructed for Savanna to get her to yell.

"My three-year-old," Savanna said.

"Oh yeah." I could see his interest wane immediately. Our instructor was apparently not a family man.

He was about to turn away. "Take a seat," I said. "I'd like to talk to you about something."

His eyebrows showed a revival of interest. In me, this time. He had a high opinion of his own allure, our instructor.

Savanna excused herself, giving me a quizzical glance out of the corner of her eye. "Don't even think it," I muttered as she slid out of the booth.

"What can I get you?" she asked Duke with a grin.

He ordered a Bud draft, and she went over to the bar. I noticed Angel looking our way. Looking daggers our way, I should say. It was pretty obvious who the daggers were for. Evidently *he* had recognized Duke Conway in spite of his sexy getup. I supposed Gina was holding down the fort in Buttons & Bows—she'd been around earlier for the lessons.

"Are we having a date, Charlie?" Duke asked with a lot of blue-eyed twinkle.

"All I offered was a seat," I said. "I don't date."

"Not at all?"

About to say never, I realized a male-chauvinist type like Duke might take that as a challenge. "Not this week," I amended, then added, hoping it would turn him off, "I'm sorry I can't host the class tomorrow. I'm having some medical work done on my inner parts."

Savanna brought his beer and another water for me and took his money for both, winking my way.

Duke's interest had waned again. That might even have been a grimace I saw on his face before he hefted his beer. His interest in female inner parts possibly had a different focus.

"How well did you know Estrella Stockton?" I threw out, watching to see if he choked on his beer. He didn't. He lowered the bottle, set it down, and gave me a cool raised eyebrow.

"What's it to you, Charlie?" he asked.

"I've been asked to look into her murder."

"Who by?"

"A relative."

Both eyebrows came up, but he didn't question me further. "I met her once before the class," he said. "After you asked me to teach the group, I put a poster in the beauty parlor where she worked. Hair Raising. It's in the Fairview strip mall, not far from the golf course."

"I know where it is." So okay, his story matched Estrella's.

"I put a poster in all the businesses around these parts," he added.

"What did you think of Estrella?" I asked.

He shrugged. I wondered if his jacket had extra padding in it. He hadn't looked that broad-shouldered in his black pajamas. "A tad too aggressive," he said. "I'm not sure she needed self-defense classes."

"She seemed eager to learn all the maneuvers she could."

He nodded.

"So you didn't see her outside the classes?" I asked.

He shook his head, and I scolded myself for poor technique. Surely it would work better to make a positive statement, or an accusing one. I imagined Chris Noth who used to be on *Law and Order*. *Where did you meet her apart from CHAPS?* That's what I should have said.

I couldn't believe I was thinking of using TV police techniques. I'd be imitating Sheriff Lazarro next.

I waited until Duke lifted his beer bottle again, then I said, "Estrella told her husband she was having an affair with you."

This time he did choke. He also spluttered. "Cheesh, Charlie," he exclaimed when the fit was finally over. "What possessed you to come up with a statement like that?"

"Is it true?" I asked.

A frown appeared between his smooth dark eyebrows. "You're serious."

I nodded.

"Why would Estrella tell her husband that?" he asked. "Are you making this up?"

I shook my head.

"Who told it to you? Her husband?"

I nodded again. The cool and cunning investigator, letting the subject take control of the conversation with the hope that he'll blurt out something useful.

"Well, that explains it," he said. "The guy imagined she was having an affair with every man in town."

Cool and cunning had worked.

I pounced. "How do you know that?"

He took another swallow of beer. To give himself time to think?

"Hi," Gina Giacomini said, appearing alongside our table.

Not good timing.

Duke apparently disagreed. Sliding over, smiling broadly, he patted the booth seat, and Gina slid in next to him. I had to force myself not to look at Angel. I imagined his hot gaze shooting like a laser beam across the room, illuminating all the dust motes, incinerating Duke.

"Hello, Charlie," Gina said brightly, looking at me. She must have had a recent haircut—her hair looked even spikier than ever. Still magenta-and-blond stripes. She'd varied her makeup though—her lipstick and nail polish were dark red. So was her eyeliner.

"Hello yourself," I said in my best schoolmarm voice.

Duke alternated a couple of lustful glances at her— I hate when people do that in public—with a brief, but fairly hopeful peek at me. I could almost hear him thinking: *okay Charlie, you can leave now, you don't want to date, you want to ask dumb questions, that was okay for a while, but show some tact can't you?*

"Well, I guess you two would like to be alone, huh?" I said.

Gina looked uncomfortable, as well she should. Duke nodded. "Nothing personal, Charlie."

"Good. I'll vamoose as soon as you finish your answer."

He laughed. "I don't remember the question."

"You said Estrella's husband imagined she was having an affair with every man in town." Sometimes I have instant recall.

"You *knew* Estrella?" Gina gasped, staring with wide carmine-banded eyes at Duke.

He lifted his gaze to the ceiling and sighed audibly. "No more than you did, honey. That's what I'm trying to tell Charlie."

Honey?

"One time," he said, shifting a little on the seat. "After the first class. Just before Christmas. I stopped for a smoke outside CHAPS. Several of the people in the class do that. It's become a social occasion—chatting, smoking."

"I didn't know you smoked," Gina said.

"Once in a while," he said. He gave her a dippy look. "Never around anyone who doesn't like it, though."

"So?" I said.

"Estrella asked for a light. We talked."

Now that he'd said that I remembered seeing them standing at the foot of CHAPS' steps as I locked the front door behind the last person to leave.

"And out of the blue she confided that her husband was insanely jealous?"

He took another swallow of beer. "She hit on me," he said. "Told me she was ... interested. Then she commented that her husband was the jealous type, so we'd have to be discreet. Kinda took my breath away."

"And you said?" I prompted.

"That I didn't date married women. I'm no home breaker."

Gina believed him. Her bloodred lips were smiling at him very sweetly. Far as I was concerned, the slightly self-righteous tone in Duke's voice didn't quite ring true.

I wondered if he was the one who had made the first move and Estrella who had turned him down. He'd been ready to make a move on Savanna, and maybe even on me just a few minutes ago. And now he was all over Gina. I realized suddenly I couldn't see his left hand or her right.

"Estrella got kinda mad at me for turning her down," he said. "I think that's probably why she ..." He broke off, and Gina and I exchanged a wincing glance. I imagined she was remembering, as I was, Estrella's knee coming up into Duke's groin.

I saw that Sundancer was in his booth, putting his headset on over his wispy hair, peering my way through his Coke-bottle glasses. I slid out of the booth. In a way, I hated to leave Gina with Duke, but it wasn't any of my business what two consenting adults did with their time. Obviously, something had gone wrong between Gina and Angel, and there probably wasn't much I could do about it.

Which didn't mean I wasn't going to try.

I wandered over to the deejay booth and talked to Sundancer for a few minutes. Sometimes on Sundays we ran an extra lesson or two, but we decided there wasn't a big enough group to worry about, and we'd just go with general dancing unless we had some special requests.

After which I strolled over to the bar in the main corral and hitched myself up onto a stool. "Hi, Angel," I said.

He nodded. Beneath his Pancho Villa mustache, his mouth looked glum. Usually whenever Angel was behind the bar he was busy washing glasses, wiping down the counter, hooking up a new keg, dusting bottles—bar stuff. But right now he was just standing there idly drying off a knife, staring fixedly over at Duke and Gina, who were talking animatedly.

Oh, it wasn't a switchblade or anything like that—just the small knife he used to slice lemons to go in the mineral water. It had a serrated edge, which hardly qualified it as a deadly weapon. Though it did have a wicked-looking point to it.

"Was that prearranged?" he asked.

"What?" I asked, though I knew perfectly well he was talking about the meeting between Gina and Duke.

He looked at me.

"Not as far as I could tell," I said hastily. "I wanted to ask Duke some questions, and while we were talking, Gina came over and joined us."

"Questions about what?"

"Estrella Stockton."

I'd surprised him.

"He knew her?"

"Not outside our self-defense class, except they smoked a cigarette together once, outside CHAPS."

He frowned, probably wondering why that would be a basis for questioning. I wasn't about to tell him Estrella had told her husband she was having an affair with Duke. Not while Gina was sitting in the same room and Duke was making eyes at *her*.

Gina did seem extra vivacious tonight.

"You and Gina not hitting it off?" I asked.

Angel shrugged.

I studied him for a minute or two. He's the strong, silent type, our Angel. Very strong, very rugged-looking. Super clean. His white cowboy shirts always look as if they'd just come off the store shelves. Under his white-straw cowboy hat, his black hair, hauled back and tied in a ponytail at the nape of his neck, always looks freshly shampooed. His drooping mustache is always neatly trimmed and groomed, the rest of him clean-shaven.

As I've already mentioned, Angel appears to be a very gentle man, but I was often aware of hidden undercurrents when I was around him. The undercurrent was more of a riptide right now, according to the vibes that were coming at me over the bar while Angel stared narrow-eyed across the main corral.

"What color's Duke's aura?" I asked, hoping to lighten him up a bit.

"Black," he said without hesitation, then muttered, "It's not Gina's fault, Charlie. It's me."

How come? I wanted to ask, but I was conscious of

a barrier between us. Maybe he didn't want to talk about it. I was his friend. I should respect his wishes.

"How come?" I asked.

One of our more recently hired waitresses came over with an order that took a few minutes to collate. She was humming along to the Doug Stone song Sundancer was playing for our patrons to slow-dance to. "These lips don't know how to say good-bye."

It seemed fitting.

"How come?" I said again, the minute the waitress left.

Angel shook his head.

I sighed. "I hope you can work it out," I said.

He shrugged as if he didn't care, but there was misery in his dark eyes.

Another waitress came over and stayed to chat, then one of our faux cowboys asked me to show him how to do the Texas ten-step. I wasn't feeling that exuberant, but when you work at a place like CHAPS and you are a part-owner you learn to smile all the time, even when it hurts your face.

By the time I returned to the bar for something to replace my electrolytes, Angel had evidently decided to ignore whatever situation was developing on the other side of the main corral.

"What's this about you going into the hospital tomorrow?" he asked, as I poured Gatorade into a glass.

Savanna had certainly been spreading the word. "Not the hospital, Angel. The Women's Clinic over on Cavenaugh Street." I shrugged in what I hoped was a lighthearted manner. "It's just a biopsy."

"For what?"

"Just a precaution."

"For what?"

I sighed. "To rule out cervical cancer. I expect it's just a false alarm. Dr. Hanssen's the cautious type."

His big hand covered mine on the bar. Which brought a lump to my throat. Angel is not normally a touchy-feely person like Zack.

"I'll be fine, Angel," I said.

"Sure," he agreed.

The dancers were returning to their tables. Angel glanced one more time across the main corral, then drew himself a beer and took a long swallow. I bit my tongue to stop myself from commenting. We had an agreement, the four of us. No drinking on the job. After the doors were closed, sure. Private occasions, okay. Otherwise—no way.

He caught me looking at him. "*Salud*, Charlie," he said, taking another swig.

Your health.

"I'll drink to that," I said.

CHAPTER 15

Zack gave me a proper movie-star sendoff with a kiss that heated up every red corpuscle in my body. I was almost tempted to raise one leg behind me from the knee, the way female movie stars used to do in like circumstances.

"I'll be right here waitin' for you, darlin'," he said. Releasing me, he looked sternly at Matilda, Dr. Hanssen's office manager, who was holding the door to the clinic's inner regions open. "You take good care of her, hear?" he said.

I felt like a soldier going off to war as I marched bravely through the doorway. I took with me the impression that Zack didn't really expect me to survive, but would mourn appropriately.

It was something of an anticlimax that I had to wait in the hall several minutes until Matilda recovered from the trance she'd swooned into. As she showed me into the treatment room and turned me over to one of the nurses, her face was bright pink and damp-looking. Possibly she was having a hot flash. I often had one myself around Zack, though menopause wasn't due to claim me for quite a few years.

"You're so lucky," she murmured.

"Zack and I are just good friends," I assured her.

"Uh-huh."

There are many women of my acquaintance who totally understand why my self-esteem won't allow me to get involved sexually with Zack Hunter. These are the intelligent women who know all about the argument that goes on between women's bodies and brains in the presence of a gorgeous hunk who has "Don't fence me in" written all over him. They agree, even though they may be smitten by our man-in-black themselves, that no sane woman would choose to be just one of the many on the conveyor belt of love that doubles as Zack's king-size bed.

(How do I know it's a king-size bed? I've passed through his bedroom on the way to his swimming pool. What did you think?)

Most men do not understand this dichotomy that women go through—this intelligence versus hormone conflict. That's because most men obey the dictates of their hormones without consulting their brains.

There are also women who think I'm out of my mind for not basking in the sunlight of Zack's charms while I have the chance. Matilda was evidently one of these.

"Zack?" the nurse queried.

"Zack Hunter is in our waiting room," Matilda said in tones of reverence.

The nurse followed her out, zombie fashion. And took ten minutes to return.

The biopsy was a bit of an anticlimax. Don't worry, I'm not going to give you a blow-by-blow description. I'll just mention that it wasn't as bad as it had sounded.

Usually, when a doctor or dentist tells me, "You may feel a little discomfort here," I brace myself for agony.

I complained about this to a dentist's assistant once, and she told me it would hardly be beneficial to the patient's psyche to say, "The pain is going to send you right through the ceiling." I conceded she had a point.

But in Dr. Hanssen's case, he had not spoken with forked tongue. Mostly the procedure was boring, though uncomfortable. Lying flat on my back on a paper-covered examination table, knees jackknifed, feet in stirrups, wearing a thin cotton gown that's open all the way down the back and pushed up in front, is not one of my preferred situations. Fortunately, Dr. Hanssen is not a motor mouth, and my mind, though slightly befuddled by the tranquilizer the nurse had pressed on me, was free to roam as I gazed at the ceiling.

Naturally, it chose to roam among the various tidbits of knowledge I'd come up with while inquiring— *snooping*, Bristow would call it—into Estrella Stockton's murder. Most significant of these was the bit of information provided by Detective Sergeant Bristow himself.

I rolled it around in my mind while Dr. Hanssen explained what he was going to do next. The explanation had something to do with cutting and a wire and electricity and cauterizing tissue. I had no interest in any of it. There are some things a patient is better off not knowing.

It was much easier to think about Estrella's first husband. Carlos Rosales. Somehow he had fallen through a window while on the tenth floor of a hotel.

Was it really possible for someone to fall *through* a window? Accidentally?

Maybe he'd been drinking. Maybe he'd been pushed. A detective had been involved. Which would seem to suggest there had been some suspicion of evildoing. The detective couldn't come up with enough evidence, Bristow had said. *Enough* evidence.

The trank was making me drowsy. I had a feeling there was something about the death of Carlos Rosales that could be significant, but I couldn't seem to get my mind to concentrate—it kept wanting to flutter aimlessly.

"All done," Dr. Hanssen said, startling me. I must have dozed off.

The nurse provided me with pads and told me I could get dressed. "So what's the result?" I asked, yawning. I hoped I'd start feeling a little more wakeful soon.

"We'll let you know in a week or so," she said. "Would you like me to tell Mr. Hunter you're ready to go?"

"Sure," I said, and she raced out of the room.

A week or so. I had to worry about cancer for another week?

Served me right, I supposed. I'd put the biopsy off over and over. I could have known the truth about my condition months ago. Probably I could have been cured then. By now, cancer was probably spreading throughout my body.

Do other women get these morbid thoughts every time they go through something like this? I wondered.

I dozed all the way back to CHAPS. I could imagine

the nurse's and Matilda's reactions if they knew that. Wasting my time dozing and yawning while I was alone with one of our country's major sex symbols was probably un-American.

I began to snap out of the trank-induced stupor as Zack escorted me up the stairs to my loft.

I heard voices. "Ssh," I said to Zack. "Someone's in there."

"I know," he said. "They all said they wanted to be here, so I called from the clinic to let them know we were on our way."

All?

Savanna had brought me daffodils and had made chicken soup. Savanna's chicken soup is the stuff gastronomic heaven is made of. As soon as I smelled it I was hungry.

Detective Sergeant Bristow was at ease on my falling-down sofa, holding Benny. Angel was standing around near a wall looking awkward, but concerned. He'd brought me Armenian cracker bread from Lenny's Market—gorgonzola cheese to crumble on it—my favorite things to have with soup.

There were hugs all around. Somewhat constrained from Angel, but a hug nonetheless.

I felt my eyes tearing up. The three times in my life I'd taken a tranquilizer it had depressed my spirits, but that wasn't the sole reason for the tears. It was the realization that somehow in the past twenty-one months our little gang of loners had become a family.

After I'd petted Benny in all his favorite places, I handed him back to Bristow. I couldn't put him down on the floor. Little rabbits tend to get nervous around too many feet.

Savanna, aka Earth Mother, got me tucked into my rocker and served everyone a bowl of soup—mine on a bed tray she'd brought with her. The most thoughtful caring person in the universe, my friend Savanna.

"You didn't bring Gina?" I asked Angel, unable to resist.

He shook his head and didn't offer any excuses, stoic as ever.

"You want to call her? Invite her to come over and have soup with us?" Savanna asked.

"Nope," he said.

"She was at the self-defense class this morning," Savanna said.

Angel shrugged, his lips tightening. Savanna and I exchanged glances, then gave up for the time being. "How did the class go?" I asked.

Savanna smiled. "Great. We learned how to attack all the vital strike points. How to think of an attacker as a collection of targets. Stuff like that."

Bristow cast his gaze upward to the ceiling. "We do pray for mercy," he declaimed in his lovely vibrant voice.

"I've been thinking," I said.

"The brain that never rests," Bristow said, switching to genial mode. He seemed to be feeling jocular today.

I made a face at him—the soup was waking me up—and continued my thought. "I was thinking about Estrella's first husband falling out of a hotel window."

"I remember a scenario like that on *Prescott's Landin'*," Zack said.

I was going to interrupt him, but then I remembered how kind he'd been, driving me to the clinic, kissing me good-bye, hanging around until Dr. Hanssen was through with me. I put an interested expression on my face and spooned soup into my starving mouth.

"Bessy Mae Starlin'," Zack said. "The postmaster. She hired her second cousin Wilbur to bump off the dude who'd raped her granddaughter. Wilbur got the dude drunk then hauled him up to the landin' of some old house and tossed him through a tall window. Defenestration, they call it."

"They do indeed," Bristow murmured.

"They didn't use real glass of course," Zack added. "Anyhow, nobody knew Bessy Mae even had a second cousin. She'd made damn sure she had an alibi, singin' with the church choir. She almost got away with it."

"Almost?" I queried.

"Wilbur felt bad, afterward. He confessed, and he and Bessy Mae went to prison for life."

Bristow snorted. "TV always makes that seem so easy. Get a confession, it's all over. Rarely works that way. Somebody confesses in real life, any defense lawyer worth beans is going to say the confession was coerced by the police. And the jury's going to halfway believe him. Halfway is enough to make for a shadow of a doubt, so the guy usually gets off."

"It's not a bad theory, all the same," I said reluctantly. "The part about someone hiring someone to push the guy through the window."

Why reluctantly? You must understand that admitting that Zack's reliance on *Prescott's Landing*'s plot lines in order to solve a mystery was a workable method, was not easy for me.

But it made Zack happy. He smiled smugly, then leaned back and combed through his black hair with his fingers. The hair, of course, fell immediately into its proper, carefully casual disorder. Heck, if I paid a hundred dollars for a haircut even my hair would ... nah.

"Isn't it possible Estrella hired someone to kill her first husband?" I suggested to Bristow.

"The detective I talked to already looked into that, Charlie," Bristow said. "Again, no evidence."

"But let's suppose there *was* someone. Some guy Estrella knew. A lover even. Felicia said Estrella was at Paulie's Place with some dark-haired guy. Estrella seemed excited. Estrella told Candy the man was an old friend from the Philippines. She said it was fun talking about the old days. She told Maisie the guy was her lover. And that she was a little afraid of him."

Bristow nodded. He'd heard all this when he visited Hair Raising.

"If Estrella *was* having an affair with this Filipino guy," I said, thinking it through while my mouth was in motion, "maybe she got *him* to push her first husband out of the window. Maybe later he heard she'd married a rich American and he tracked her down then came here to blackmail her and that's who she drew the money out of the bank for and that's who killed her."

"Or maybe the first husband's death was an accident," Bristow said. "Did I ever tell you he went through an *open* window?"

"Oh." Well, that did change the picture a little bit, I supposed. It made the possibility of an accident a little more likely.

I pondered for a while, noticing that Bristow had become distracted watching Savanna as she bustled around my loft, collecting dishes, running water over them, stacking them in my dishwasher.

Of course I have a dishwasher. Just because I don't believe in owning a surplus of "things," that doesn't mean I don't appreciate modern conveniences. The dishwasher is the greatest invention since the washing machine and dryer.

I didn't want Bristow distracted while I was laying out a possible plot for him, but at the same time it seemed to me there was even more than the usual dorkiness in the glances the two of them were exchanging.

"It seems a bit of a coincidence that Estrella's first husband should fall to his death in the Philippines and then later Estrella should be tossed off a bridge in a sleeping bag," I mused aloud.

Bristow's eyes narrowed, and he passed Benny over to Zack. That would please Ben. He liked Bristow okay—but he *adored* Zack. Almost immediately he hunkered down and started vibrating.

"Go on," Bristow said.

"Well, there is a similarity isn't there? Although Estrella was dead before she was thrown off that bridge. All the same ..." I broke off. Suddenly my scenario seemed unsubstantial.

I started off on a new track. "If Estrella could persuade the guy to kill her first husband, he must have been highly motivated on her behalf. And he got away with it, so why would he kill *her?* What I really wonder is if there *was* a guy doing the pushing, if there's any way he could be Domingo. I just know that man lied to me a couple of times. And he is a Filipino. Maybe he did come here thirteen years ago, and maybe Big John whoever can vouch for that, but can he also be sure Domingo didn't take a vacation trip to Manila and while there help out his good old friend Estrella, whom he'd known since he was in kindergarten?"

"Hey," Zack said.

We all looked at him.

"I saw that Domingo dude yesterday when I was in Lenny's buyin' a few groceries."

I hadn't known he ever bought any food outside a restaurant but I wasn't about to interrupt him when he was leaning forward, his green eyes glinting with something that could be excitement.

"I wouldn't have recognized Domingo if he hadn't asked could he get an autograph for his friend—kid a few years younger. Soon as he spoke I knew who he was. He sure looked different out of uniform though— baggy pants hangin' off his butt, crotch down to his knees, hat on backwards, sloppy sweatshirt hangin' off one shoulder."

A little red flag poked up in my brain and waved at me. What? I asked it crossly. What was so significant about the way Domingo was dressed?

Bristow was saying something to Zack, questioning him about the "friend." I couldn't concentrate. Then I had it. "Whoa!" I exclaimed, almost making Benny jump out of Zack's hands. "What about what Rory said? Roderick Effington III, the homeless guy—didn't he say the guy who got in the car with Estrella was wearing baggy jeans and a sweater?"

Zack nodded, his eyes glinting some more. "He said it was dark in the parkin' lot and he was peerin' out of the Dumpster. He said the dude had short hair."

"Felicia said the man with Estrella in Paulie's Place had short dark hair. Not very well cut. Domingo has short dark hair, but it's styled and has inscriptions cut in it."

Zack pondered. "Maybe Estrella cut them in for him, after that night."

We were on a roll.

"What guy who got in what car?" Bristow interrupted with danger in his voice.

Uh-oh.

"Didn't we tell you about that?" I asked with as much sweetness as I could cram into my voice.

Zack got up and took Benny to his cage in the bathroom, then came back and sat down.

"Slipped your memory, no doubt," Bristow said, glowering at both of us.

I leaned forward to show how earnest I was in my regret, and felt a twinge of pain.

Apparently, Bristow caught my grimace. He took a breath and let it out slowly to show he was perfectly calm, not about to go off any deep ends.

I told him about Rory Dumpster-diving behind Hair Raising, hearing Estrella greet the man as though his sudden appearance had shocked her, seeing her face when the man lit her cigarette. "They got in a car and drove away," I added. "Felicia told me Estrella had borrowed her old Ford about that time, and Rory said the car they drove away in had an old engine, so I guess . . ."

"*When* did this take place," Bristow asked with infinite patience.

I shrugged. "Rory said two to three months ago. Felicia said three months. I would think Felicia's calendar is a little more reliable than Rory's."

"Yeah, well, your friend Rory also has short dark hair, which looks as if it was cut with a Weed Eater, and his clothing could be described as baggy. Maybe *he* was the one got in the car with Estrella, and he's just acting out. Or trying to confuse the picture. Maybe he and Estrella were getting it on and then she ended it and he killed her and gave me that whole story about the sleeping bag coming down off the bridge."

I don't think he believed Rory was a killer any more than I did. "What's Rory's motive?" I countered.

"Estrella had drawn a considerable amount of money out of the bank the previous day."

"You think Rory's a thief, or a blackmailer?"

"I think Rory is a homeless person. When you are homeless you tend to think of your own survival first." He gave me a tired smile. "Here's another possibility for you, Charlie. I would say you are right about your friend Domingo being gay—if he's not he's missing a good opportunity—so it's not likely he was involved with Estrella. But she might have hired him in the Philippines as you say. And if she saw him socially here and Stockton found out about him and thought his wife was boffing him, then maybe *that's* why he killed Estrella."

"You're always trying to bring this around so it comes back to Thane Stockton," I complained.

"I like things to be tidy," he admitted.

I gave him a jaundiced look. "Do you remember the last time I got involved in one of your cases?"

"Engraved on my memory," he said.

"Well then, you'll remember telling me in regard to Detective Sergeant Reggie Timpkin that sometimes a law-enforcement officer gets obsessed, decides a certain person is guilty, hates to let go of that belief, neglects to look for anyone else."

"Point well taken," he conceded.

"Did Mr. Stockton have Estrella insured?"

"Apparently not."

"How about this then," I said. "How about if Estrella was setting Thane Stockton up to be murdered, and it backfired? It might be worth checking to see if *he* was insured. You said she collected insurance from the first husband's death."

He smiled broadly. "If that theory is correct, Ms. Plato, then maybe our friend Thane found out about Estrella's plan and killed her before she could kill him."

We both laughed. "I think we're getting punchy," I said.

"I think it's time you gave this up," Savanna said to Bristow. Such a fond note in her voice. Things must be going real well there. "Charlie's had a busy morning," she went on. "She should rest up."

"I'm fine," I protested. "Brain-dead, but otherwise perking right along."

Bristow shook his head. "That's all very well,

Savanna, but I wanted to tell her and Zack and Angel ..."

"We can tell them tomorrow," Savanna said, but she looked disappointed.

"Now," I said firmly, sitting up straight, already suspecting from the looks on both their faces what news they wanted to impart.

Bristow smiled his full-dress Michael Jordan smile. "Ms. Savanna Seabrook has done me the honor of agreeing to become my wife," he announced.

We all cheered. Then hugged all around again. Well, the guys didn't hug each other. They are great guys, but they aren't *that* liberated.

"I'm a good matchmaker, I am," I crowed.

"You think I could not have won my fair lady without your help?" Bristow asked.

"I did tell each one of you that the other one liked you," I pointed out.

"We would not have noticed for ourselves?"

"All right, you two," Savanna interrupted. God, she looked wonderful. A radiant Savanna was almost more than anyone could bear to look at. Bristow had a glow of his own.

"For what is wedlock forced, but a hell, an age of discord and continual strife?" Bristow quoted, causing us all to look at him questioningly, until he finished ... "Whereas the contrary bringeth bliss, and is a pattern of celestial peace."

"We'll have the wedding at CHAPS," I said. "I'll make all the arrangements."

"We'll all make the arrangements," Angel corrected.

We all loved Savanna and respected Bristow. This was a good match.

"Maybe a wedding here will take the bad karma off this place," Angel continued.

There he went again, going mystical on us. We all looked at him, and his cheekbones reddened slightly. "I mean it will be a good thing to have a wedding to think about instead of a murder."

That cast a pall over the proceedings.

Angel apologized. "This is a happy occasion. I shouldn't have said anything."

I patted his arm. "It's okay, Angel—I suppose you could call it karma—finding bodies in the neighborhood, or the body of someone who's been in the neighborhood. But you don't really think CHAPS is responsible, do you?"

"No, of course not," he said quickly. Too quickly. "We should have some champagne," he said, looking at Zack. "Do we have any in the wine captain?"

Zack nodded. "We do. At its proper temperature. Not Dom Pérignon, but a couple of good labels." Once in a while, Zack sounds less like Sheriff Lazarro and more like Zack Hunter from Beverly Hills.

"Isn't it a little early in the day for champagne?" Savanna asked.

"One glass," Angel said. "How often do we have an occasion like this? None of us has to work tonight. It's Monday. Except maybe the happy groom here."

Bristow shook his head. "I'm on R and R until tomorrow. Charlie's friend Sergeant Timpkin is on the job for me today."

We all groaned, then they started heading for the door. I sat down in my rocker fairly abruptly.

Savanna squatted in front of me at once. "Oh, Charlie, how selfish of us. We forgot you were hurting."

"God help me if I have to have an operation," I said. "You'll all have me laid out in my casket before I draw my last breath. It was only a biopsy, Savanna. It's just the suspense that's nerve-racking. I'm feeling perfectly okay, just fading fast."

Actually, I *was* hurting a little bit, but why spoil everybody's fun by admitting that. "You all go ahead," I said. "I'll celebrate with you later. Right now, I'm in the mood for a nap."

She leaned down for a hug. "I'm delighted about your news," I told her.

She gave me her killer smile. "Hey, me too, girlfriend. So is Jacqueline. She's already calling him Daddy Taylor." She straightened. "I've an idea being a cop's wife may not be too stress-free, though."

"The downtime is magnificent, however," Bristow said, beaming at her.

"Listen," I said, rallying. "Are you going to check up on Domingo with your Manila connection?"

"To see if he took a vacation in his hometown and just happened to hire himself out as a killer while he was there?"

"It's possible," I said. "You've got to admit it's possible."

"There are more things in heaven and earth, Horatio, than are dreamt of in your philosophy," he intoned.

One of these days that man was going to learn to take my hunches seriously.

"Charlie?" Zack asked, looking back from the doorway, the last to leave. His green eyes were dark with concern. "You want me to stay? Keep you company?"

There are times when I could cheerfully take after that man with a baseball bat, other times I'm consumed by affection for him. This was one of the latter.

I shook my head. "I'm fine, Zack. Truly."

The door closed. I heard their footsteps on the stairs. Then silence. I leaned back in the rocker and closed my eyes and let go.

CHAPTER 16

After I made sure Bristow was working on Wednesday afternoon, I suggested we hold our usual partners meeting at Paulie's Place. "I have a right to celebrate this engagement, too," I declared.

It had occurred to me after I got all rested up that maybe someone who worked at Paulie's might be able to offer a better description of the guy who had accompanied Estrella there. I didn't know if Bristow had made inquiries at Paulie's, but I thought maybe the bartender might talk to me more readily than to the police.

I was wrong.

Once the business part of our get-together was done with, I left the others at the table, Savanna drinking wine, Zack drinking beer—Angel was our designated driver—and went over to the bar on the pretext of finding out if they had any healthier snack foods than beer nuts and potato chips. What I really intended to do was grill the bartender.

"I don't remember," was all the bartender would say after I told him the approximate month and gave him a description of Estrella. He wouldn't even say if he'd already talked to the police.

The name tag on his shirt said Warren. "Would Paulie remember?" I asked.

He looked blank.

"Paulie," I repeated, thinking maybe he was a little slow on the uptake. "This *is* Paulie's Place, isn't it?"

"There isn't any Paulie," he said, his tone of voice telling me I was pretty dumb not to know that.

"Well, the owner then."

"Owner never comes near the place."

"Another bartender?" Warren appeared to be the only one on the job, though the place was fairly busy. There were a couple of lone men at separate tables, a few scattered couples, one woman reading a paperback novel with one of those tiny, battery-operated booklights clipped to it. (I hate when someone reads in public and I can't see the cover. I always want to know the author and the title in case it's a mystery by someone I haven't read yet.)

The rest of the tables had been put together to make one large table for the benefit of a bunch of local office workers who had been celebrating someone's birthday ever since lunch, or maybe instead of lunch. They had hardly stopped laughing uproariously since we got there, though I hadn't overheard anything that sounded the least bit funny. I guess you had to have been there.

"Listen, lady," Warren said, leaning forward in a mildly threatening manner. "Nobody in here remembers nothin'. Nobody in here *never* remembers nothin'. That's the best kind of bartender to be."

You might have gathered that Paulie's Place was not in the best part of Bellamy Park. Even an upscale town has its pockets of imperfection.

"You're in the way, lady," Warren added while I was pondering a way to open him up. Looking at his scowling face, I decided he was a lost cause and turned around, almost bumping into the sole waitress. She was as tall as me, but with curves where I had bones. Naturally, life being unfair, along with her curves she'd been endowed with wonderful hair—the fat, tawny, shaggy kind that women who get illicitly involved with politicians always seem to have. The kind of hair I would have been born with if life was fair.

The waitress was wearing a lot of sooty eye shadow, a black turtleneck sweater with two cone-shaped bulges in it, and the skimpiest, tightest, white-leather skirt I'd ever seen. She was holding a tray filled with used glasses, and I realized I'd been standing at her station.

She shrugged unsmilingly when I apologized. Probably her feet hurt. With the stiletto heels on those shoes they had to hurt. There's a name for those kind of heels.

"The staff here's not much on *joie de vivre*," I said as I joined the others. "Maybe we should have done our celebrating in our own bar."

Savanna laughed. "Who do you think you're kidding, Charlie? We know what we're doing here."

"Snoopin'," Zack added, in case either Angel or I hadn't got the point. I gave him an imitation of the bartender's scowl and he laid one of his thin-lipped bad-boy smiles on me.

"Oh my God, it's Zack Hunter!" the waitress exclaimed, materializing beside me, her gaze fixed on our man-in-black. Evidently she hadn't had a good look under Zack's cowboy hat before now. She was made of stern stuff though. She didn't swoon. "We haven't seen you in here for a long time, Zack," she said.

Ah, that explained the lack of hysterics—she had met the sex symbol in the flesh on a previous occasion.

How much flesh? my inquiring mind immediately wondered.

"Been doin' a little shootin', Mandy," Zack explained modestly in his best Lazarro drawl. "*Prescott's Landin*'s bein' revived. Sheriff Lazarro along with it."

It was an actor's duty to do a little self-promotion whenever the opportunity presented itself, he'd told me once. Nowadays you couldn't just make a good movie and rest on your residuals—you had to get out there and hustle. Do the talk shows and the print interviews, have someone maintain a web site on the Internet for your fans, show up in the right places at the right time, drop a sound bite whenever opportunity was listening.

"*Prescott's Landing*? Oh my God!" Mandy said.

"Did we want another round?" I asked, thinking that might possibly be the reason Mandy had come to the table.

Zack and Savanna nodded, Angel said he'd take another black coffee.

Mandy returned with the drinks, stood back, and stared at Zack some more. Without turning her head, she spoke to me out of the corner of her mouth, proving her vocabulary wasn't as limited as I'd begun to think.

"What was that you were asking Warren? Something about a Filipino gal?"

I hate the term "gal," but this was no time to debate semantics. "Estrella Stockton," I said, feeling a rush of adrenaline. "Do you know her?"

"She's the one got herself killed, right?"

I nodded. It was no time to debate responsibility either.

Zack gave Mandy an encouraging smile. "God!" she said again.

"Don't overdo it, Zack," I murmured.

He ran his booted foot up my leg.

"I saw the story in the *Gazette*," Mandy said, after shaking her head a couple of times like a dog with water in its ears. "She had great-looking hair. I guess that's what made me recognize her."

"You'd seen her before?" I asked.

She nodded. "She came in here a couple of times. With a guy."

"When?"

She shrugged, squinching up her eyes. I glanced over at the bar. Warren was watching television. The sound was turned down so low and the office party was so noisy I didn't see how he could follow whatever was going on, but I was glad to see him occupied.

"October 18," she said firmly. "That was the first time. I remember the date because it was the day I made my last payment on the credit card bill my ex stuck me . . ." She broke off. "Water under the bridge," she said. "What did you want to know about her?"

"We're more interested in who the guy was," I said.

"I hadn't seen him before," she said, speaking

directly to Zack even though I'd asked the question.
I'd had this experience before. "He was an average
kind of guy," she went on. "Thirties or forties. He had
a cap on. Like a ball cap. What I could see of his hair,
it was dark. Brown or black. These lights, it's hard to
tell."

She was right about that. The bar had track lighting.
No windows. And the bulbs had an odd look to them.
One of the women in the office party had a dress on
that had a raised design on its white collar and lapels—
it was glowing with a faint green color as if it was
phosphorescent. The partygoers thought that was
hilarious. "Get the Geiger counter," someone had said.
"Kimberly's gone nuclear."

"Black light," the waitress said, following and interpreting my gaze.

"Could you tell if he had inscriptions in his hair?"
She frowned.

"Designs cut into his hair."

Her face cleared. "Oh, I know what you mean." She
shrugged. "He kept his cap on."

"Was he white? Black?" Zack queried.

"He wasn't black, I don't think. Seems to me his
skin was maybe brownish though. Hard to tell. Might
just have had a dark tan."

"Filipino?" Zack asked.

"I don't know. Oh hey, I just remembered—he had
shades on. Aviator shades. He kept them on both times.
Some guys do that."

Aviator shades had struck some kind of chord, but
I didn't know why. Had I seen someone wearing them

recently? A lot of people wore aviator shades. I had a pair myself. So did Zack.

"They sat over there in that corner," the woman told Zack, pointing. "They seemed to be having a good time the first time, not the next time."

"When was the next time?" I asked.

She considered. "Sometime during the holidays. New Year's Eve, maybe. They argued about something. It was noisy in here. I don't listen in on customers anyway. I wouldn't have paid any attention except he yelled at her once that she'd promised. He sounded real bummed, but she calmed him down." She shrugged. "That's about it. I didn't notice when they left. We were busy."

"Do you use the Bellamy Park Bank?" I asked her.

She looked a little surprised by the change of subject, then shook her head. "I live in East Dennison," she said. "I go to a bank there."

"Do you ever go into the Bellamy Park Bank?"

"Why would I do that?"

"There's a guy in there, a guard. I wondered if you'd ever met him. His name's Domingo." I hesitated, wondering how I could ask her to take a look at him to see if he was the guy who'd been with Estrella. In view of the questions I'd been asking, it wasn't going to take a genius to figure out I also wondered if he'd killed Estrella. Which would be enough to spook anyone.

Maybe I ought to consult with Bristow on this one. In any case, about then Warren's attention drifted our way, and he yelled for Mandy to get over there.

"Domingo?" Zack echoed. "You're right, Charlie, his

skin is goin' on brown. 'Course, so's a lot of Californians. Exceptin' yours."

I swallowed the last of my Chardonnay—which tasted as if it came out of a screw-capped bottle. "Did Domingo wear shades?" I asked Zack, then shook my head before he could reply. "No. Who did? Did anyone?"

I was talking mostly to myself.

"How 'bout Rory?" Zack said.

I looked at him blankly.

"Rory didn't sport shades around us, but when I asked him if he got his Air Force clothes from a Dumpster he said they were his own. He must have meant he was in the Air Force some time or other. Way back, by the look of that jacket. But Air Force types wear aviator shades. Tom Cruise in *Top Gun*, remember? 'Cept he was a Navy pilot."

"This isn't a movie, Zack," I said.

Zack went right on ruminating. "Aviator shades. Tanned skin—yeah, Rory looks like he's spent a lot of time outside. Didn't someone say Estrella's old boyfriend had a bad haircut? That would surely fit Rory."

"But Rory's not a Filipino, Zack. And Felicia and Candy and Maisie all said Estrella told them her boyfriend, lover, whatever, was an old friend from the Philippines. It's got to be Domingo. He fits the whole description, except the guy with Estrella didn't have his hat on backwards. But there's no law says a guy has to wear his hat the same way every time."

"But the dude's gay," Zack reminded me.

"So? He could be bisexual."

"That's a fact," Savanna said flatly.

Oops. Savanna's ex-husband was—is—gay. She

caught him in bed with a truck driver—that's how she found out. And, of course, he was also Jacqueline's father.

"Sorry, Savanna," I said. "But there it is," I added to Zack. "It may not seem likely, but it's possible. I'm definitely leaning toward Domingo as the guy we want. Besides—can you imagine Rory as anyone's lover, smelling to high heaven the way he does?"

"You two surely meet the most interesting people," Savanna said. "Don't you think you ought to let Taylor take care of this whole mess?"

Zack and I exchanged a glance, and both looked at Savanna. "You aren't going to tell him we were here asking questions, are you?" I demanded.

"You're asking me to keep secrets from my new fiancé?" she asked.

"I'll tell him myself in my own way," I promised.

She laughed. "Sure you will, Charlie."

"All we're trying to do is find out the truth," I said. "Your fiancé, superman though he is, has the fixed idea that Thane Stockton is the guilty party. Maybe he is. He says he's not. Zack and I think he might be telling the truth. He went through a terrible time with Estrella. We don't want to see him go through some more. If he's innocent. That's why we've been talking to Domingo and Rory and Dr. Hutchins and Felicia and her gang. That's why we're talking to Mandy today."

"I don't think I'm up to speed on all these names," Angel said.

I was pleased to hear Angel join in the conversation. He'd been very subdued for someone who was supposed to be at a party. Not that Angel had a big party

personality, but he was a truly nice, good-natured guy
most of the time, and he had certainly been known to
crack a smile on special occasions. I was quite sure I
knew what the cause of this long-lasting grim mood
was, but I didn't know what I could do about it. Unless . . .

"Why don't you ask him what's happening with
Gina?" I murmured to Savanna after Zack had been
updating Angel long enough to get his attention fully
engaged.

She nodded. "I was thinking I might if an opportunity comes up." Savanna doesn't have my inquiring
mind, but she does like for everyone to be happy.

"An opportunity for what?" Zack asked.

While Savanna scrambled to find something to say,
I spoke up. Sometimes my mouth takes over from my
brain, but this time I made an effort to be tactful. "We
were just wondering if either of you had seen Gina
Giacomini lately," I said. "We miss her. Don't we,
Savanna?"

Savanna darted a "why didn't you let me handle
this?" glance at me.

Angel squinted my way and tugged on his mustache,
something he does when he's perturbed.

Zack looked at him and canted his eyebrows. "You
and Gina have a bust-up?" he asked. Like I said, no
subtlety.

"That's about the size of it," Angel said.

So okay, sometimes the direct approach works.

"What happened?" I asked.

"Charlie," Savanna chided.

"Angel's our friend," I pointed out. "I'm concerned about him. He's obviously not happy."

"I'm fine, Charlie," Angel said.

"Then why have you been acting like a gorilla with a bellyache the last couple of weeks?"

"Maybe he has PMS, darlin'," Zack said. "Certain people act middlin' sour at such times."

I would have kicked his shins, but his comment had brought a smile out of Angel. Not much of one, but enough to show some teeth.

"Charlie can't stand anyone clammin' up about their love life," Zack told Angel. "She's always goin' on at me about mine. Reason bein' she's wild for me. Maybe she's wild for you, too, ever think on that?"

I blew them both a raspberry.

Angel was smiling all the way now. "So come on, Angel," I coaxed. "Tell us what's happening?"

He shrugged. "We had a difference of opinion," he said. "It was my fault, like I told you."

"It didn't have anything to do with our esteemed self-defense instructor?"

"Duke Conway was a result, not a cause."

Zack grinned. "You've done it now, Angel. That answer was just ambiguous enough to get Charlie comin' at you with both barrels."

I ignored him.

"What do you mean?" I asked Angel. But he just shrugged again, and said, "Let it go, Charlie." Then he glanced at his watch, picked up his cowboy hat, and put it on. "It's time we were getting over to CHAPS."

CHAPTER 17

I felt frustrated all the way back to CHAPS. Not only was I a flop as a detective, I was a failure as Miss Lonely Hearts.

All was not bleak, however. I might not be able to get any further as far as Domingo was concerned— for the present, anyway, but I could maybe pursue the Angel-Gina problem. Even in the middle of a murder investigation other people's lives have a way of going on, sometimes merrily, other times with difficulty.

Accordingly, once everything was in readiness at CHAPS and I'd had a bite to eat, I popped into Buttons & Bows, the country-western concession store in CHAPS' lobby. The one Gina Giacomini is the manager of. I had half an hour to spare before starting line-dancing lessons.

"Hey," I said, idly glancing around as if deciding what to look at.

"Charlie," she said warily.

She's another one who knows me.

"Heard you had some new cowboy hats," I said.

"Uh-huh."

I wandered over to the display and selected a black

one with a beaded band. It was my size—I'd take a size smaller if I didn't have all this hair. It looked pretty good. I like a hat with a low crown—I think it's sexier.

"Why don't you go for a white one, Charlie?" Gina asked, getting interested. "It would make a change for you. And it would look good with your blue eyes."

"You think so?"

"I could have your old hat cleaned for you," she said as she hunted down a white one. I tried it on. It didn't look bad. It sure wasn't cheap though.

I checked myself at different angles in the full-length mirror. "Angel always looks good in *his* white hat," I mentioned casually, with a sidelong glance to check her reaction to the sound of his name.

"Why don't you just come right out and ask, Charlie?" Gina said with a glint in her hazel eyes. She'd gone back to black eyeliner, I noticed. It was an improvement over the red.

"I feel bad for Angel," I said. "He says your breakup is all his fault. He's miserable, Gina."

She inclined her head to one side. "Good. I want him to feel miserable."

"What on earth did he do?"

"Nothing," she said. "That's the problem."

"It is?"

She went behind her counter as though she needed something to lean on. I leaned on the other side and gave her what I hoped looked like a sympathetic and encouraging smile.

"Angel's not ready to make a commitment," she blurted out.

"North American men never are," I said. "It's a

'give me liberty or give me death' gene passed down from Patrick Henry. You have to coax them into it. Look at Taylor Bristow. He wasn't doing any committing for a long time, but then all of a sudden he decided he needed Savanna around full-time forever, and boom, next thing you know they're engaged."

Gina managed a smile, but it was a small one. "You think I haven't coaxed Angel? I've tried everything. I even went off the pill, but that didn't do any good. Angel used a contraceptive every time, Charlie."

I muttered something about safe sex, and she gave me a look. I apologized. "I take it you wanted to get pregnant?" I said.

"Doesn't your biological clock ever tick?" she asked.

"This isn't about me, Gina."

Time out for some history. When I was married, I was blessed every holiday by visits from my husband Rob's two children, Brittany and Ryan, whose aim in life was to make *my* life miserable. They succeeded admirably. Any maternal urges I'd ever felt had been lopped off inch by inch during those holidays. If my biological clock started ticking, I was prepared to drown it in a bucket of water. Always supposing I didn't die of cancer first.

"I *want* children," Gina wailed. "I want to settle down, quit work, have babies. I want to be a wife and mom, Charlie. I want to cook and clean and wash diapers and have a man all my own to love and live with. It's all I've ever wanted."

People are constantly surprising me. Who'd have thought a woman who went around with spiky hair dyed all the colors of the spectrum depending on her mood, wearing tight sweaters and skirts that showed her rear when she bent over, alternating with ripped jeans or fatigues with Doc Martens and rock-band-tour T-shirts—a woman who usually wore several gold studs and rings of various designs in each ear, for heaven's sake, not to mention numerous strings of beads hanging around her neck, would harbor the soul of June Cleaver.

Here was the wife Thane Stockton should have had.

"So what you're saying is that Angel has a problem with all that domesticated stuff?" I asked.

"He wants things to go on the way they did before. Dating, spending all our spare time together, staying over once in a while, but living separately, living free."

"And that isn't better than nothing?"

"I didn't think so. Now I'm not so sure."

About then Gina's assistant, Stacie Hogan, came in, said hello, and went on through to the back room. Stacie's a Stanford student. A very pretty young woman, twice Gina's size. Gina had recently hired her to help out a couple of hours a night. So she could pursue her relationship with Duke Conway, I supposed.

No sooner had that thought crossed my mind than Duke popped his cowboy-hatted head around the door. He said "Yo!" to me, then raised his eyebrows at Gina. "You want I should go on in to CHAPS and get a table?" he asked.

She nodded. "I'll be there in half an hour."

I had to admit the guy wasn't bad to look at. Especially in Western gear. Every man becomes better-looking the minute he puts on the hat, shirt, jeans, belt buckle, and boots. Tuxedos have the same mystical effect.

Duke gave me a mini-salute and a cocky grin. "Cool hat, Charlie," he said, then went on his way.

"So you think a macho guy like Duke Conway is going to be more amenable to your baby-making plans?" I asked. I could hear the disbelief coming through clearly in my voice.

Gina's mouth tightened. "Of course not, Charlie, I'm not that dumb. Duke likes me. He likes taking me places. He likes coming to CHAPS. I enjoy the attention, but mainly I'm just trying to make Angel jealous."

"Well, I think you're succeeding," I told her. "He's been in a rotten mood for weeks."

She nodded, looking as if her own mood was way beyond miserable. "I know." She shook her head. "It's one of the few things I do know. I love Angel, but after all this time he's still almost a stranger to me. I don't know any more about him than I did when I met him."

"He's not too chatty, is he?" I put my hands over hers, which were clasped on the counter. "None of us knows much about Angel, Gina. All he's ever let on is that he worked on a ranch in Texas at one time and took part in rodeos. From his appearance I know he's Hispanic with maybe a little Indian thrown in to cause those great cheekbones, and he's a Catholic—I've seen him cross himself—like the time we found the skeleton in the flower bed. He fainted then and said it was because when he was little he'd found a dead body, and the skeleton had reminded him of that."

Gina was tearing up. I wasn't helping a whole lot, obviously. "I didn't even know that much. I don't even know where he's from. It isn't normal to be that secretive."

"I think he might be from Mexico," I told her. "At least he lived in Mexico sometime or other. He told me about a schoolfriend he had in Mexico. He'd lost touch with the friend and wanted to know if I had any ideas on how to find him."

"So did he tell you *where* in Mexico?"

I shook my head.

"You see what I mean? People ask me where I'm from, I don't say I'm from the United States, or even that I'm from California. I say I'm from San Diego." She pulled a box of tissues out from under the counter, mopped her eyes and blew her nose. "I laid my feelings on the line with Angel," she said. "He said he couldn't make a commitment, so maybe it would be better if we stopped seeing each other. He said I should look for someone else to make babies with because he was never going to do that. I said okay, I would. Because I was upset. So when Duke showed he was interested in me, I went along for the ride. But now I'm even more miserable. Talk to Angel, would you, Charlie? Tell him Duke doesn't mean anything to me at all, except for companionship. I just wanted to make Angel jealous. Tell him we could at least be friends, see each other, talk to each other. He doesn't even help me with the window displays anymore. I miss him, Charlie. I really, really miss him."

I'm never averse to interfering, so I promised I'd do what I could and started toward the exit. As I pushed the door open I could hear that Sundancer had started up some music—"God Blessed Texas."

"Were you going to buy that hat?" Gina asked.

I came back in, laughing. "Almost got away with it." I took the hat off and looked at it, put it back on, and preened in the mirror behind the counter. It did look good. "Okay," I said. "I'll leave my black one for cleaning, and I'll bring my credit card in on my break."

"Bring your card in tomorrow, Charlie," she said. "Talk to Angel on your break."

I nodded. I'd opened her up, I told myself. It was my responsibility to see what I could do.

This is the way I rationalize when I'm interfering. It works for me.

Zack had come back to CHAPS with Savanna and Angel and me and wasn't doing anything too useful, other than standing around looking like a famous sex symbol, so I asked him to take over the bar in the main corral during our break. Young Patrick works the main bar when Angel and I are doing line-dancing lessons, but he wants a break when we're through.

Zack obliged, which meant most of our female patrons suddenly decided to get their own drinks from the bar. Quite a few males are starstruck, too, so pretty soon you couldn't even see the bar for bodies.

"What's going on, Charlie?" Angel asked when he returned from the men's room.

For a minute or two I debated canceling my plan for some dialogue. Angel's face always looks as if it was carved from mahogany with a chain saw. Tonight—more precisely—since Duke Conway and Gina Giacomini had settled into one of the booths on the other side of the main corral and had talked intimately and joined in the dancing, his features seemed cast in bronze, immovable and grim.

"Don't knock it, Angel," I said, injecting as much lightness into my voice as I could manage. "Zack's actually working. It's good for his character." I'd ordered up a couple of mineral waters before the rush started, and I handed him one and suggested we go out and sit on the plaza steps—get some air. Unspoken was the other reason behind my suggestion—he wouldn't be able to see Duke and Gina.

It wasn't all that warm out, but the coolness felt good after a couple of hours of dancing. Line-dancing looks smooth, but it's fairly athletic.

There was a full moon, and Adobe Plaza was almost as bright as day. The great-spreading branches of the California live oak trees—the kind Oakland got its name from—cast long shadows over the ancient pavers and the flower bed where we once found a skeleton. I still shivered when I looked at that strip of soil, and I was compulsive about looking at it.

It's not too busy in the plaza at night, especially during the winter. There was a trio of cowboy wanna-bes over to one side, smoking—we're a smoke-free building—and a young couple wandering hand in hand toward Casa Blanca, the Mexican restaurant across the way. Otherwise it was just Angel and me, leaning on the wrought-iron railing at the top of the steps; we'd decided the steps were too cold to sit on.

"You heard anything from your doctor?" Angel asked.

I shook my head. "Don't expect to until Monday."

He nodded.

"How d'you like my hat?" I asked.

He gave me a brief once-over. "Why do I think that's a loaded question?"

"I bought it at Buttons & Bows."

"It's nice, Charlie. Looks good on you." His lips hardly moved, each word sounded chopped off before its time.

This was not going to be easy—I might as well just plunge on in. "Gina's very unhappy, Angel."

He averted his eyes and swallowed visibly.

"She says the problem is that she wants to get married and have kids, and you don't want to do that."

He sighed. "That about sums it up, Charlie. Especially the part about kids. I'm never going to have children."

I didn't ask. I wanted to. But heck, I'd made that decision myself, and I'm never sure I want to tell people why. It always sounds like whining.

One of the three smokers said something that made the other two laugh and glance our way. I guessed they were probably speculating about Angel and me. Which didn't bother me in the least. Some men can't understand the concept of a man and woman being friends. But that's what Angel and I were, even if I couldn't get him to talk.

"Gina says she doesn't care about Duke Conway one bit. She just wants to make you jealous. She's succeeding, isn't she?"

"Maybe we ought to go in," he said. "Getting chilly out here."

"I'm just going to keep after you until you talk to me," I pointed out. "You know what I'm like."

"A dog with a bone, yes."

Hardly a flattering description, but I let it pass and let the air fill with silence.

The three smokers came up the steps, smiled at us, and tipped their hats to me. That is so cool. I think all men ought to be required to wear cowboy hats.

"So is it just Gina, or marriage itself that's holding you back?" I asked Angel after the guys had gone inside.

"I cannot make a commitment to anyone," he said.

Another long pause. Then he added, "I have something I must do first."

Progress.

I tried to think of a casual way of asking what he had to do. "What?" I blurted out when nothing else came to mind.

"When someone makes a solemn promise, Charlie— a vow—he must keep it."

I waited through several minutes, but it seemed he felt that was more than enough to say. "Does it seem likely you might get through with that in the fairly near future?" I asked.

He straightened up. "I think it would be best for our friendship if we go inside now," he said.

"Well just tell me this. If you don't mind. I've always wondered. Where exactly are you from?"

"I came here from Texas," he said. "I told you that."

"Yes. You also told me you had a schoolfriend in Mexico. So were you born there? Is that where your family is from? I always took it for granted you were from Mexico. Maybe because of your Pancho Villa mustache."

"I was born in Mexico," he said. A straight answer for once, spoiled by what followed. "What matters is that I am here now. That is all you need to know."

His voice had stiffened. I stole a glance at him. In the moonlight his dark eyes glinted coldly. His strongly carved features were set and unsmiling, his mouth a straight line.

"I'm sorry, Angel," I said. "I wouldn't have pushed, but I'm really worried about Gina—she seemed so upset. She asked me to tell you she's lonely for you. She's willing to go back to the way it was between you and not ask for anything more."

He looked out at the tree-studded plaza for a few more minutes. A man and woman came out through the plaza door and down the steps without paying any attention to us. They stopped at the foot of the steps and lit cigarettes. I hoped they'd use the sand-topped canister we had there. I hadn't noticed if the former bunch had done that.

"Sometimes a person can't go back," Angel said at last, very softly, beginning to turn away. "Sometimes a person is afraid of becoming soft, forgetting his purpose."

"Will you tell me about this promise of yours someday?" I asked.

He looked at me directly. His eyes had darkened even more than usual. Maybe it was a trick of the light, but I didn't think so. Looking at him I had the ominous sensation you get when you hear distant thunder. "When the time comes, you will know," he said.

I hate ambiguous answers; they make my head ache.

But at least I'd learned a couple of interesting things, I thought as I followed Angel's ramrod-straight figure into the main corral. Someday, in a year or two perhaps, maybe Angel would trust me enough to tell me what Paul Harvey calls "the rest of the story."

CHAPTER 18

Visiting Rory was interesting. It was like going back to the days before telephones, before voice mail or e-mail or even snail mail—when you wanted to talk to someone you just had to go to where the person was.

Rory wasn't living in the attic anymore, his ex-landlady and still drunken friend Bonnie informed Zack and me when we went looking for him on Thursday. "Said he had closetro—claushtro—said the walls were closing in."

It seemed possible Rory might have moved back to his old home under the bridge, but he wasn't there either. Gateway told us my guess was right though—he'd taken up residence in his packing case after Gateway acquired a tent.

I wondered but didn't ask how Gateway defined "acquired."

We found Rory "working" along a nearby highway and gave him and his sacks of recyclable litter a ride back to base camp, both of us holding our breath until our lips were blue, even though we had the windows rolled down all the way.

With a princely flourish, Rory pronounced us wel-

come to his humble abode, but after I'd presented him
with the down pillow Zack and I had bought him, the
omnipresent odor persuaded me we'd prefer to sit on
some of the sizable rocks in the old creek bed. There
was a light breeze, and Zack and I waited until Rory
was seated, then carefully positioned ourselves
upwind.

"Bonnie told us you'd moved out," I told Rory to
get some dialogue under way.

"Bonnie's drinking has become something of a problem," he said sadly, shaking his head. "Twice in the
past three days she left a pan on the stove until it
melted. On the most recent occasion it started a grease
fire under the burner. I have a fear of fire, and it seemed
to me indoor living was becoming hazardous to my
health." He showed me his gap-toothed smile.

"You aren't worried about being mugged again?" I
asked.

"One can only hide for so long, my dear," he said.
"Life must go on."

"Cigars holding out?" Zack asked.

"Oh my yes. I'm rationing them to one a week. Not
only because of my cash-flow problem. They aren't good
for you, you know, no matter how fine or how much
pleasure they give. Rather like a woman, wouldn't you
say?"

"Not in front of Charlie, I wouldn't," Zack said.

Fortunately for him, his rock was some distance
from mine.

"We'd like to go over your story about the night
you saw Estrella get in a car with a man," I said.

"When I was peering out of my Dumpster like a spy in a comic strip," Rory said with a twinkle.

I laughed, picturing the scene.

He closed his eyes and sat in silence for so long I thought he might have gone to sleep, but then he started talking and told pretty much the same story as he'd told before. Though not in precisely the same words, which might have seemed suspicious.

When he mentioned the man's cap, I stopped him. "It was a baseball cap?"

He shrugged, opening his eyes. "It was of that general type and shape," he said. "It was dark, remember. I did not have my infrared-vision glasses with me."

His chuckle was gentle. "It could have been the kind of cap that features a slogan or place name. Or one like my own—the kind of cap a military type wears with fatigues. Other than that, the mysterious stranger was wearing baggy pants and a jacket—a parka perhaps, an anorak, whatever it is trendy to call such a jacket this year."

"Did it zip up the front?" Zack asked, frowning in concentration, jawline tensed Lazarro-style.

"Possibly. Though it might have been a pullover."

"Did he wear the cap backwards?" Zack went on.

Once again I found myself looking at him admiringly. He'd mentioned seeing Domingo wearing a cap like that and had remembered it.

Not that it helped much. Rory was already shaking his head. He looked thoughtful, however. "He might have been dressed in that disreputable manner some young males affect. The pants were definitely baggy."

"Might the jacket have been a sweatshirt?" Zack asked.

"Also possible, if it was loose-fitting."

This description was getting more and more vague. "You said before that the pants were jeans," I pointed out.

"Did I?" He closed his eyes again. "They might have been, probably were. I suppose it is their very bagginess that confused me a little. One expects jeans to fit."

"Yours don't," I said.

He nodded, smiling. "True, Charlie, but the previous owner of my jeans was evidently built to a more generous frame. One takes what one can get from Lord Dumpster's bounty."

"Did you notice anything about the way the man spoke?" I asked. "We're wondering if the man with Estrella might have been a Filipino guy we've met. Once in a while he goes into a distinctive way of talking. Kind of singsong, and he raises his voice at the end of sentences."

"After Estrella exclaimed 'Mother of God, what are you doing here?' all the man said was, 'I was looking for you.' It's a little difficult to judge speech patterns by such a brief statement. I didn't notice any particular accent."

"You said before that the man said 'Looking for you, *sweetheart*,' " I reminded him.

"Did I indeed? Then I suppose he must have said that. The last time you and I spoke, the scene was fresher in my memory."

Uh-huh. Or was he trying, for purposes of his own, to muddy the waters?

"Domingo said 'you know' a lot, at the end of sentences," Zack offered.

Rory shrugged. "All I recall is that the man I saw said he was looking for the woman. It's possible I may have blanked out a 'you know' or two. My brain doesn't do as well as it used to."

Uh-huh. "Have you ever been inside the Bellamy Park Bank?" I asked.

Rory chuckled. "Not since the last time I checked my safety-deposit box."

It took me a minute to realize he was joking.

"I'm not sure Rory was being totally open with us this time," I said to Zack, as we drove back to CHAPS. "That memory-failing thing struck me as a convenient way of not answering any more questions. I don't really think he killed Estrella though—we don't know of a motive for one thing."

I mulled for a while. "I think I'm becoming as convinced that Domingo murdered Estrella as Bristow is that Thane Stockton did it," I said to Zack as we drove back to CHAPS. "He's the only Filipino male we've run into since we talked to the women at Hair Raising. And I keep coming back to the way he sort of closed up and didn't want to talk anymore that day we talked to him at the bank—right at the last. Remember? When I asked if he knew of any other Filipino male Estrella might have been involved with, he went real quiet. That *could* be because he knew there wasn't another man."

Zack nodded.

After a moment, he said, "Domingo seemed antsy when I saw him in Lenny's that day. It was the friend's idea to ask for an autograph, he said. Seemed like Domingo didn't really want to spend any time talkin', to me."

"Antsy?"

"Restless. Like he wanted to be somewhere else. Jiggin' from foot to foot. Like he was short of time."

"Maybe he was. Or maybe he was afraid you'd ask him more questions. Which would seem to indicate he might have some answers he didn't give us yet. Maybe we should go back and talk to him some more."

"Not today," Zack said.

I looked at him. A particularly smug smile was curling around the corner of his mouth. "Why not today?" I asked.

He sent me one of his zinger glances from under his eyelids.

I sighed. "You have a date, I take it? One of your usual dollies, or someone new?"

He didn't answer right away.

"Not Candy?" I said, horrified.

He shook his head. "Candy's too young," he said. "I'm no cradle snatcher."

"Oh yeah? What about Adorin' Lauren?" The nineteen-year-old in question had gone out of our lives some months ago, but for a while there she had followed Zack around like a lonesome puppy.

"There was never anythin' goin' on between me and Lauren Deakins," he insisted as he had insisted before.

I still wasn't sure I believed him.

I also realized he hadn't answered my question. "Your date wouldn't happen to be at Paulie's Place, would it?"

His mouth twitched.

Mandy. Dandy Mandy instead of Candy.

"You're incorrigible," I said.

"Your fault, Charlie," he said. "You break my heart every day refusin' to come home with me. What d'you expect me to do?"

"You can't have a date tomorrow," I told him, pointedly ignoring the last comment. "We're all supposed to get together after CHAPS closes. We still haven't celebrated Bristow and Savanna's engagement with all parties present. She and Bristow are picking up her ring tomorrow. She had to have it sized."

"I haven't forgotten. I've put some Dom in the wine cabinet."

Bristow rarely drank, but he had once expressed a liking for Dom Pérignon. I liked the stuff myself, though I couldn't afford to buy it. "That was thoughtful of you," I told Zack.

"So you wanna come home with me after we finish the champagne? I could show you how thoughtful I can be."

I ignored him. As usual. At least my brain did. My body yearned. Also as usual.

To hear Savanna tell it, her engagement ring would qualify as one of the seven wonders of the world. When she proudly held out her hand for inspection on Friday night I had to agree that the ring was certainly magnificent—a wide gold band supporting an emerald-cut

ruby flanked by shoulders that contained enough dia-
monds to act in place of a mirrored ball on a dance
floor.

I should have known Savanna would go for a ruby—
she always had some touch of red in her clothing—
fringed red shirts were a particular favorite. She even
had a pair of red cowboy boots that she wore on special
occasions. She was wearing them tonight. Her face was
luminous. Bristow looked pretty puffed up himself. He
was even wearing a starched, long-sleeved shirt and
slacks instead of his usual jeans and polo shirt.

We were all sitting around a table in the little corral.
It was right on closing time. A few stragglers were
drifting out. We still needed to do our picking up—
the janitorial service would take care of the rest when
they came in before dawn. But we'd decided to have
our little party first, chores later.

There were just Zack and Angel and me besides
the happy couple. And Benny. I'd brought his cage
down, so he could join in the celebration. I'd provided
a romaine leaf for him to pig out on, some hummus
and pita chips for the grown-ups.

Savanna had wanted to invite Gina, arguing that
she was still our friend even if Angel had dumped her.
But we'd decided it would cast a pall on the party if
Angel got upset. Actually, Angel was sort of upset
already because Gina and Duke were still sitting in a
booth in the main corral, talking intimately, as if they
hadn't noticed the place was closing around them.

If they didn't leave in the next five minutes, I was
going to roust them out, I decided. As if they'd heard

me they stood up. They were evidently having a small argument. Nothing dramatic, but Gina was holding back, shaking her head.

While Zack was getting out the Dom Pérignon, Duke came toward us. Gina headed for the exit. Apparently, the argument must have been about coming over or not coming over.

"Hey," Duke said to Savanna. "Gina told me you got engaged. Great news. I just wanted to offer my congratulations."

"Thank you, Duke," Savanna said warmly.

I could feel vibrations coming out of Angel's body— he was sitting next to me. I put my hand on his arm, and he glanced sideways at me and nodded tersely. Translation: *Don't worry, Charlie, I'm in control.*

The vibrations didn't go away.

We all looked up as the wagon-wheel light fixtures jittered and clinked. Another reminder that human beings hadn't succeeded in taming all forces of nature. The tremor lasted twenty seconds or so. A fairly long time when the ground feels as if it's about to go out from under you. But this time it didn't.

"I'd like you to meet my fiancé, Detective Sergeant Taylor Bristow," Savanna said to Duke when we'd all let out the breath we'd been holding. "Taylor, this is Duke Conway, he teaches Charlie's self-defense class. He taught me to yell 'back off' real good."

"I'll remember that," Bristow said with a mock scowl.

The two men shook hands. "All the best," Duke said, then apologized graciously for intruding. "I've taught classes to several police departments," he added.

"So I've heard," Bristow said. "Maybe you should talk to the training officer at Bellamy Park PD."

"I'll do that." Duke sent his cocky grin around the circle, said, "Great hat, Charlie," then took his leave.

Angel's tension dissipated like air out of a balloon. I was suddenly furious at him for just letting Gina go. Why couldn't he just explain his promise *to* her, ask her to hang in there? Why make such a big deal out of it, like he'd taken a monk's vows or something?

"Okay," Zack said, coming out from behind the bar. "Looks like we've finally got the place to ourselves. Give me two seconds to lock up."

He was setting a new record in helpfulness tonight. When he returned, he set a flute in front of each of us. "Let the festivities begin," he said, and began removing the foil capsule from the top of the first bottle. He was about to work on the wire hood when Bristow's pager beeped.

"No, no, no," Savanna wailed.

Bristow said a word that wasn't Shakespearean, then gestured at the bar. When Zack nodded he got up and used the telephone to call in. We all sat silently waiting, but couldn't make anything out of his cryptic comments. The only thing that came through clearly was, "I'm on my way."

"Sorry, sweetheart," he said after he hung up. He put his hands on Savanna's shoulders, gave a regretful shrug, and launched into one of his store of Shakespearean quotes. " 'Good night, good night! parting is such sweet sorrow, that I shall say good-night till it be morrow.' "

"Is it something bad?" I asked.

He had a cop expression on his face. Which is to say unreadable. "Some kind of incident out at Pillar Point," he said airily, which meant he wasn't going to tell us what it was.

Pillar Point Harbor is on the Pacific Ocean side of the peninsula—the main embarkation point for deep-sea fishing trips, whale-sighting cruises, bird-watching expeditions—and even burials at sea. It was Zack's favorite place to go fishing. "Macintosh and I were out there fishin' for rock cod a few weeks ago," he said now.

"We-ll," Savanna said, drawing out the syllable— "I guess I might as well start rehearsing my upcoming role." She raised her eyebrows at me. "What kind of cop's wife should I be, Charlie? Should I play the neglected martyr and pretend I don't mind spending large chunks of my life alone? Or yell and scream and accuse Taylor of loving his work more than me? Or make him take up basketball for a living?"

"Kick his shins," I said.

"Charlie purely enjoys kickin' shins," Zack said, having had his own attacked on several occasions, never without justification.

The party definitely fell flat after Bristow's departure. "What d'ya say?" Zack asked, still holding on to the bottle of Dom. "Should we open it anyway, or save it until we're all present and accounted for?"

We voted to save it and get our picking-up chores

over with. No sense having too late a night if it wasn't for a good reason.

A half hour later I locked up after everyone and carried Ben upstairs in his cage, cleaned out his litter box, and covered him up for the night. Then I slept blissfully, having no knowledge of what Bristow was up to.

CHAPTER 19

The report was on the noon news on Saturday. Well, it might have been on earlier, but that was the first report I saw. I often switch TV news on while I'm eating lunch—it's the one time in the day I have a chance to catch up with what's going on in the world outside CHAPS.

Benny was lunching, too, in his cage nearby on the floor. His little green pellets of rolled barley, alfalfa, and soybean meal looked more appetizing than the soup I was eating. I only eat canned soup once in a while when I get tired of cooking for one. I'd bought some in the local health food store. Non-fat. Some foods *need* fat, I decided after a couple of spoonfuls. I set the bowl aside and started on my tuna sandwich, still keeping track of the news.

At some time on the previous day, a car had been driven or had rolled down the boat ramp at Pillar Point and into the water. My ears pricked up. This had to be the case that had called Bristow away from our celebration; there'd hardly be two incidents in that small an area in such a short period of time.

A tow-truck driver who had been called to the scene

had thought at first it was an abandoned car that someone had jettisoned. But as he hauled it out of the water, bystanders had yelled up to him that the driver was still strapped in his seat belt.

The tow-truck driver had ceased recovery at once and someone had called the local police.

Local police. Interesting. Detective Sergeant Taylor Bristow could hardly be called local to that area. Why would a Bellamy Park detective get involved in something that happened on the other side of the peninsula, way out of Bellamy Park's jurisdiction?

It could be a tragic accident, or a suicide, the reporter on the scene speculated. Newspeople love to speculate. They can do it for hours, then finally come up with a few facts, then spend more hours talking to experts who supposedly specialize in whatever the facts turned out to be.

No one had witnessed the accident. Most people who used the parking lot went out fishing in the morning and returned hours later. There was no other reason for anyone to use that particular parking lot. The only thing there was the boat ramp. No one had even known about the accident until eight-thirty Friday night, when a couple of sports fishermen had started to bring their boat into the first ramp of three after a day of cod fishing. They were late coming in because of engine trouble, which they had eventually managed to fix. They had no particular reason for choosing that ramp except that they had left via that ramp shortly after dawn.

The fishermen had meant to tie up to the dock, then hike up to the parking lot for their car and boat trailer.

Instead, they had run afoul of something pretty solid, managed to back away and come in on the next ramp. Investigating the source of the entanglement, they had spotted the submerged car.

Eight-thirty Friday night. Bristow had been called out around midnight, right at the beginning of our aborted celebration. When he was supposedly off duty.

More and more interesting. If this was the case that had pulled Bristow out of CHAPS, then whoever had been working on it had discovered something, three and a half hours into it, that had caused Bristow to be consulted.

The TV station showed some footage of the automobile being hauled up the ramp, water streaming from it. The cable was attached to the rear bumper of the car. Evidently the car had gone forward down the ramp. But if the driver had intended to pick up or drop off a boat, he would surely have gone down the ramp in reverse.

Dumb, Charlie, nobody had mentioned a boat. Either the driver had deliberately driven down the road from the parking lot and followed the curve of the road into the ocean, or, perhaps waiting for a pal's boat to come in, he'd gone to sleep at the wheel and the car had rolled down on its own, taking him to a watery grave. In which case, what happened to the pal with the boat? Forget the boat. Forget *him*. Nobody had mentioned gender either. It could be a woman. That must have been some nap. Maybe s/he'd had a heart attack or a stroke and died at the wheel just as s/he arrived at the top of the ramp and *then* the car had rolled down.

I can speculate pretty good myself.

The identity of the driver was being withheld pending notification of the next of kin, the reporter said.

There was another brief shot of the car. It looked quite a bit like Felicia's, I thought.

I debated calling Savanna to see if she'd heard from Bristow, but that would really be nosy. I didn't want her thinking that when she was married I'd be sticking my nose into every case her husband got involved in. This one really wasn't any of my business. If Bristow hadn't mentioned Pillar Point the previous night, I wouldn't even have paid that much attention except to wonder how it had happened. No doubt more details would be forthcoming later in the day.

Having finished my sandwich, I switched off the television. Reluctantly, I must admit. I needed distraction the closer I got to Monday and the possibility of Dr. Hanssen or Matilda calling with my biopsy results.

I thought of calling Thane Stockton, but was afraid I'd blurt something out about his dog being alive after all. So then I thought about Hair Raising. Probably because of the similarity of the car in the TV story to Felicia's. The brain makes these links for a reason.

Next thing I was calling Hair Raising to see if I could get an appointment. This seemed as good a time as ever to get my hair seen to.

Maisie had had a cancellation, Candy said. Could I get over there in twenty minutes?

Perfect. I could and did.

We started with shampoo and conditioning, followed by what Maisie called a light slide cut, done from the inside out, which was supposed to "open up" my curls.

"We don't want to *fight* your hair, Charlie," Maisie explained. "We want to enhance its natural assets."

I'd been fighting my hair all my life—I hadn't known it *had* any assets. Oh well, if this didn't work, I'd just keep my new white cowboy hat on all the time.

"Estrella said she'd use an antihumectant on it," I told Maisie, whose eyes filled immediately. At the mention of Estrella, I supposed.

"I already did that," she said, her lips quivering. "Have you heard anything, Charlie? Have the police made any progress?"

"Not that I know of," I said. I certainly wasn't going to discuss any of *my* discoveries. I might risk a question though. "This Filipino boyfriend of Estrella's you told me about," I murmured. "Do you happen to know if he worked in Bellamy Park? Did Estrella ever mention his job? Like if he worked at Lenny's Market, or one of the gas stations?" See how cleverly I omitted mentioning the bank.

She thought for a while, still snipping. "No, Charlie, I don't think she ever did. Estrella wasn't a confiding sort. The things I told you about she sort of blurted out one day when we were celebrating Candy's birthday with a lunch at Mario's. We had a bottle of Chianti—you know—those adorable bottles in straw holders? Estrella was just the least bit tiddly."

"Great word," I commented.

Her smile was watery around the edges. "I drove Estrella back here because she wasn't sober enough to drive—and the penalties are really quite severe in California—and she talked a bit more than usual. That's how I knew about the snuff-film thingy."

She had lowered her voice to a whisper even though the other stylist was wielding a blow dryer over her client's head. I could barely hear her. After a brief silence, she shook her head. "No, I think I can say without fear of contradiction that she never mentioned the man's job."

Dang—as Zack would say.

Another thought occurred to me. "Did Estrella ever give this old boyfriend from the Philippines a haircut?"

Maisie's forehead furrowed. "She never said so. The only Filipino person I remember her giving a haircut to was a fellow she knew who worked at a bank. The Bellamy Park Bank, I believe."

For the first time I fully understood the expression, "she jumped out of her skin." I did it. "Estrella did Domingo's inscriptions?" I exclaimed.

Maisie nodded calmly. "Domingo, yes, that's the fellow's name. A *young* man. An acquaintance of Estrella's. She wanted to practice, and he was willing. He came in one evening. I was fascinated. You hold a stencil against the hair and use battery-operated clippers, cut out the hair in the stencil." She shook her head. "Wouldn't want to try it myself, but it was interesting to watch."

"I had no idea you knew about Domingo," I said excitedly. "Don't you see, Maisie, Domingo must be the old boyfriend from the Philippines."

She shook her head again. "Oh no dear, that's not possible; Domingo's gay." She whispered the last word the way she'd whispered "sex" when I talked to her before.

"Maybe he discovered he was gay *after* he was

Estrella's boyfriend," I suggested. "Or maybe he was bisexual." I thought for a minute or so. "Was Felicia here when Estrella cut Domingo's hair?"

"No, dear. She had the evening off. Estrella was the only one with a client. She trimmed my hair when she was finished with Domingo, that's why I stayed until she was done."

"So did Felicia ever meet Domingo?" I asked.

"Not that I'm aware of."

"Where's Felicia today?" I asked, suddenly realizing I hadn't seen her yet.

"Oh, she had to go to—she had an errand," Maisie said. "She should be back soon."

"If Felicia didn't ever meet Domingo, then she wouldn't recognize him in Paulie's Place," I went on. "She said the man with Estrella in Paulie's had a bad haircut. That could have been Domingo before Estrella had a go at him."

"He was very shaggy," Maisie conceded. "But you know, Charlie, I can't say I like some of these styles young men are favoring these days. Some of them are ever so peculiar."

I stopped listening. My mind was racing along, thinking that Estrella cutting Domingo's hair implied a little more intimacy than Domingo had indicated. He hadn't even mentioned that she'd cut his hair.

Maisie was still snipping. Every once in a while she would hold out chunks of my hair to each side and frown at them in the mirror, evidently checking that the lengths were equal. Then she'd spritz with water and snip some more.

"I have a meeting at CHAPS at three o'clock," I ventured after a while.

"You'll be through in plenty of time," she said, then gave me a sly little grin in the mirror. "Do you have a date, Charlie? With Zack Hunter perhaps?"

"Be still my heart," the other stylist said, having cut off her blow dryer in time to hear Zack's name.

"It's a partners' meeting," I explained.

"Of course it is," Maisie said. Her cheeks turned a little pink, then she gave me a shy smile. "I have a date myself tonight," she said. She tipped my head down, moved half my hair forward so that it hung over my forehead like a curtain, and started snipping away at the back.

"That's great," I said, hoping she'd tell me about it. I love hearing about other people's doings, whatever they are.

"I'm very nervous about it," she added, but didn't say any more. After a minute, she said, "I've been doing some thinking about that nickname Estrella called her Filipino boyfriend, Charlie."

My ears jumped to attention, but then I felt a change in the air as the outer door blasted open. Bent over, blinded by my own hair, I couldn't see who came in and slammed the door closed. It wasn't until I heard her voice that I realized it was Felicia.

"Boy, did I get a runaround," she exclaimed.

"No luck?" Maisie asked.

"They'll get back to me as soon as they have any information," Felicia said in a parrotlike tone.

"Is anything wrong?" I asked Maisie, as Felicia stormed past and went into the back room. I could just barely see her legs from under my hair. She was still wearing those killer heels.

"Felicia's car was stolen yesterday," Maisie said. "She didn't notice it was missing until we closed up. I took her to the police station to report it. How we didn't hear it leave, I've no idea. That motor could awaken the dead. Probably we were operating blow dryers, or else Felicia had the stereo on. She *will* play it at full blast."

She flipped my hair back and told me I could straighten up. In the mirror I looked like a fish, my mouth hanging open, my eyes wide enough to show white all around.

"Felicia's car was *stolen?*" I echoed. "*Yesterday?* You're sure it was yesterday? Who stole it?"

"Well now, Charlie, we don't know that, do we?" Maisie chided. "All we know is that it disappeared from the back parking lot somewhere between noon and seven o'clock, which is when we left. You can see how we wouldn't notice it was gone even if we glanced outside—there are a lot of cars in that back lot when the mall is open."

She sighed. "I drove Felicia to the police station, and an officer filled out a report and said he'd be in touch. So today Felicia decided she needed to push the police along a bit. Seems as if she didn't get any new information. I don't know why she's so upset—the car's not *worth* anything. Felicia prefers to spend her money on clothes and jewelry. She got really shirty with the police because she didn't feel she was getting any satisfaction."

I was still in a state of shock.

Maisie was evidently through cutting. My hair didn't look any shorter, she'd barely taken a half inch off the ends, but I supposed it had to be a little thinner; there was quite a mound of carroty curlicues on the floor.

She worked some kind of lotion into my hair. "Frizz-Free," she told me, as she combed it through. That in itself was an improvement, she was actually getting a comb to go through. Picking up a blow dryer with a large round appliance on the end of it—a diffuser, I guessed, she started lifting hair and drying it carefully, molding it with her fingers, telling me I should do it like this.

Yeah, right. Charlie the patient person.

Felicia came storming out again. "Damn cops," she said, almost spitting. "I asked did they start looking for my car yet, and all they did was look at one another. Then they disappeared in the back for a while—two of them—just left me standing there. Then they came back and said they'd be in touch in the next twenty-four hours and to keep myself available. Like I'm going somewhere without a car? I'm going to get something to eat, okay?"

I swallowed. If the police hadn't known where her car was, or at least hadn't told her, I certainly wasn't going to. But it seemed obvious that was Felicia's car I'd watched being hauled out of the Pacific Ocean this morning. The car whose driver had been strapped inside. The car whose driver was dead.

Felicia wasn't sticking around for any comments anyway. "It's the principle of the thing," she muttered before slamming out of the door again. "It might not be much of a car, but it was *my* car."

I called Savanna's number the minute I got back to CHAPS, but the baby-sitter said she'd already left her apartment. I was waiting for her when she came in CHAPS' main entrance. Angel and Zack were right behind her. "Hey!" Zack said. "Lookin' good, darlin'!"

"Yeah," Angel said. "What did you do to your hair?"

"It's gorgeous. *You're* gorgeous," Savanna said.

"Never mind that," I said, though inwardly I was preening like a peacock. A peahen. No, peahens don't have anything to preen about. My hair was still orange, but it definitely looked better. And felt great. It actually bounced when I moved my head. Rather nice-looking crinkles had replaced the usual frizz.

"Curly-*locks*," Zack said.

I gestured them all into the office and closed the door, in case Sundancer came in early to play with his electronics.

Then I told them what I had seen on the news and what I had heard at Hair Raising.

"I saw part of that newscast," Zack said. "I didn't have the sound on though—I was—well that isn't germane. I didn't get that it was happenin' at Pillar Point."

Why would he have his TV on without sound? I could think of one scenario. Billing and cooing with a member of his doll brigade while idly watching the news, not wanting to be disturbed if the billing and cooing became more intense.

Savanna had her eyebrows up. "Dandy Mandy?" she mouthed. We thought alike on Zack's doll brigade. Well, not completely, we were both amused by it, but

Savanna's amusement was edged with indulgence, mine with irritation.

"That's where Taylor went chargin' off to last night?" Zack asked Savanna.

"Haven't seem him since," she said. "He called to say he'd be tied up for a while, he'd maybe get back to me tomorrow morning. Evidently there were some businesses broken into over the weekend, and all the merchants are up in arms wanting to know where the police were. Sergeant Timpkin and a couple of patrol officers are out with 'flu, so things are in turmoil."

"But he *is* handling the accident or whatever it is over at Pillar Point?" I asked.

Savanna frowned. "He mentioned it, said that was what they'd called him in for, but he didn't really have much time to talk, Charlie."

"So what do I do now?" I asked. "I don't want to talk to anyone else. Especially if Bristow's handling the drowning case, though I don't see how he can be in charge of it when it's clear over in Pillar Point. I think it's important I tell him about Estrella giving Domingo a haircut and Domingo not mentioning that fact. And I want to be sure the police know that's Felicia's car they pulled out of the harbor."

"They most probably do know," Zack said, his jaw-line assuming its Lazarro slant. "Sounds to me like they were stallin' Ms. Felicia until someone in charge decided what to do."

"Lucky she reported it stolen before it showed up where it did," Angel said. "Though I suppose someone could do that if they *knew* their car was going to be used by someone else for . . ." He broke off. "This lady—

Felicia?—would hardly know if someone was going to commit suicide or have an accident in her car, would she?" He showed one of his rare, but always beautiful smiles. "Guess I'm not as good a sleuth as you and Zack, Charlie."

A chill went down my spine. What if it wasn't an accident *or* a suicide?

I was getting ahead of myself. A habit of mine, jumping to conclusions and riding off in all directions. "We're not doing too good lately, Angel," I admitted, filing the question away for future pondering. "We've asked a lot of questions about Estrella and we've been given a lot of answers, but none that spells the murderer's name."

I looked at Zack. "Does it seem like a heck of a coincidence to you that a car belonging to a woman who worked with a woman who was murdered should be fished out of the harbor with a dead body in it? The same car that the dead woman once borrowed? The same car her old boyfriend from the Philippines rode in and commented on?"

"You're sayin' Estrella's murder and this drownin' might be linked?"

"I'd be very surprised if they aren't."

"We don't know for sure that was Felicia's car," Zack pointed out.

"I only saw it on TV, but my first thought was that it looked a *lot* like Felicia's car. An hour later, I heard Felicia's car had been stolen the day before. Now the police don't seem to want to discuss it with her. That's enough for me. Especially now we know Bristow was called out on the case."

I mulled for a while. "I guess it's possible the Bellamy Park police might *not* know it's Felicia's car. The accident or whatever it is was over at Pillar Point. Bristow would know if the license plate on the accident car matched Felicia's license, but I doubt Felicia saw *Bristow* when she went to the station to inquire about her car. It's also possible whoever stole the car from the parking lot might have taken the license plates off it."

"Yeah," Zack said, nodding slowly. "One time on *Prescott's Landin'* we did a story about a scam where some dudes were stealin' trucks and paintin' them different colors, strippin' off the plates and then sellin' the vehicles."

Prescott's Landing had used every story line that was ever invented. Five or six to an episode sometimes. It had always amazed me how people had managed to keep track of who was who and what they were doing.

"The question is," I said, "*if* the stolen car and Estrella's murder *are* connected, whose body is that in the car?"

I turned to Savanna, who was sitting in one of the swivel chairs, looking wide-eyed and horrified. "Did Bristow say if he knew who was driving the car that went into the water?"

She shook her head. "I think he's trying to establish a pattern where he doesn't bring his work home."

"We'll have to change that," Zack said with a glint in his eye. "Charlie's goin' to have a conniption if she can't use you as a pipeline to what's goin' on."

"I've no intention of *using* Savanna for anything," I said with dignity.

Which brought me Zack's bad-boy smile and its accompanying *Whomp!* to my stomach. Plus a lingering—and fond—look from those famous—and sexy—green eyes.

When we got through with the business part of our meeting, and the others went off to get CHAPS ready for the influx of Saturday night dancers, I found myself reaching for the telephone. I wanted to touch base with everyone who was in any way connected with Estrella's murder. I punched in Thane Stockton's number first.

Nobody answered. He was possibly out working in the grounds, or playing chess with Adler Hutchins. He'd have to come in soon, it was beginning to get dark.

Was it worth calling Adler Hutchins? To ask him what? If he'd seen Thane Stockton today.

The doctor was still staying with his daughter. The baby was still wailing in the background. No, he hadn't seen Thane or talked to him since Thursday. Was anything wrong?

"I just wanted to talk to him," I said lamely. I could hardly say I wanted to find out that he was still alive so I could cross him off my possible corpse-in-the-car list. "He's not answering his phone," I added.

"He does that," the doctor said. "Doesn't answer I mean. I made him buy an answering machine so I could leave a message, but he forgets to switch it on."

Rory didn't have a phone, and I couldn't drive over to the creek now—I had a lot of chores to do before CHAPS opened.

No use calling the bank on a Saturday. I looked for Romero in the local directory and found a whole slew.

No Domingo, but I called them all anyway in case Domingo was related to one of them. Only one woman knew a Domingo Romero. He was her uncle, and she was perfectly willing to give me his phone number in Tijuana, but he was an old man of ninety and somewhat deaf, she said, so he might not hear the telephone if he didn't have his hearing aid in. I finally convinced her I didn't think her uncle was the man I was looking for.

If Domingo *was* gay and living with a man, the man would have another name, of course. Maybe the friend he'd been with when Zack met him at Lenny's.

I went in search of Zack. He was doing an inventory of the wine captain. I saw he'd replaced the Dom Pérignon. It looked as though we wouldn't be doing our official celebration of Savanna's engagement for a while—at least until Bristow had some time off.

"You still stewin', darlin'?" he said, when I posed my question. "Thought we'd be waitin' for word from Taylor Bristow. If that is Felicia's car—he knows our interest in the Hair Raisin' salon—he'll be sure to tell us about it." He shook his head. "I didn't get Domingo's buddy's last name, Charlie. Didn't even get his first name. 'Shakey' was his nickname. Wrote the autograph to Shakey."

I wandered back to the office, thinking about nicknames. Maisie had said *she'd* been thinking about the nickname Estrella had given her Filipino boyfriend. Which I couldn't remember. We hadn't got back to it. Felicia's arrival and the story about her car being stolen had driven everything else out of my mind.

Maisie had been about to tell me something.

I searched my brain for Maisie's last name. I wish someone would come up with a computer search program that would work on a human brain. I gave up and went into the main corral to help the others.

People were beginning to filter into CHAPS before "Ridley" appeared on the tip of my tongue.

I dashed back to the office and hauled out the telephone directory again. There were eight Ridleys. I called every one of them. None of them was Maisie. None of them knew Maisie.

Detecting can be a frustrating business.

CHAPTER 20

Around nine o'clock, just as we were getting through with line-dancing lessons, I thought of calling Felicia Godfrey. Her husband answered and said she was out. "She always goes out on Saturday nights," he said in a voice that sounded as frail as cobwebs.

I dismissed the idea of calling Paulie's Place to see if Felicia was in the bar, then thought to ask Mr. Godfrey if he knew Maisie Ridley's phone number. He didn't, but offered to look it up in Felicia's address book. It took a while. "I think I need new glasses," he said at one point. "Ever since that second cataract operation . . ." His weak little voice trailed away.

And then he came up with a number for Maisie.

An answering machine turned on with the fourth ring. It featured some serious bonging, a snatch of "Rule Britannia," and Maisie's recorded voice, which sounded more British than the Queen. She did the whole message from the answering machine manual, from the "Hello, I can't come to the phone right now," and "Your call is very important to me," all the way through to giving explicit instructions on how to leave a message—like nobody knew by now.

I left my name and CHAPS' number. *I have a date tonight*, Maisie had said, turning rosy.

I supposed the date must be working out.

Sunday morning, I tried again to reach Maisie. Big Ben and "Rule Britannia" answered. I called Thane Stockton again. No response. I thought of going to see Rory but couldn't figure out how that would turn out to be helpful. If Rory wasn't "home," it wouldn't mean he was the guy in the car; it would just mean he was off doing other stuff. Likewise for Thane and Domingo—the only way to eliminate any of them was to see them or talk to them.

In any case I hated to leave my loft in case Bristow came by or tried to call me. He might, if Savanna had passed on my message that I had news for him, as I'd asked her to. I didn't really want to go to the creek area by myself. When I called Zack to see what he might think of such a jaunt, I got *his* answering machine.

I tried Maisie off and on without success. The Sunday paper offered a rehash of yesterday's TV news. Police were still attempting to notify the dead driver's next of kin. Autopsy results had not yet been released. TV news had nothing new to offer.

Bristow telephoned shortly after noon. I hit him with everything I had learned and heard and thought since Friday night, except that I didn't say anything about Felicia's car. I wanted a face-to-face meeting, so I could get some information. I hinted that I knew something else but didn't think my cordless phone was all that secure, then finished up by telling him about Maisie's apparent disappearance.

"She may not *want* to answer her phone," he said soothingly.

I hate when people soothe me.

"Okay, Charlie," he said, when I'd vibrated across the line without saying a word for a minute or two. "You're right. It's not all that good an idea to talk on the phone." He hesitated. "What I need most right now is a good workout. Why don't you get hold of Zack and meet me at Dandy Carr's? It shouldn't be too busy this time of a sunny Sunday. We can put my stuff together with your stuff and see what comes out of the mixture and get some exercise at the same time."

Dandy Carr's was the most popular gym in Bellamy Park. Real bodybuilders used it. Everybody who was anybody worked out there. Except me. One, I don't care for the monstrous all-in-one weight-resistance machines the place is full of. Two, I don't want to hang out where people wear spandex. And three, I don't like Dandy's gym for personal reasons connected with a previous owner. Not Dandy Carr—it's gone through a couple of owners since Dandy moved away.

"How about we meet at my gym in Condor?" I suggested. "It will probably be empty."

Bristow had met me there once before when I didn't want anyone to see me talking to him—the first time I involved myself in one of his cases.

"There's a reason for that gym being empty, Charlie. It was most likely furnished in 1940."

"I *like* that gym," I said.

Bristow laughed, but agreed to my suggestion.

I'm willing to admit the gym I work out in has out-of-date machines—a bench press, knee machine, leg press, rowing machine. But I like that each one performs a single function, and that none of them hooks up to monitors to tattle on pulse and blood pressure and how many calories the user has burned up in how many minutes. Besides which, membership is dirt-cheap.

I called Zack expecting to get his answering machine again, and got the man himself, sounding as if he was barely awake. I'm not a morning person, but Zack beats me hollow in the staying-up-all-night department. You can read that "staying up" part anyway you like.

Just as I'd expected, my gym was empty. It was also stuffy and smelled of BO. I elected to start on the rowing machine, Zack squinted at me and got a puzzled frown on his face. "Your hair doesn't look as good as it did," he said.

"I know that," I snapped. As I mentioned earlier, I don't have Maisie's patience. "I'm not a hairdresser," I pointed out.

"Still lookin' good, darlin'," he said soothingly. "Lookin' better than it did before, for sure."

That was supposed to be a compliment?

He hopped on the treadmill and started hiking. When Bristow arrived a few minutes behind us, he took a second look at me, too, opened his mouth, then closed it again without saying anything. He's a diplomat. And a survivalist. Stretching himself out on the bench press, he started pumping with long, steady strokes.

"Who was in the car?" I asked as soon as he took a break. I was ready with all kinds of arguments if Bristow refused to divulge information, but I didn't need them.

After glancing at the door to make sure he had closed it, he said, "Domingo Romero."

"Whoa!" Zack exclaimed.

I froze in midstroke.

"Accident or suicide?" Zack asked.

"Could be either one," Bristow said. "But it looks more like murder."

It took me a minute to recover my voice; it has a way of deserting me during times of extreme stress. "You think somebody pushed the car into the water with Domingo in it?"

"Seems possible." He did a bunch more presses, the machine squealing its need for a lube job.

"Were the car windows open or closed?" I asked.

"Open."

We all worked out without talking for a few minutes. "How come he couldn't get himself out?" I asked. "Did he panic or something?"

Bristow turned his elegant brown head on the bench and looked at me. "He was probably unconscious, Charlie. There was a lot of alcohol in his body. And I do mean a lot. There was an empty Jim Beam bottle in the car. He had drunk directly from it. The whole fifth, apparently."

I let go of the "oars." "Domingo told Zack and me he didn't drink," I exclaimed.

Zack nodded agreement. "Dude said he'd never

been to Paulie's Place and didn't ever drink, so he hung out at The Grange."

Zack was still trudging along on the treadmill. He didn't look at all like himself in grey sweats that had seen better days. I was used to seeing him in black Western gear. If he wore sweats more often, my hormones might stop leaping around like Mexican jumping beans whenever he was in their neighborhood.

"He *never* drank?" Bristow said.

I cudgeled my brain to come up with the precise words Domingo had used. "He said 'I don't drink. Ever. Hate the taste of the stuff. Makes me sick.' "

"Not barf sick—ill," Zack added.

Bristow pushed up on the levers of the old machine, wincing at the sound. "Well that would explain it then," he muttered.

"What?" I demanded.

"Trenckman said Domingo didn't die by drowning. He died because of a severe reaction to the alcohol he'd ingested."

I'd read newspaper accounts of college kids killing themselves by chug-a-lugging during fraternity hazing rituals. As far as I knew it hadn't become common in sorority houses. Yet.

"He was dead when he went into the water?" I asked.

He nodded.

I rowed some more. "When did all this happen?"

"Trenckman said he'd been in the water around six hours. Which means he went in around two or two-thirty."

"Nobody saw it happen?"

"Nobody saw nada. Boats coming in and out various times of the day, no way of checking who was where when. We've put out a media request for any information anyone can supply. No response so far."

"Did you track down Domingo's relatives yet?"

"According to John Avila, he didn't have any. Mother and father deserted him soon after they came to the U.S. At that time, John tried to track them down to help support the kid, but didn't have any success."

John Avila. Big John—the Condor police officer who had taken Domingo under his wing—"Like Mother Goose, you know?" Domingo had said.

Nausea flapped around in my stomach like a trapped bird.

"You talked to Big John then?" I asked when I was able to speak again. "Was he able to tell you anything about Domingo? Did he know if he ever went back to the Philippines? Did he know how well he was acquainted with Estrella?" I suddenly remembered I'd been holding back a bit of information. "You do know it was Felicia's car Domingo was in?"

Bristow turned his head on the bench and scowled at me. "How did *you* know that, Ms. Plato?"

When Bristow calls me Ms. Plato it usually means he's losing patience. I explained hastily about almost recognizing the car on television, subsequently going to Hair Raising to get a haircut. "Felicia was going on about her car being stolen and the police not seeming to care," I finished.

Bristow sat up. "Ms. Johnny-on-the-spot, that's you!" He rubbed the back of his shapely bald head and sighed. "Okay, Charlie, tell me exactly, *pre*-cisely, what Ms. Godfrey said."

"Is she a person of interest?" I asked.

The jaundiced look he gave me persuaded me I'd better give some information before asking for it. I told him everything from the time Felicia slammed in to the hair salon to when she stomped out.

He lay down and did a few more bench presses before commenting, then he asked in a thoughtful tone, "Are you sure she said, 'It *was* my car.'"

I frowned, got up from the rowing machine, and went over to the knee machine. It was set at an impossible-to-move weight. I moved the lever down, then squinted at myself in the spotted mirror on the wall and replayed the scene in my mind. "She didn't use that emphasis," I told him. "She said, 'It's the principle of the thing. It was *my* car.'"

"But she did speak of her car in the past tense?"

I looked at him with admiration. "It would seem more natural to use the present tense wouldn't it? 'It is *my* car.'"

"Possibly." He glanced over at me—I was on the other side of him now. "Do you know of any animosity between Estrella and Ms. Godfrey?"

I shook my head. "Felicia said she and Estrella weren't all that close, but I didn't get the impression she was hostile. You could maybe talk to the other women in the salon. They'd know, working close together the way they do. Maisie especially seems willing to talk."

I paused. "I thought I had this whole thing figured out," I said. "Are you *sure* Domingo didn't commit suicide? Why don't I tell you what I thought, and you tell me if it sounds logical."

"A Plato is never illogical," Bristow said—a reference to the philosopher my late father had insisted belonged somewhere on my family tree. I had my doubts about that, but I was willing to accept any compliments on Dad's behalf, especially if they rubbed off on me.

"First of all, three months ago, Felicia lends Estrella her car," I said. "Which Estrella then uses to transport a man, a man she was surprised to see, a man wearing baggy jeans, a sweater or jacket, and a ball cap. All of which is according to Roderick Effington III. Somewhere around the same time, Felicia sees Estrella in Paulie's Place with a dark-haired man wearing aviator shades and a ball cap. This is confirmed by Mandy, the latest member of Zack's doll brigade . . ."

"Hey!" Zack protested when Bristow shot him a questioning glance.

I ignored the interruption, but amended the description out of a sense of fairness. ". . . Zack's *friend* Mandy, a waitperson at Paulie's Place. Mandy sees Estrella and the dark-haired man together on a couple of occasions, on the second of which—New Year's Eve—they are arguing. Something to do with Estrella breaking a promise. Later on, Estrella tells Candy that the man who was with her in Paulie's Place is her old boyfriend from the Philippines, and they had talked about the good old days back home. She told Maisie she and her old boyfriend were having an affair and that sex with the man was exciting, because it was a little dangerous."

I squinted at Bristow, who was sitting up squinting quizzically at me. "Stay with me, okay? Domingo was gay, right? Maybe when Estrella said sex with the man had an edge of danger, she was referring to him being gay and the prevalence of AIDS. If we accept that Domingo was Estrella's old boyfriend in spite of being gay, then everything fits. He could have killed the first husband, then followed Estrella here when he found out she'd married a rich man . . ."

I held up a hand as Bristow seemed about to interrupt. "I *know* Domingo was supposedly in the U.S. long before Estrella, but he could have gone back to the Philippines and done all that in a fairly short time. So then Estrella comes to the United States and Domingo gets cozy with her again, and maybe she wants him to kill *this* husband for her. Thane Stockton, I mean. Maybe she pays Domingo the money for that reason, or maybe he refuses to kill Thane but wants the money not to tell about the first husband. But then he and Estrella have another falling-out and he rapes her, then kills her and tosses her body over the bridge."

I gave Bristow a second to comment, but he waved me on with a courtierlike flourish. Definitely Shakespearean. And reeking of sarcasm. "Well, I'm a little vague after that. As we haven't heard of or run into any other Filipino man apart from Domingo, it would seem to me Domingo *must* have been Estrella's old boyfriend. She could have been referring to old school days. Maybe he was her boyfriend before he admitted to himself he was gay. That happens, you know. So maybe they picked the relationship up again when Estrella came here, even if by then Domingo had decided to come out of the closet. If he *was* the old boyfriend, then he knew about Felicia's old car and where it was usually parked because Estrella had driven him to Paulie's Place, possibly in that very car. Maisie said the boyfriend had joked about the old car, then was blown away when he saw the Mercedes. So he comes back to the parking lot and steals the car again yesterday—he's despondent, afraid you're getting close to arresting him for Estrella's murder."

I paused, searching for possible holes in my argument. Bristow was looking negative. "I guess he needs a key. Maybe he hot-wires the car, whatever that means, then drives it to Pillar Point and drives himself into the water."

"The alcohol?" Bristow asked.

I'd forgotten the whiskey. "He drinks to give himself courage, then passes out, and the car rolls into the water."

"A second ago, you said he drove into the water," Zack said.

"Details," I said.

Bristow had turned around on the bench to face me. He had such a knowing smile on his face I could tell I was about to get trounced. Zack must have sensed it, too. He got off the treadmill and leaned against the barre, giving me his thin-lipped smile accompanied by puckishly slanted eyebrows and a glint in the famous grass green eyes. I had to revise my former thought about his wearing apparel making a difference to his charisma. He could be dressed in rags and smile that smile and every corpuscle in my body, white or red, would do the wave.

"I had a talk with John Avila a few days ago," Bristow said. "That's how come I was called in. John was called to Pillar Point on Friday because one of the first officers on the scene recognized Domingo and remembered seeing him with John and his family on various social occasions. John in turn knew that Domingo was a person of interest in the Stockton case, so suggested I should be contacted."

"So what did Big John say?" I asked.

"Domingo did indeed come to Condor thirteen years ago when he was sixteen," Bristow continued. "He'd had a couple of run-ins earlier with the Manila police, but it was only adolescent mischief. As was the trouble he got into when he arrived here. John took an interest in him, helped get him through school, then got him a job at a major San Francisco restaurant as a waiter. Sometime later Domingo transferred into hotel security and worked his way up. According to his former employers he was a reliable and responsible employee. Which is also the verdict of his current employer at the Bellamy Park Bank. Domingo Romero might dress funny when off duty and act spaced-out on occasion, but he was evidently a responsible citizen."

"But is Big John sure Domingo didn't return to the Philippines at all?"

Bristow bowed his head in mock submission. "I will concede that according to John Avila, Domingo returned to Manila a couple of times."

"Well then?"

"I have instituted inquiries, as they say."

I went back to lifting the leg weights while I thought. "Even if Domingo wasn't the old boyfriend, he might still have murdered Estrella," I pointed out. "Maybe he committed suicide out of remorse."

"You would pluck out the heart of my mystery," Bristow declaimed in the vibrant voice he used whenever he was quoting the bard. Then he went on in his normal tone. "After he was dead, Domingo was moved from the passenger seat to the driver's seat," Bristow said.

"Oh." That put a serious dent in my scenario. About to ask how he could be sure of that, I remembered that at the moment of death sphincters let go. The trapped bird fluttered around in my stomach again.

"I'm still watching Thane Stockton closely," Bristow went on. "Even as we speak, I have someone questioning him about his movements yesterday."

"He didn't answer his telephone around five o'clock," I conceded. "But don't forget it's almost impossible for him to bring himself to leave the grounds. And I can't think of any way he'd know about Felicia's car. Though I suppose Domingo could have driven it somewhere to meet him ... even if Domingo wasn't Estrella's boyfriend, he might have known about the car. He mentioned giving Estrella a lift to work himself while her Mercedes was in the shop."

I sighed. "I still like my scenario best. But if the body was moved ..."

"It would seem to me that you perhaps perceive Thane Stockton as needy and previously ill-treated, and you are forming these complex theories in order to protect him."

"I am *not* forming theories," I said. "I was laying

out a scenario that fitted all the known facts, until you came along and blew me out of the water. So to speak."

Bristow scowled and seemed about to snap something back, but Zack stepped in as peacemaker. "Nobody's sayin' anythin' about Rory," he pointed out. "Seems to me anyone wears an Air Force flight jacket and cap is more'n likely to wear aviator shades."

"Zack came up with this idea from watching Tom Cruise in *Top Gun*, except he was a Navy pilot," I told Bristow.

Bristow looked justifiably confused.

"Dandy Mandy the waitperson said the man with Estrella wore aviator shades," I reminded him. "What Zack failed to take into consideration was that Roderick Effington III is definitely not a Filipino."

Wait a minute. There was something worth pondering there.

Bristow was looking at his watch. "I'm off," he said. "I'll try to catch you later at CHAPS, but I may not make it."

"I'm still savin' that Dom Pérignon, waitin' for party time," Zack said.

"It may be well and truly aged before we get to it," Bristow said.

They both looked at me. I was still sitting on the knee machine, brooding. "Wait a minute," I said.

They waited.

"I've been taking it for granted that Estrella's old boyfriend was Filipino," I said slowly. "Mainly because that's what Maisie said. But what Candy originally told Zack was that Estrella said the man with her in Paulie's

Place, the man Felicia saw her with, was her old boy-friend from the Philippines."

"So?" Zack asked.

Bristow's eyes were showing their friendly amber color. "Go on," he said.

"All that means is that the man was Estrella's boy-friend in the Philippines," I said. "Maisie interpreted it to mean he was Filipino, but she said she'd never met him. So she didn't *know* he was Filipino, did she? And if he wasn't, if we turn that around and *say* he wasn't, then I'm thinking about Rory maybe being in the United States Air Force, and the United States Air Force having a presence in the Philippines until fairly recently, so Rory *could* have been the old boy-friend from the Philippines."

"Rory said he was 'almost' a policeman," Zack contributed.

I nodded. "He said he wasn't in favor of anarchy—he respected law-enforcement officers because he was almost one himself," I recalled.

Bristow was shaking his head, his eyes glinting with amusement now. "How you two amateurs do build a case," he said. "I'm afraid it has a muddy bottom in this instance. I've looked pretty thoroughly into Mr. Effington's background."

Zack nodded wisely. "Old Lazarro used always to be highly suspicious of the person who found the body," he said.

"What did you find out?" I asked Bristow.

"He worked for a few weeks some years ago as a night watchman, at one of the businesses in Silicon Valley. That may be what he was referring to when

he talked about almost being a policeman. He did catch
a would-be burglar once and turned him over to the
local police. His employer was quite happy with him—
seems he'd stay after hours and chat about the state
of the world with Effington, said he was a wise man.
Unfortunately, the wise man decided steady work was
too draining on the health and intellect and handed in
his notice."

"Did you find out if he did any military service?"
Zack asked.

Bristow nodded. "Evidently, he wanted to be a pilot.
He was accepted, but after a few months he showed
up with some kind of heart murmur. Nothing life-
threatening but enough to get him discharged. Honor-
ably discharged."

"So he might have taken to aviator shades during
that period," Zack said. He was never one to let go of
an idea once he had one.

"I can't imagine Effington in the military at all,"
Bristow said.

Wait a minute.

"What?" Bristow asked, though I hadn't spoken.

I shook my head. I didn't want any more snide
remarks about amateurs building a case, or me making
up complex theories in order to protect Thane Stockton. Besides, the idea that had come to me was so
unexpected that I didn't think I could even put it into
words until I'd thought about it for a while.

CHAPTER 21

I tried Maisie's number again the following morning. Once again, her answering machine picked up. My imagination painted in an image of her empty apartment.

After I hung up, I kept hearing her voice saying, "I've been thinking about that nickname," and "I have a date tonight, Charlie." That was on Saturday. This was Monday.

When it was time for the self-defense class, I watched the entrance from the main corral as anxiously as a mother bird awaiting her fledgling's return from its maiden flight.

I saw P.J. enter—she'd gone back to wearing sweats. She'd evidently noticed Duke's attentions to Gina and had given up on him.

As if she'd heard me think her name, Gina came in. She cast a glance at the bar where Angel had lately taken to making busy while the self-defense class was in session. I saw disappointment crease her face and almost, but not quite, well up in her eyes before she smiled bleakly at me and wished me good-morning. For a moment, she hesitated, and I was afraid she was going to ask me if I'd talked to Angel. I didn't want to tell her what he'd said.

Savanna came in soon after Gina. She was wearing grey sweats and bright red sneakers. A red ribbon kept her hair tied back neatly out of her way. I wondered if that glow was going to last her the rest of her life. I hoped it would.

By twos and threes the rest of the group strolled in. And finally, so did Duke.

"Did you hear anything from Maisie Ridley?" I asked him. "She hasn't shown up."

He raised his dark eyebrows as he shrugged out of his parka, folded it, and placed it neatly on a barstool. "Maisie who?"

"Ridley. The Englishwoman who comes to the class. Blond, kind of plump. Late forties. Fifty maybe. I've been trying to reach her all weekend, but she wasn't home, and she hasn't turned up this morning. She's usually the first one through the door."

He shrugged, his expression showing that he didn't really remember Maisie too well, and wasn't all that concerned if she was among those present or not. As usual, he was dressed in a black loose-fitting top and black baggy pants. His dark hair had been neatly combed, but was a little ragged around the edges. He needed a haircut. I thought of Estrella.

"Ready for action, ladies?" he called out, and the women, who had split up into little conversational groupings, gathered around.

"You up for some action, Charlie?" he asked with a quirk of one eyebrow. I supposed that was a reference to my medical procedure—the one I didn't want to think about today, or I'd find myself sitting staring at the telephone, willing it to ring.

"Sure," I said.

What I wanted to do was go call Bristow and find out if he'd followed up on Maisie. That led to another thought, and I shook my head. "Give me a minute, okay? Do some warming up or something." Without waiting for a response, I took off to the office.

"No, Maisie is not here," Felicia said, sounding irritated. "I have three ladies here waiting for her. You'll have to schedule some other time, Charlie."

"Did the police find your car?" I asked.

"I don't know," she said after a pregnant pause, which told me they had probably told her what had happened but asked her not to talk about it.

"Ready?" Duke asked when I returned to my place in the circle. His voice was edged with impatience. What was he in such a hurry for?

"I guess," I allowed. I was more worried about Maisie than ever. She might not answer her phone on a weekend, sure, but to not turn up for work when she had clients scheduled . . .

I'd call Bristow as soon as the class was over, I decided. Insist he put out an APB.

"Charlie?" Duke asked, evidently noticing I'd drifted off.

When he was sure he had my attention he did his drill-sergeant walk around the circle, discussing what to do if someone attacked. Evidently the class had gone over this the week before while I was on the bench, so to speak. They kept nodding as he enumerated options.

"One: Run, if possible. Often, retreat is your best

defense. If you think someone's following you, go to the nearest building that looks occupied. Knock on the door. If the individual won't open the door, ask him or her to call the police. 2: If you are cornered, talk to the attacker, try to de-escalate the situation. 3: Yell for help if anyone is nearby. 4: Try to stay calm. 5: If attacked, do something. Fight back with whatever weapons you have. 6: On the other hand, if robbery is obviously the motive, don't fight, give him whatever he wants. 7: If he's armed, get yourself out of the line of fire if possible, or try to confuse the attacker. If you can't do that, try to slap the gun aside, into his body. Don't try to grab it. We'll go over all the techniques again in a little while. The main thing is to try to relax. Breathe in through your nose and out through your mouth to oxygenate your blood. If you stiffen up, you won't be able to move."

He turned on his heel to look all around the circle again. "What do we yell?"

"BACK OFF!" we shouted.

The wagon-wheel light fixtures clinked in response. But just as I was thinking our vocal cords had come a long way from that first lesson, I realized those tectonic plates beneath the earth's crust were jostling each other again.

This was not a serious tremor, but it wasn't quite minor either. We all stood very still as the floor rolled and trembled and the electric power fizzled. A couple of bottles of Pellegrino water fell off the main corral bar. Somebody cussed. It might even have been me. I had planned on watching Duke all through the lesson, hoping for something I could give to Bristow, something positive, something physical, instead of just my own deductions and a play on words. Now it looked as if the class was going to be terminated.

"We'd better go outside, just in case," I suggested, as the emergency lights came on.

The women grumbled good-naturedly but headed for the plaza door, which was the nearest exit. I looked around for Duke and didn't see him at first, but then picked him out near the bar, where he was retrieving his jacket. In the dim light, his black "pajamas" made him well-nigh invisible. Even his jacket was black.

No doubt about it, his kung-fu outfit could definitely be described as baggy, I thought as he came toward me. I added this to the information I'd put together the previous night.

As we emerged into the bright cool sunshine, Duke unzipped the left hand pocket of his parka, pulled out a pair of sunglasses, and put them on. Aviator sunglasses.

My peripheral vision picked up a number of people in the plaza, outside the bank and Leah Stoneham's physical-therapy clinic, the Casa Blanca Restaurant and the Granada apartments across the way. But I couldn't pull my gaze away from Duke Conway's sunglasses. They weren't enough physical evidence for Bristow, but they were enough to convince me my imagination hadn't been running wild.

Duke had noticed I was watching him. He was smiling sexily in a way that indicated he thought I was interested in him.

If he only knew *how* interested.

Best if he didn't know, I reminded myself as I

averted my gaze. I certainly wasn't going to pull any foolish stunts while he was among those present. I wasn't going to do a damn thing to make him think I suspected him of anything. I was going to wait until everyone went home, then wait for Angel and Zack to arrive—Angel had promised to come in around noon to practice a new line dance with me. Zack was supposed to show up, too. He never taught lessons, but he liked to keep up with the latest dances. We had some other chores to take care of after practicing.

As soon as Zack and Angel arrived, I'd tell them what I was thinking, and if they agreed it seemed possible, I'd put a call into the police station, tell Bristow what I suspected, and let him take it from there.

In spite of myself I found my speculative gaze going back to Duke's face. "Maybe we ought to call it a day," I suggested when a few minutes went by without further earthquake action. "There's not much point hanging around waiting for . . ." I broke off as Duke gestured at the bank's windows, where the lights had come back on. The employees started going back in.

"Okay," I said. "I guess we can give it another go."

"Didn't you tell me you were in the Army?" I asked Duke as we all trooped back into CHAPS. So much for all my good intentions.

"I may have done," he said. "I *was* in the Army, that's for sure."

"I believe you said you were a military policeman?"

He nodded.

My heart had started beating rapidly. I had to quit right now before I blurted out some stupid question that would give me away. "Where were you stationed?"

my mouth asked, with, I swear, no intention on my part.

"Europe mostly," he answered readily enough. "Germany for a while. What's with the interrogation, Charlie?"

I managed a smile, though my cheeks felt as if they'd been sprayed with starch. "I have an inquiring mind, Duke."

Behind me, Savanna laughed. "Everybody knows that, Duke," she said. "Charlie's the nosiest person was ever born."

Excusing myself, I ran up to my loft to check on Benny. He was trembling a little, and I held him and petted him until he felt better, then put him back in his cage with a treat to munch on. I hesitated, looking at my telephone, wondering if I should call Bristow now. No, it was much better to wait until the women were safely out of the way and Duke was out of the building. See how sensibly I was thinking?

I trotted back down the stairs.

A military policeman could have traveled anywhere in the world, I thought as I picked up the broken glass from the floor beside the bar and mopped up the mineral water.

A military policeman. An M.P. With Estrella's slight speech impediment, her hesitation on the letter "p," it *could* have come out sounding like empty. She'd had an affair with "the instwuctor man," she'd teased Thane. "The M.P. man," she might have called her "old boy-friend from the Philippines." "The empty man," Maisie had heard.

Maisie.

Obviously, Maisie had realized the significance of the nickname, too. Had she *known* Duke had been an M.P.? Yes, he'd announced it to us all at the beginning of the first class.

Had Maisie called him up, arranged to meet him, to question him, I wondered as I took my place in the circle. Was that who her date had been with? "He *is* good-looking, isn't he?" she'd said after the first lesson. "And so well built." Had she confronted him?

No, I was not going to ask Duke if he'd been stationed in the Philippines. Though maybe I could ask him if he'd ever been based in the West Pacific? Nah, that would be totally dumb.

The class seemed to last forever. I kept goofing up, my mind unable to concentrate on the complicated maneuvers Duke was teaching us. I kept remembering disconnected things that were suddenly becoming connected.

Estrella had told Thane Stockton that she was having an affair with the instructor. "Sometimes Estrella told the truth, sometimes she lied. So I never knew when to believe her," Thane had said.

He should have believed her on that one.

The class ended at eleven-forty-five. As usual, the women lined up for mineral water. I put out bottles and glasses and a tub of ice.

Duke left right away. I felt tension drain from me as he strode off toward the lobby. It wasn't that I'd been afraid of *him*—he hadn't known what I was thinking, after all—I'd been more afraid of what my big mouth might blurt out that would give my thinking processes away.

Savanna was the last to leave. She'd begged off learning the new line dance today. She had some kind of special lunch at preschool with Jacqueline. "I'll be here as close to three as I can get," she said.

Today was Monday, so normally none of us would have been working, but it was also the last week of the month, and we needed to update the events board. The board advertises the live bands who'll be playing for the following month. It's a real pain to do—we have to take down the top band and move the next three up and add in a fourth. And then we have to do it all over again on the inside signboard.

I waved her away, telling her Zack and Angel and I could manage the boards, and I'd teach her the new dance in no time the following evening. When it came to dancing, Savanna was a very fast study. "You're sure it's Jacqueline you're having this special lunch with?" I teased as she turned away.

She blew me a raspberry. Savanna's the only person I know who can look beautiful doing that. "Taylor's on duty," she said. "He's still working on the Pillar Point thing."

I flashed on an image of Domingo strapped in a car that was spewing water as it was dragged out of the harbor.

A picture of Maisie's plump and rosy face followed. Would someone be fishing her out of the water next?

"I have to call Bristow," I said.

"Why?"

I shrugged. "Just a question that came up."

She frowned a little suspiciously, but then smiled and went on her way.

I waited until I heard the outer door close, then glanced at my watch. Angel and Zack were late. They might even have forgotten they were supposed to come in. Maybe I shouldn't wait any longer. I reached for the telephone—just as the lights went off again.

Damn. I held on to the bar and waited for the shaking to start. But it didn't. Possibly the sudden surge of electricity coming back on after the last shock had been too much for the power company. Few people remembered to switch everything off when the power failed. I was surprised when the emergency lights didn't come on automatically. Had anyone checked them lately, I wondered.

I fumbled underneath the bar until I came up with a flashlight and turned it on, then crouched to look for the battery-operated lamp Angel kept in the cupboard.

Damn again. We'd still be able to do the outside events board, but it was going to be impossible to practice the line dance without lights or music. We could do a few walk-throughs in the front foyer with the outer door open, maybe. Or out on the plaza. Perhaps I could get Zack to sing. Along with all his other accomplishments, he had a very pleasant croony sort of tenor voice.

As I put the little lamp on the bar, I became aware of movement in the shadows behind the deejay booth. Sundancer must have come in for some reason, I thought. I turned the flashlight in that direction and saw Duke Conway instead. My stomach tied itself up in a pretzel knot and sank like a chunk of concrete in a pond.

"Yo, Charlie," Duke said.

The flashlight glimmered on something he held in his right hand. A gun. Black and matte. I recognized it right away. I even remembered the name of it. Walther PPK. One of the guns Duke had passed around during one of the lessons. The lightweight 9mm pistol I'd felt most comfortable holding.

Stupidly, the first thing I thought was, *Well, of course.* In every mystery story if you show a gun, you have to use it.

I froze. All those self-defense classes, and I couldn't get my brain to function properly. It kept chanting about the fight or flight syndrome, and I wasn't doing either. I was just standing there like some stupid wild animal caught in a car's headlights.

"I guess we had another power failure," I said as Duke came closer, the gun held very easily, very steadily, in his hand.

I suppose I thought if I ignored the gun, I could fool him into thinking I hadn't noticed it, and he'd put it away before any harm was done.

"I turned the power off, Charlie," he said. He pointed with his left hand. "Turn the lamp on and the flashlight off, Charlie. Set the flashlight down on the bar, okay?"

I did as I was told.

He picked up the flashlight and stuck it in his jacket pocket. I supposed he was afraid I might throw it at him. I wished I'd thought of doing that.

Apparently, I wasn't functioning on all cylinders. The only instruction I was receiving from my brain was a repeat of one of the options Duke had listed earlier: "If you are cornered, talk to the attacker, try to de-escalate the situation."

"What's this all about, Duke?" I asked. My voice was supposed to come out sounding soothing—why did it choose this moment to crack? I didn't think it was any use trying to yell "Back off!" Duke probably wasn't going to pay much attention even if I succeeded in getting the words out.

His grin was as cocky as ever. "What gave me away?" he asked.

I gave it one more try. "About what?" I asked.

He kept on grinning. "You have a very honest face, Charlie. It shows what you're thinking. Maybe it's the freckles. One look at you, and I knew you knew."

Okay, here was something to talk about. Not the freckles, the *knowing*. I was dying to know the answers. *Nice turn of phrase, dying to know,* I complained to my brain. "You knew Estrella in the Philippines, right? You were the old boyfriend from the Philippines?"

"Estrella always did talk too much," he said with a grimace that gave his sharp-featured face a mean cast. "Soon as you mentioned her telling that husband of hers we'd had an affair I knew she was at it again. She never could keep things to herself."

He glanced at his wristwatch. I tensed, and he lifted the pistol a fraction of a centimeter, just enough to remind me of its presence. As though I needed reminding.

"I heard Savanna say she'd be back at three. Is that when you all get together around here?"

I nodded, not feeling it was necessary to tell him

Zack and Angel should be arriving any minute. I hoped. They had both been known to be tardy. Especially Zack.

"We'll hang around here a few minutes, make sure all the smokers get clear," he said. "Last I looked there were still a couple of women hanging out in the parking lot."

"Then what?" I asked.

"Why then we'll take one of those little rides bad guys talk about in old movies," he said.

I had a strong feeling of déjà vu. I'd taken one of those rides a few months ago. And had sworn I'd never feel that helpless again. That was why I'd organized the self-defense class in the first place. It was difficult for me to appreciate the irony of the situation, but I could certainly see it.

"I suppose you shoved Estrella's first husband through that window, huh?" I asked.

Okay, it probably wasn't a good idea to show that I knew about his previous homicide. I should have continued to play dumb. I *was* dumb, obviously. But even at this extremity, I couldn't resist finding out for sure what had happened.

"It doesn't take a lot of effort to push someone through an open window," he said bluntly.

"Did Estrella hire you to kill Carlos?" I asked.

He laughed shortly. "No way. I did it all for love, Charlie, would you believe that? Estrella and I met at some social function, years ago. We might have married, but we both had this fatal flaw—we wanted to be rich, and neither one of us had any money. I was an M.P. doing automobile repair on the side, she was a hairdresser."

"You met *before* she was married?"

"Sure—it was a setup right from the start. Carlos wasn't all that rich, but he was willing. Estrella came up with the idea of taking out an insurance policy on him. It was touch-and-go for a while, because the policy wouldn't pay on a suicide. We hadn't thought of it looking like suicide. We just didn't want it to look like murder."

He laughed again, and hitched a hip onto one of the barstools, as if he was relaxing into his story. But his gun hand was still rock-steady. "Estrella was supposed to split the insurance money with me, of course. After a while, we'd get married. She promised that. But somehow the money didn't arrive. She kept putting me off, telling me the check hadn't come through yet, the insurance company was still suspicious, we shouldn't see each other. Blah, blah, blah. Like a sucker, I was taken in. I believed her. Next thing I knew she'd vanished, and all I could find out was she'd married some American she'd met on the Internet. Took me a while to find out who and where."

"She must have been surprised to see you again."

There was something diabolical about his laugh. It had a self-satisfied sound to it. "Yeah, she was surprised, came up with all kinds of stories about how she had been abducted by this Stockton guy, hadn't had a chance to let me know where she was, how she was scared to death of him because he beat her up all the time, how she'd really like to be rid of him, just like the other one, and how she had him covered with an even bigger policy than Carlos."

"So you agreed to do him in?"

Where were Angel and Zack? They'd have some explaining to do if they didn't show up before this maniac took me off at gunpoint. I didn't want to examine that thought too closely. Like, who were they going to explain to?

I wasn't going for any little ride, I decided. If Duke really wanted to shoot me, he could shoot me right here and maybe get caught doing it.

"What?" he asked, suddenly looking at me with great suspicion. I must have changed my posture, shown some backbone, something.

"I asked if you agreed to do him in. Thane Stockton."

He glanced at his watch again. "Sure I went along with the *idea*, but I'm not that dumb, Charlie. I wasn't about to get in that situation again. She said she'd give me half the insurance she had on Thane, plus the money she got from the first guy, *and* she'd marry me. Like I wanted to marry her after the way she'd treated me. I told her I'd off the guy if she gave me the money first."

The cocky grin flashed again. "Guess what—she was the sucker this time. Soon as she paid me off, good-bye Estrella. She had it coming, Charlie, you must admit, she had it coming."

"You raped her," I said before I could stop myself.

He nodded. "Yeah well, she had that coming, too."

He unhitched himself from the stool. I felt myself stiffen and tried not to. I needed to be completely relaxed but alert, ready at the first opportunity to . . .

To do what? My brain scurried around, and produced a hopeful thought ...

"Before we go, Charlie, you have to tell me how you caught on to me. I might need to know if I get in this kind of situation again."

I debated refusing to tell him, but the longer I could keep him here, the more chance there was of Zack or Angel showing up. And getting shot?

"I remembered you were in the Army," I said. "I remembered you were a military policeman. I'd heard that Estrella called her old boyfriend the empty man. I realized she'd been saying the M.P. man." I swallowed. "Actually, at first I thought *Domingo* was the old boyfriend from the Philippines."

"He tried to blackmail me," Duke said indignantly. "Stupid little fruitcake. Seems Estrella told him about her friend from the Philippines, too, *and* gave him my name. Said she was going to pay me off, but if anything happened to her, he should tell the police it was me. He didn't want to get involved, but then I guess he saw the implications of the situation. If she'd paid me off before I killed her, I'd have money and might be willing to part with it. Or else he'd go to the police. That's what he said when he telephoned. Little dweeb actually had the nerve to threaten me."

"You agreed to pay him, I take it."

"Absolutely, no hesitation, glad to do it." He laughed that creepy laugh again. "Told him to meet me at Pillar Point at the boat ramp. Told him I was going fishing off the pier. He didn't suspect he was going to join the fishes. He did insist on meeting in broad daylight though. Guess he thought he'd be safe then."

"So you stole Felicia's car?"

He looked at me with something close to admiration. Which I didn't want from him. "You figured that out?"

"Someone saw you and Estrella get in that car one night, out back of Hair Raising. You're an auto mechanic, you'd find a way to start it without a key when you wanted it again."

He shook his head. "Nah. I took the car back for Estrella when she picked up her Mercedes. I automatically pocketed the key." He frowned. "Someone saw us? Who? I didn't see anybody around that parking lot."

I shrugged. "I just heard about it. I don't know who." I might not survive this, but I wasn't going to put Rory at risk.

"Yeah, well, I didn't want to chance someone seeing my van in the boat-ramp parking lot. It's recognizable. And I figured it would confuse hell out of the police if Domingo went down in Felicia's car. I had to think of something when he told me he'd be riding a motorbike. It wasn't going to be easy to prop him on a bike and get him rolling down that ramp." He laughed. "He made the mistake of getting in the car when I gestured him over. Not too swift, our Domingo."

His eyes narrowed as he remembered the scene. "I took a bottle of Jim Beam along—Estrella had told me her friend Domingo didn't drink. Figured it was a kind way for him to go. Not that he wanted to drink the whiskey, but he didn't have a whole lot of choice, with this baby pointing at him."

He jiggled the gun again. "Didn't really take him long to pass out. Nothing to it to move him over, give the car a push. Had to look like an accident. Drunk out of his skull, didn't know where he was or what he was doing."

I certainly wasn't going to tell him it hadn't looked like an accident at all. Obviously he hadn't realized Domingo was dead before he pushed him into the water.

There was some relief in knowing Domingo hadn't been killed by one of the people I'd mentioned him to. Though if Zack and I hadn't questioned him, he might not have thought of blackmailing Duke. I took in a much-needed breath of air.

Something changed in Duke's eyes, and his lips tightened. "Okay, Charlie, I doubt any of the ladies will still be hanging around outside. Let's get this show on the road."

I shook my head, but kept my eyes fixed on his face. I was about to make a move, and I didn't want him watching my hands. "I've been there, done that," I said. "I don't intend doing it again."

See how well I remembered what he'd taught me? *Try to confuse the attacker.* I couldn't quite see me vaulting over the bar and slapping the gun out of his hand, but I did have a plan.

And he did look confused.

And then the phone rang.

I don't know which of us was more startled, but I kept my cool better than he did. I picked up the receiver in my left hand, and, as his surprised gaze followed the action, I used the other hand to reach under the bar and grab the canister of pepper spray I'd made Angel put under there.

A split second later, I pushed down on the plunger and sprayed the stuff in short bursts right in Duke's startled face.

The effect was instantaneous.

His hands went to his face and he began coughing and choking uncontrollably. The gun was still in his right hand, and it seemed a good idea to dispose of that, so I pivoted smartly in a proper line-dancing manner, yanked open the wine captain, and grabbed the neck of the first bottle to come to hand.

As Duke staggered around, obviously blinded, his chest heaving as his lungs fought for air, I slammed the bottle against the back of his gun hand. The gun went flying. I flew after it and grabbed it, hopped smartly back behind the bar, and hung up the phone, which was squawking my name in a shocked but familiar voice.

Then I picked it up again and punched in 911.

The instructions that came with the spray had said the effect would last for thirty minutes, but Duke started coming out of it after ten. I thought I might write a letter of complaint to the manufacturer. I thought I was maybe suffering from posttraumatic shock. At the same time I felt tremendously powerful and proud of myself.

And terrified.

I had to zap Duke two more times with the spray to persuade him to stay down. I wasn't taking any chances.

I was still standing over Duke with the gun in one hand and the pepper spray in the other when Detective

Sergeant Bristow and a couple of officers hurtled in through the main entrance.

I thought Bristow was going to have an apoplectic fit. To tell the truth I wasn't sure if he was laughing or choking from leftover fumes as he bent over Duke and read him his rights.

The two patrolmen escorted Duke out. He was still bent over, still coughing. "Water," he kept saying, but nobody was paying any attention. Well, his voice was hoarse; maybe they couldn't understand him.

It was at that moment that Zack and Angel finally arrived. I glanced at my watch. They were half an hour late.

"No gold stars for punctuality for you guys," I said crossly. "I might have been dead for all you cared." My voice was a little hoarse. I'd inhaled some of the fumes myself.

Zack and Angel looked a little confused, which was fairly understandable, I supposed.

Bristow briefly filled them in, embroidering a little at the end. Something about dashing in to find me holding a smoking gun, with one foot on Duke's prone body.

He held out his hand. "Maybe you'd better give me the gun now, Charlie."

I couldn't seem to let go of it, so he very carefully pried it loose from my grip.

"Charlie," Zack said, coming up behind me. "Are you okay, darlin'?"

And wouldn't you know it, I immediately did the woman thing again and started shaking. He put his arms around me, which felt very very good. I decided

I wasn't going to move for several hours. Everyone needs a little cocooning from time to time.

I felt Bristow pry the spray canister loose from my left hand. "I hit his hand with that bottle," I told him, gesturing at the bar where at sometime I had set the bottle down. "That's how I got the gun away from him."

"D'you know what a chance you took?" Zack exclaimed.

I was moved by the concern in his voice. He did care about me, he really did. "That was Dom Pérignon in that bottle," he said. "Couldn't you have socked him with something cheaper?"

I would have kicked his shins, but he was holding on to me pretty tight.

CHAPTER 22

I have this recurring dream in which I follow Estrella Stockton out to her Mercedes on that cold January morning and talk her into going to a marriage counselor.

I don't know why my subconscious thinks this would do any good. She had already persuaded Duke to kill her first husband before I ever met her. Carlos Rosales would have been just as dead. Duke would still have demanded his money and probably killed her anyway. Domingo might still have remembered Estrella's "old boyfriend from the Philippines," and gotten himself murdered.

So why am I dreaming about Estrella? I guess, subconsciously, I feel that if I hadn't interfered, fate might have changed direction and given everyone a happy ending.

"I'm making a solemn vow here and now," I told Zack when he came around to see how I was holding up the following afternoon. "From now on, I'm not going to get involved in anyone else's life or death."

Sitting at ease in my old rocker, Benny cradled in his long-fingered, beautiful hands, Zack greeted my statement with his wry, slanted eyebrow smile. "Great idea, Charlie."

"If I even come close to poking my nose where it doesn't belong, I want you to remind me of this conversation," I went on.

"Sure, Charlie." His face sobered. "You really did take an awful big chance, darlin', and I'm not talkin' about the potential damage to the Dom Pérignon this time. You up to tellin' me exactly what happened yesterday?"

I sat down on the sofa. I'd been puttering around picking up my loft, stuffing newly laundered underwear in drawers, hanging shirts and jeans in the closet, sorting knives and forks in the cutlery drawer; the adrenaline rush from the previous day had been slow to subside. Domesticity might be boring, but it's also calming.

Like the ancient mariner in Coleridge's *Rime*, once I got started there was no stopping me. I told Zack everything, starting from the time I realized Estrella's old boyfriend's nickname must have been "the M.P. man" rather than "the empty man," and went straight on through my worries about Maisie, Duke's arrival, and the subsequent action, until I reached the part where the phone rang and distracted Duke just enough to allow me to zap him with the pepper spray.

Then I stopped. Abruptly.

"What?" Zack asked.

I guess my jaw had dropped. I couldn't believe it hadn't occurred to me to think about that phone call again until right now.

The voice squawking on the other end had sounded

familiar. As well it should. I'd been waiting for that
phone call all week, worrying about it, dreading it.

"It was Matilda who called," I exclaimed. "Dr. Hanssen's Matilda."

Sheriff Lazarro's deliberative frown appeared on
Zack's face. "The office manager? What was she callin'
about?"

"I didn't give her a chance to say. I dropped the
phone as I picked up the pepper spray. Then I hung
up on her so I could call 911." I swallowed dryly. "She
had to be calling with the results of my biopsy."

"She didn't call back?"

"I unplugged the telephone last night. I wanted to
be sure of a good night's sleep."

I got up and checked. Yep, the phone was still
unplugged. I plugged it in and checked that it had a
dial tone.

"Aren't you goin' to call her back?" Zack asked.

"Later," I said.

He carried Benny across the room and put him in
his cage, then came over to me and handed me the
receiver. "What's the number?" he asked, finger at the
ready.

I told him.

Matilda was glad I'd called. She'd tried to get me
a couple of times this morning, she said. "That tavern
of yours gets pretty wild sometimes, I guess," she said.
"I called yesterday and someone picked up the phone,
but all I could hear was a lot of heavy breathing and
somebody cussing."

"We had a bit of a ruckus," I said feebly, then took

a deep breath and asked "Were you calling with the results of my tests?"

"Everything was negative," she said right away.

For one long stupid moment I remembered a *Seinfeld* episode in which George Constanza called his doctor to get the result of a medical test and was told it was negative. "Negative? Oh God, why me, why me," he'd whined until he was informed a negative result was good, he was going to live.

"Thank you," I said, when my eyes uncrossed. I hung up and considered that lately I was making almost as many references to TV series as Zack. Maybe I should get rid of the television set. Could a single American nineties woman manage without a television set, I wondered.

I also considered the possibility that I was suffering from some kind of silent hysterics.

"I'm okay," I told Zack. "I don't have cancer." He'd been standing by. He was always ready and willing to comfort and console any damsel in distress. He was also quite happy to celebrate good news. The end result was the same. Lickety-split, I was in his arms, doing the woman thing one more time, sobbing my heart out—with relief this time.

His gentle kiss on my cheek brought me out of it. Following his usual pattern, my mouth was scheduled to be next, and in my weakened state, my body would probably not want to listen to my brain telling it to repel all boarders.

If you're wondering why I couldn't just relax and enjoy one more of Zack's kisses, which were after all pretty wonderful and memorable, not to mention soul-stirring, I will remind you that getting involved with a man who loved women as much as Zack does would be akin to skating on thin ice, playing with fire, dancing on a razor's edge, sitting on a barrel of gunpowder, going to sea in a sieve, throwing caution to the wind, and hanging by a hair—all at the same time.

"My nose is running," I announced.

I've learned how to shatter a potentially romantic scene. It's one of my automatic defense mechanisms. It works very well.

"I guess I should tell you the rest of the story," I announced when I returned from mopping myself up in the bathroom.

Zack had reseated himself. His answering grin was wry. The danger had passed one more time.

"So I dropped the phone and reached for the pepper spray the minute Duke's attention was distracted," I said, picking up where I'd left off and seating myself at the end of the sofa that was farthest from Zack. "I sprayed it just the way he'd showed us in class. . . ."

When I was all through with my tale, I felt empty, cleaned out, but very glad to be alive. "You know what's the best part?" I said, and went on without waiting for an answer. "I had almost convinced myself that phone call from Dr. Hanssen's office was going to be a sentence of death. Instead of which it saved my life. Isn't that something?"

"Sure is," Zack agreed.

He was silent for a long time, apparently thinking it all through. "So what happened to Maisie?" he asked at last. "Did you or Taylor ever track her down?"

I shook my head. "I don't *know* what's happened

to Maisie. She's been on my mind through all of this. I called her again this morning, but all I got was Big Ben and 'Rule Britannia.' I'm afraid something awful's happened to her. Don't you think it seems suspicious that she'd disappear right after saying she'd been thinking about the boyfriend's nickname?"

Zack's jawline assumed its wise and pensive slant, but he didn't come up with any ideas.

It wasn't until the following evening, when Bristow came over just as CHAPS was closing, that I found out what had happened to Maisie.

"Seems all that talk about old boyfriends got her to thinking about one of hers from grammar-school years," Bristow told me. "She remembered hearing that he'd emigrated to Canada, so she made a few phone calls and discovered he was a widower, rich beyond the dreams of avarice, living on Vancouver Island. After talking to her on the telephone, he flew down here in his private plane and they fell into each other's arms. Evidently he remembered her as fondly as she remembered him, and they spent the next few days at the Saint Francis Hotel in San Francisco making whoopee, or whatever the Brit equivalent is. Last I heard, they were holed up there still."

We were sitting at our usual table in the main corral—Bristow, Zack, Savanna, Angel, and I.

"How did you find all this out?" Angel asked, curious as always about methods of detecting.

"My experience, hairstylists are talkative people," Bristow said. He ran a hand over the back of his elegant brown head. "Not that I often have dealings with hairstylists," he added, then grinned at Angel. "In this case, it was a manicurist. Maisie had confided in Candy. Candy confided in me."

Feeling extremely relieved, I nevertheless checked Zack's eyes for any signs of reminiscent gleam at the mention of Candy's name, but they were quite contented-looking. He did catch *my* glance, however, and gave me back one of his specialized zingers from under his eyelashes.

I caught my breath and saw Savanna smile mischievously.

"I went to see Thane Stockton today," I said, to show her my equilibrium was restored. I glanced sideways at Zack. "I told him Champers was alive."

Bristow frowned. "Champers? Who's Champers?"

"It's a shaggy-dog story," Zack said. He smiled at me. "I take it Thane was a happy camper?"

"Extremely happy. When I left he was already talking on the phone to Dr. Andersen. He was so excited he could hardly get the words to come out straight."

I looked at Bristow. "Mr. Stockton said he was inclined to blame himself for Domingo getting killed, thinking he should have stood up for himself early on and thrown Estrella out of the house, but I got him to see that this whole thing started with Duke and Estrella deciding to kill Carlos Rosales. I told him he was just a sort of way station along the road they chose, and pretty lucky not to be dead himself."

Bristow nodded. "According to Duke's confession, Estrella definitely had him slated for a tragic accident." He leaned forward, his amber eyes glinting. "Your friend Roderick the Third had a narrow escape, too."

"It was Duke who mugged him?" Zack asked.

Bristow nodded.

"I told you Duke's aura was black," Angel said.

"To think that man had his hands around my throat," Savanna said with a melodramatic shudder, then added, "I'm always amazed when people confess to such crimes. Surely they'd be better off waiting for the State to prove them guilty."

"There's a tremendous pressure to tell someone," Bristow said. "It builds and builds until the guilty party can't stand to keep it inside anymore. Usually after they confess, they feel tremendous relief."

He laughed shortly. "Until they talk to their lawyer, that is. Then they start yelling about coercion and denying the whole thing all over again. I'm looking for that to happen with Duke."

He threw me a suspicious glance. "You're very quiet all of a sudden, Ms. Plato."

"I was thinking about Rory," I said. "I went to see him, too. I wasn't sure if you'd told him about Duke, and I thought as he was in on the start, he had a right to know how it ended."

"I gave him a rough outline," Bristow said. "I didn't tell him Duke had deliberately come looking for him after seeing him on TV though. Seems Duke hadn't known about the camp down there in the old creek bed, had no idea anyone was down there until after he'd tossed the sleeping bag over with Estrella inside it."

He hesitated. "Duke explained the sleeping bag by the way. Seems it just happened to be handy. Sometimes he's asked to give self-defense classes in out-of-the-way places. He charges for lodging expenses but

camps out in his van for a few days while he's going
through the course."

"His lodging will be paid for by the taxpayers for
a while," I said. "Maybe he can teach self-defense tac-
tics to the prison guards."

Bristow laughed. "He said the van also came in
handy as a love nest when a situation called for it.
Seems he made a practice of never taking a ladyfriend
home. Anyhow, when Mr. Effington went hopping
around yelling about the sky falling, it startled Duke
into looking over the bridge, and he was afraid there
might have been enough light for Effington to see him.
After thinking it over for a day or two, he decided he
might as well finish him off just in case, who was going
to care? But he didn't hit him hard enough. Your friend
Rory is fairly hard-headed."

"He's a very good-natured and entertaining person," I said defensively. "It seems a shame he has to
live the way he does. I don't know why we couldn't do
something about housing for him."

"He smells, Charlie," Zack reminded me, as if anyone could forget Rory's aroma.

"We could find him a place with a bath," I said.

"You want us to rent an apartment for him?" Bristow asked.

"We could club together," Savanna suggested.

"I think he'd feel lonely in an apartment," I said.

"He's not movin' in with me," Zack said. "I'm sorry,
darlin'. I like ole Rory myself, but I do value my pri-
vacy."

Meaning he needed a house to himself to entertain

whatever member of his doll brigade was on call, I supposed. "I wasn't thinking of asking *you*," I said.

"Who then?" Angel asked.

I was glad to see him join in the discussion. As usual he'd been pretty quiet so far. I'd hoped he might have made up with Gina after everything that had gone down, maybe offered her some comfort. It had to be pretty traumatic to find out you'd been dating a murderer. But he was still holding out. Men can be so damn stubborn.

"Well," I said. "I did get to thinking about Thane Stockton, because after all . . ."

"Whoa, darlin'," Zack interrupted. "You told me to remind you not to interfere with people. Charlie's made a solemn vow," he told the others. "No more getting involved with other people's lives or deaths."

"This is not interfering, this is just common sense," I pointed out. "There's poor Mr. Stockton living all alone in that huge mansion of his, afraid to go outside the grounds, and there's Rory, who's not afraid of anything, but doesn't have a home. Rory would be really good company for Thane, don't you think? They are both cultured men."

"Don't tell me you've suggested this to Effington?" Bristow exclaimed.

"All I did was set up a chess match between them," I said. "I asked Rory if he played chess, and he said he used to be pretty good. He was very intrigued by the idea of an outdoor chess set. And you know, now that Adler Hutchins is so taken with his new grandson, he might not have as much time to spend with Mr. Stockton. Whereas Rory has all the time in the world.

I did explain to Mr. Stockton that it might be a good idea to invite Rory to have a bath before they start the match. He has eight bathrooms in that house. Eight!"

Nobody seemed to have anything to say. Probably they'd been struck dumb by the logic and wisdom of my plan.

"Rory's also very fond of cocker spaniels," I added brightly. "I asked him, and he said so."

Savanna was laughing, Angel shaking his head, Zack smiling fondly.

After a moment, Bristow sort of shook himself, and said to Zack, "It's my understanding that bottle of Dom survived Charlie's use of deadly force. Maybe this would be a good time to open it? While I try to put all this together with Charlie's vow of noninterference, I believe I feel a need for some kind of libation."

Zack rose at once and retrieved the bottle, which I had placed back in the wine captain. We all waited while he smoothly removed the wire hood—the *coiffe*, they call it in France, he informed us, and poured the lovely bright liquid into five flutes.

Zack proposed a toast to Taylor Bristow and Savanna Seabrook, and we all raised our glasses. I hoped no one would notice that I didn't drink.

While the others talked and laughed and discussed wedding plans I studied the ascending bubble-streams, not at all sure I could drink any of the champagne, considering the last time I'd handled this bottle.

Eventually Zack noticed that I was pondering the situation and brought out another bottle, removed the foil, the hood, and the cork, and poured me a fresh glass.

Sometimes our man-in-black is so sensitive and thoughtful, not to mention virile and all-out attractive, I'm tempted to put my brain on hold, grab him by the hand, and drag him up to my upstairs lair, there finally to allow my body to win out over my brain and ride off into the sunset as so many women have ridden ahead of me.

Zack's green eyes had assumed their "squinting into a dust storm" mode. "I've heard tell that new restaurant on San Pablo Avenue is very classy," he said, speaking only to me. I could feel the others looking from Zack to me and back again, maybe exchanging a glance or two in between.

"French cuisine," Zack murmured. "Each plate a work of art. Sensual surroundings, too. Soft lights. Softer music. Sofas instead of chairs. A waiter for every customer. I've heard they serve the food covered with glass domes, then the waiters remove the lids at precisely the same moment."

"Classy indeed," I murmured back.

"I guess you'd probably be too chicken to try it out with me," Zack said.

"That restaurant is booked up until midsummer," I told him, not without regret. "There's no way anyone can get a reservation. Doc Hanssen told me he even offered the maître d' hotel a bribe, but the man is incorruptible."

Zack smiled his bad-boy smile.

Silly me. Imagine you owned a restaurant and one of the major sex symbols of the twentieth century called wanting a reservation for himself and a friend.

Would *you* say no?

"We could schedule a proper celebration," Zack continued. "Next Monday maybe when we aren't so exhausted." He paused. "They say couples who dine there come out crazy for love."

We were still looking at each other.

Sometimes Zack's smile starts way back in his eyes, then moves forward slowly.

"Is this celebration going to include any of us?" Savanna asked the table at large.

"Looks to me like Zack's suggesting a much more private affair," Bristow said.

"What d'you suppose Charlie's going to say?" Angel asked.

"This is a very dramatic moment," Savanna said.

"Sparks flying to a fare-thee-well," Bristow said.

"Say something, Charlie," Angel said.

"Say yes," Zack said.

I took a sip of my champagne, then smiled at Zack. "To be continued," I said.

AUTHOR'S NOTE

Meg Chittenden's web site is at
http://www.techline.com/~megc
email: megc@techline.com

Please turn the page for
an exciting sneak peek of
Margaret Chittenden's
newest Charlie Plato mystery
DON'T FORGET TO DIE
now on sale wherever
hardcover mysteries are sold!

Every once in a while I get twisted up in my sleep, wake up with a crick in my neck, and take myself off to my chiropractor, who fixes me up in no time. Actually, I go even when I don't need to. Regular adjustments keep a person healthy.

Dr. Yarrow's clinic is conveniently situated on Cavenaugh Street, in one of those upscale medical malls that have huge skylights and a jungle of tall plants everywhere you look. The mall houses everything from a dentist to a physical therapist to a heart surgeon. It also features a great health food restaurant and I usually manage to time my appointment so I can take advantage of it.

Feeling totally well adjusted as I climbed down from my Wrangler in CHAPS's parking lot, I was further relieved to see Angel sitting on the steps that led up to the tavern's streetside door. I'd been worried about our missing partner. He hadn't been seen or heard from since the wedding two days earlier. Judging by the either dejected or exhausted way he was sitting there—shoulders slumped, hands dangling uselessly between his knees, head drooping so that his straw cowboy hat shaded his face—he had not benefited from taking Sunday off without notice.

As I lifted out the bag of grocery items from Lenny's Market, and the daily newspaper I'd picked up after seeing that there was a follow-up story on the body in the storage facility, I noticed a new-looking though dust-covered black dualie parked a few slots over. Cowboys love a dualie, I'd learned since I'd "gone country." A dualie's the cowboy's cadillac.

"You get a new set of wheels, Angel?" I asked, admiring the truck over my shoulder.

"Excuse me, ma'am?" he said.

That's when I realized he wasn't Angel. His voice was deeper and throatier and the Texas accent was stronger.

I swung my head back around. He was around Angel's height and had Angel's black hair and high cheekbones. Now that he'd straightened out of his slump and was standing, I could see that he didn't have Angel's mustache or ponytail. Lean but sturdy, he was wearing black jeans stacked over dusty black boots, a T-shirt with a bucking bronc on it, a white straw cowboy hat that was a little grimy around the beaded hatband. Angel always looked as if he'd just emerged from a Western clothing store wearing the top of the line. This man looked as if he'd been traveling on horseback through the desert. He also looked tough.

"Miguel Cervantes," he introduced himself, clasping my hand with a solid grip that came close to mangling my fingers. His hand was callused, hard. His eyes flicked me over, not in an insulting way exactly—more of an assessment. "If I was to guess I'd say you had to be Charlie Plato."

"You're related to Angel?" Stupid question. He was the spitting image.

He appeared to examine the question for hidden traps before answering. "He's my little brother."

"I didn't even know Angel had a brother. I thought you were him. You really do—"

"Look just like him," he finished for me.

"Did you come to see Angel? He hasn't been around the last couple of days."

His eyes were even darker than Angel's. Almost black. Angel's eyes were gentle. Kind. Miguel's were expressionless, hard. As he studied my face, I was aware of tension in his body. "Since when?"

"Since Saturday, during the wedding. He had a phone call and took off. Was that you on the other end?"

He didn't answer. I supposed he figured it was none of my business.

I tried an indirect route. "You drove all the way from Texas since then?"

"Nope."

"Where then?" See how difficult it is to keep from being nosy sometimes? It's the only way to find out anything when you run into these closemouthed types.

His chin came up. There was a hard edge to this man that wasn't present in his brother. He seemed coiled and wary. I thought he would probably refuse to answer, but he surprised me.

"Seems like Angel mentioned a time or two you had an inquisitive nature, Miz Plato." He considered for a moment, then evidently decided to let loose some information. "I've been calling Salinas, California, my hometown for a while. 'Cept when I'm taking part in some other rodeo. At the California Rodeo in Salinas they call it ro*day*o, but what I do is *ro*deo. Had a rodeo going on last couple days. Couldn't get away. Drove up here this morning but Angel's not home. Thought he might be here at SHAPS."

I must have blinked.

"I guess you say it CHAPS, the way Angel does," he said. "SHAPS is the right way—as in chaparral."

"It's our tavern," I said mildly. "We can pronounce it fish if we want to."

His eyes narrowed the way Zack's do when he's putting on his "squintin' into a duststorm" look, but he didn't comment. "Do you know where Angel is?" he asked.

"Nope," I said. I could be monosyllabic too when I wanted to be. He gave me another hard look.

"You want to come in?" I asked. "We have a partners' meeting due to start in a few minutes. Angel hasn't missed one yet."

He seemed surprised when I took him into the office. "I heard you lived here," he said.

"Upstairs, yes."

Surely he hadn't thought I'd take some guy I didn't know into my loft, even if he was the older brother of my good friend and partner. I knew all about the major differences between Cain and Abel. I thought this man could quite easily pass for Cain.

"What seems to be the problem?" I asked as I dropped the groceries and newspaper onto the floor.

Sitting down at my desk, I waved Miguel to a seat opposite.

Instead of taking it, he walked over to the window, turned, and hefted one hip onto the sill. It was a very sexy pose. Zack often assumed exactly the same position. It also meant I had to look at him against the light, which cast his eyes into shadow.

I got up and switched on the overhead light.

"What makes you think there's a problem?" he asked.

"Angel seemed—well, out of sorts, I guess, after he got your call—that call—whoever. He took off shortly after and hasn't been seen since. Looks like a problem to me."

His mouth tightened. I recognize negative body language when I see it.

I sat down again. "So you're a bull rider?" I said when a silence seemed to be setting in.

He inclined his head slightly.

"Why would anyone want to ride a bull?"

"It helps if you have an ornery disposition." A glint appeared in his dark eyes. "You'd have to look back at history, Ms. Plato. Cowboys on the ranch, on cattle drives, working hard, competition arising naturally out of the day-to-day business of ranch life. Roping, riding, horsebreaking. Who can ride the wildest horse, stay on the longest, take the falls, get back up, and do it again. Then when you got really good, looking for a bigger challenge—hey, how about a bull? Bull or horse, the animal's instinct is to throw off anything gets on its back. The challenge for the cowboy is man against animal, man against himself, man against man. I ride bulls because that's what I want to do. And I want to do it better than anyone else."

"Must be a worry for your family, all the same."

He pushed himself off the windowsill and came over to take the seat I'd indicated earlier. "I don't have a family," he said, leaning forward to make strong eye contact. "I'm a loner. Best way for a bull rider to be. Best way for a rodeo cowboy to be—traveling most of the time—five rodeos a week spring and summer, three a week in the fall. I heard you're a loner yourself?"

He had turned the question around on me. Fair enough. It was a method I sometimes used myself. "My parents were killed in a plane crash when I was still in school," I said.

"I believe Angel told me you were divorced?"

I was surprised Angel had told him that much about me.

"Did he?" I didn't talk to just anyone about my marriage. I'd fallen in love with and married a fairly famous plastic surgeon about the time I graduated from the University of Washington. We'd had a few happy years together, and then I'd caught him in one of his treatment rooms with his pants down around his ankles, boisterously "examining" an even more famous photographic model named Trudi. Turned out it was his usual modus operandi.

"Would you like a beer?" I asked.

Miguel nodded and I conducted him into the main corral, where we sat at the bar and talked awkward small talk about Zack's collection of microbrewery beers, each of which had its own weird and wonderful name, until Angel arrived.

The brothers went through a ritual that never ceased to entertain me. Two strong men gripping hands, jaws like steel, trying not to show the emotion that was vibrating between them. At some point in this display of machismo, Miguel lifted his eyebrows at Angel and Angel nodded ever so slightly. And Miguel's face tightened. With anger? Concern? I'm a student of body language, but with these two stonefaces it was difficult to tell what emotion was dominating.

Zack showed up about the time the brothers separated. He was carrying a small cooler, which he set down beside the bar. He, of course, had to go through the grip-testing ritual too. I love to watch male bonding.

"Zack got that scar on his face from a bull," I told Miguel.

Miguel raised an eyebrow.

Our man in black touched the zigzag scar on his left cheek and looked rueful. "An episode of *Prescott's Landin'*," he said.

Miguel nodded. "Angel told me you were on TV. Never did watch much."

"Bull was supposed to be tranquilized. Dose wasn't strong enough."

There really had been a bull? I was surprised. I'd always thought Zack's scar was much more likely to have been bestowed by a jealous husband.

"You get a ticket on the way up?" Angel asked his brother with a half grin.

Miguel shook his head. "I drove like somebody's granmaw. Didn't want to attract any police interest."

That statement definitely attracted *my* interest.

Angel looked at me. "I'm forever razzing Miguel

about his lead foot, Charlie. It's a habit of his to drive over the speed limit."

Miguel was not amused. "Going from rodeo to rodeo, I don't have time to mess around. I figure what I make from getting to the next rodeo in time to compete more than pays for the tickets I pick up on the way."

"I haven't seen my brother in a few months," Angel said when Miguel excused himself to the restroom to freshen up. Probably he'd sensed the questions that were working their way from my inquiring mind to my mouth.

"He seems a bit tense," I said.

Angel took off his straw cowboy hat, studied the sweatband as if looking for the manufacturer's name, then resettled it on his head. "Miguel is always tense," he said. "High-strung. Always looking for action. Our mother used to say she should have called him Diablo instead of Miguel. El Diablo. The prince of darkness. The devil," he explained for Zack's benefit.

His brother's arrival seemed to have loosened Angel's tongue. This was more information than he had ever given us about anyone in his family. I searched my mind for a way to keep him going. "The action he looked for wasn't necessarily legal?"

Angel sighed. "Miguel was always in trouble. Mostly kid stuff. Shoplifting. Drinking too much. Borrowing cars without permission—going on joy rides."

"Is he in trouble now?" I asked.

Again it took him a while to answer. Then he muttered, "Maybe," and asked if he and Miguel could borrow the office for a few minutes so they could talk in private.

Zack gave him permission before I could get around to it. So, okay, Zack was the senior partner, but I did more work in the office than anyone. About the only time Zack even went into the office was to use the phone to call one of his dollies, or to throw darts at the board we kept on the back of the office door. Occasionally he and Angel played computer golf, Sundancer e-mailed with a bunch of people on Country-Western music loops and Web pages. But I kept the books and did all the computer-related business stuff. I thought of it as *my* office and I also thought I might have found a way to persuade Angel to invite us into the office too.

"What?" Zack asked when I scowled at him.

I let it go, opened a mineral water for each of us, and came around the bar to sit on a stool next to Zack. I was eager to discuss this unexpected and very interesting turn of events. "Something's going on," I said. "What do you suppose it is?"

He took a few seconds to answer. For some unknown reason, he was carefully peeling the label off his bottle of Pellegrino. "Goin' on where?"

I sighed and took a swig of water. Zack's a mite dense sometimes. To be fair, though he has ceased to discombobulate my hormones, I have to admit he makes up for that by being something special to look at. He's tall and lean, with more than a hint of muscle under the all-black cowboy clothing. He has great hair—thick, untidy black hair that tousles up attractively when he takes his hat off. I've already mentioned his green eyes and the wry smile that hovers around his mouth most of the time. Add to all of that a pair of quizzically slanted eyebrows and you have the reason why most women, regardless of age, find him well nigh irresistible.

"Angel and Miguel," I said with uncommon patience. "They apparently have some kind of problem. I'm pretty sure Miguel was the one who called and talked to Angel at the wedding. Angel was all shook up, remember? So now Miguel Cervantes, who we've never even heard of in two years of knowing Angel, drives up here from Salinas a couple of days later. Why?"

"To visit Angel, I suppose. It's not that far, Charlie. 85 miles tops." He handed me the label from the water bottle, making an actor's small drama of the presentation.

"I'm supposed to save this for you?" I asked. "You're suddenly collecting labels instead of dollies? What's next, stamps?"

His crooked grin was pure mischief. No, not pure. "Tradition says if a guy gives a gal the label off a bottle it means he's invitin' her to sleep with him."

"That's one of the dumbest things I ever heard."

He shrugged. Gracefully. The way he did everything. "It's a bar game, Charlie. If the label rips when you try to get it off, it doesn't count. Mine never rip."

"Why am I not surprised?"

He grinned smugly, impervious, as always, to sarcasm. "Gal accepts it, she's sayin' yes."

I slapped the label onto the bar as if it was too hot to handle, which, symbolically speaking, it was. "What's in the cooler?" I asked to change the subject.

He reached down and hefted the container into the bar, opened it, and took out a glass jar full of dark gray blobs. "Leftover caviar from the weddin'. Seemed a pity to waste it."

Sliding off his stool, he went around the bar and rooted under it until he came up with a pack of crackers. "Should be toast points, but we'll make do," he said cheerfully, as he put the cooler back on the floor.

In some ways Zack is culturally challenged. He never heard of Plato, the philosopher my Greek father had always insisted was our ancestral relative; when Bristow quotes Shakespeare, he goes blank; when I mentioned Agatha Christie's Hercule Poirot once, he said he thought that dude had maybe had his own TV show some time back. Most of Zack's references originate in TV or movies. But the aunt who took him in when he was seventeen had lived in Beverly Hills all of her adult years and she'd taught him about the niceties of life, such as wines and caviar and which knives and forks to use when.

With a small spoon, he piled caviar on a cracker, gave it a squirt of juice from a lemon wedge he'd brought along, and held it to my mouth. "Here you go, darlin'."

A few months back, I would have said there is surely nothing more weakening to the knees and the brain than a sexy green-eyed man gazing at your mouth and offering it food. A reversal of Eve and the apple. Fortunately I was immune now. Mind over matter really works. You should try it.

The salty beads exploded with ecstasy against the roof of my mouth. This stuff was Beluga, the rarest and costliest caviar in the world. Zack had provided a generous amount of it for the wedding. I remembered my father telling me that Picasso loved Beluga caviar and bought it with cash wrapped in one of his drawings. I almost shared that anecdote with Zack, but was afraid he'd say, "Who?"

Like a baby bird, I opened my mouth for more. Two more cracker loads later, I was feeling much more kindly toward Zack than I'd felt in a while.

Fortunately, Angel showed up in the entrance about then. "We're leaving now," he called. "Okay if I take a couple more days off to get things settled?"

"Sure," Zack called back before I could ask what "things" and precisely how much time a "couple more days" meant.

Great, now there were only two of us to run CHAPS. Savanna, of course, was on her honeymoon in San Francisco with Bristow, and Jacqueline was safely stowed with her grandmother. "You'll have to help with the dance lessons on Wednesday," I told Zack.

"Happy to, darlin'." He looked thoughtful. "How about we start off with the Desperado Wrap? One of my favorites. Don't know that I've ever seen it done at CHAPS."

I shook my head. "I'm not familiar with that one." I lied. I had danced it several times before I ever came to CHAPS. I knew damn well it was one of the most intimate dances for couples you could imagine.

"Real pretty dance." His voice was as casual as could be. "You wanna try it out now?" he asked, waving the caviar spoon at the shadowy main corral dance floor.

I slid off my stool and turned away. "I have to go work on the Web site," I said over my shoulder as I headed for the exit. "You might do an inventory of the bar, as long as Angel's not going to be here to do it."

"Yes, ma'am," he drawled, using exactly the intonation his TV character, Sheriff Lazarro, would have used in his heyday—before the writers of the incredibly popular, incredibly unbelievable show, *Prescott's Landing*, killed him off. That was one character who certainly deserved to die. He was far too noble to live.

Zack didn't usually need to approach a woman, he was forever being propositioned and hadn't learned how to say no. So he wasn't used to rejection, except from me. It intrigued him, I guess. The way I saw it, Zack had caught on to the fact that my inner parts no longer went *whomp!* whenever I looked at him. So he'd started a campaign to prove he could conquer me if he had a mind to. Probably he was curious to know how long I could hold out. *Forever*, I could have told him, but he'd have interpreted that to mean I was really fighting to make it.

Which of course wasn't true.

Putting Zack out of my mind, I fixed my attention on business. With the help of some advice from my friend and computer guru, who was coincidentally named Macintosh, I was developing a site for CHAPS to go on the World-Wide Web. Today, I wanted to upload our lesson schedule. We were increasing it, trying to bring in more people through the week. We were charging for it too. Our overhead was eating up income at an alarming rate. We'd already instituted a cover charge on weekends and Wednesdays and were considering renting out the premises during the day and on Monday nights for group meetings or parties.

I pulled up short as I was about to enter the office. The front door was opening. I eased back around the stairway to see who was coming in and saw Angel and Miguel enter.

"We talked things over in the parking lot and we reckon we need to talk to you and Zack, Charlie," Angel said. His voice was so heavy I felt an answering sinking inside my stomach. Whatever the problem was, it was serious.

"I'm just heading into the office," I said. "Zack's in the main corral. Give him a shout."

When I entered the office I saw that the newspaper I'd dropped on the floor with the grocery bag had been opened out on the desk. The story about the dead man in the storage unit was uppermost.